MW01234390

WHEN WE BEGAN

ELENA AITKEN

Copyright © 2018 by Elena Aitken

All rights reserved.

No part of this book may be reproduced in any form or by any electronic or mechanical means, including information storage and retrieval systems, without written permission from the author, except for the use of brief quotations in a book review.

This is a work of fiction. The events and characters described herein are imaginary and are not intended to refer to specific places or living persons. The opinions expressed in this manuscript are solely the opinions of the author and do not represent the opinions or thoughts of the publisher. The author has represented and warranted full ownership and/or legal right to publish all the materials in this book.

Also by Elena Aitken

Timber Creek

When We Left

When We Were Us

When We Began

When We Fell

Women's Fiction

All We Never Knew

Ever After

Choosing Happily Ever After

Needing Happily Ever After

Wanting Happily Ever After

Fighting Happily Ever After

We Wish You A Happily Ever After

Keeping Happily Ever After

Finding Happily Ever After

Seeking Happily Ever After

Cherishing Happily Ever After

Ever After: Volume One (Books 1-4)

Castle Mountain Lodge

Unexpected Gifts

Hidden Gifts

Unexpected Endings - Short Story

Mistaken Gifts

Secret Gifts

Goodbye Gifts

Tempting Gifts

Holiday Gifts

Promised Gifts

Accidental Gifts

The Castle Mountain Lodge Collection: Books 1-3

The Castle Mountain Lodge Collection: Books 4-6

The Castle Mountain Lodge Collection: Books 7-9

The Castle Mountain Lodge Complete Collection

The Springs Series

Summer of Change

Falling Into Forever

Second Glances

Winter's Burn

Midnight Springs

She's Making A List

Summit of Desire

Summit of Seduction

Summit of Passion

Fighting For Forever

The Springs Collection: Volume 1

The Springs Collection: Volume 2

The Springs Collection: Volume 3

The Springs Complete Collection - Books 1-10

The McCormicks

Love in the Moment

Only for a Moment

One more Moment

In this Moment

From this Moment

Bears of Grizzly Ridge

His to Protect

His to Seduce

His to Claim

Hers to Take

His to Defend

His to Tame

His to Seek

Bears of Grizzly Ridge: Books 1-4

Destination Paradise

Shelter by the Sea

Escape to the Sun

Stand Alone Stories

All We Never Knew

Drawing Free

Sugar Crash

Composing Myself

Betty & Veronica

The Escape Collection

Vegas

Nothing Stays in Vegas

Return to Vegas

Halfway Series

Halfway to Nowhere

Halfway in Between

Halfway to Christmas

Chapter One

IT HAD BEEN a long time since Amber Monroe had stood in front of the doors of Timber Creek Elementary. It had been decades since she'd accepted her *graduation* certificate from the principal and marched out the door toward bigger and better things.

Like eighth grade. And Timber Creek High School.

But that was just the beginning for Amber. She'd been ambitious from the start. Her mom used to say she was born with an agenda.

And maybe she had been.

Amber had been nonstop as long as she could remember. Always looking ahead to the next thing instead of stopping to enjoy the moment she was in. Driven, her mother had called it. Before she'd died, when Amber was barely thirteen, she'd made Amber promise never to lose her drive and she hadn't.

In elementary, she'd organized a bracelet club in grade two, appointed herself leader and had run meetings at recess where they made friendship bracelets and sold them for charity to the other kids. It lasted two weeks before everyone quit because Amber wouldn't allow them a day off to play four square.

Once she was in high school, it was a lot easier to find roles she could excel in. Student body president in the eleventh grade, a role she gave up her senior year to concentrate on college admissions; editor of the newspaper; co-chair of the graduation committee; and countless other committees. Amber was in her element when she was in charge of something. When she had a plan. When she had control.

Which was why she didn't hesitate to take control when her best friend Drew Ross put off her son Austin's first day of pre-kindergarten…again.

Austin was already two weeks late starting the year. It was understandable, considering he'd just lost his dad to cancer. But the boy needed normalcy. He needed routine. He needed to get on with his life. What he didn't need was his mother holding him close while she cried into his hair every night instead of reading him a bedtime story.

Which was exactly why Amber was back in Timber Creek. Her best friend needed her. And that's also why she was once again standing outside of Timber Creek Elementary school with Austin's tiny hand clenched tightly in hers. Once upon a time, she'd promised that she would never set foot inside that school again until there was such a time she was asked back to speak to the students about women's rights in business. Or equal wages, or whatever it was that she was passionate about at the time.

She'd never been asked back. Despite the fact that she was a successful lawyer at a huge law firm in San Francisco. So successful she'd made partner.

Correction. *Almost* made partner.

She shook her head and straightened her shoulders. It wasn't the right time to think about what *almost* was.

"Auntie Amber?"

Amber blinked hard and looked down at Austin, who was staring up at her, wide-eyed.

"Are we going in?"

Amber forced herself to be present in the moment. She didn't need to think about the past or home or anything at all. She just needed to get through today. And then tomorrow. And then—

Focus.

She squeezed the boy's hand, forcing herself to be in the moment. There was nothing else.

Just Austin.

She smiled and hoped the boy believed it was genuine.

"Absolutely," she said. "Are you ready for your first day of school?"

Austin nodded readily. "Yes. Mommy said I didn't have to go. But I want to go."

"That's good." Amber squeezed his hand. "You'll have fun." She took another step forward toward the school, but Austin tugged on her hand.

"Auntie?"

Amber looked back into his troubled face. He was only a little boy. He should be smiling and laughing. But he'd lost so much for someone so young, it broke her heart. "What's up, kiddo?"

"Do you think I should stay home? Mommy wanted me to stay home. Will I have friends? What if the kids don't like me? What if the teacher is mean?"

He fired the questions at her like popcorn in a hot pan, but Amber grabbed each kernel as it popped.

"I don't think you should stay home. Your mommy is just sad right now, but she wants you to go to school. Of course you'll have friends. The kids will love you and I happen to have it on good authority that your teacher is super-duper nice."

Austin grabbed onto the last detail. "She is? What's her name?"

Amber bent to give him a kiss on the cheek. "Why don't we

go find out?" Before he could answer, she started to walk again and this time he followed along.

Walking through the heavy doors was a blast from the past for Amber. Not much had changed since she'd been a student there but there were a few new touches. Including the young female principal who greeted her the moment they stepped inside.

"Mrs. Ross, it's nice to—"

"Monroe," Amber corrected. "I'm Amber Monroe. Mrs. Ross couldn't be here." She gave the woman a look that she hoped was understood. The school had been briefed on Austin's situation and Amber had called and spoken with the principal personally when Drew only stared at Amber blankly upon the suggestion of Austin starting school.

The woman's face changed, and her face split into a smile. "It's nice to meet you, Amber." She turned her attention and extended her hand. "And you must be Austin."

The little boy, suddenly way too old for his age, took the principal's hand and shook it seriously. "Nice to meet you."

"Well, aren't you the sweetest thing?" The principal straightened up and grinned at Amber. "He's very sweet."

Amber nodded in agreement.

"I'm Principal Foster. Maggie Foster. It's nice to meet you both. Did you want to go with Austin to his class and see him settled in?"

Amber looked to the boy. She knew he was nervous but she also knew he was trying to be brave. He'd never admit that he wanted her to go with him. "You know what." Amber looked back to Maggie Foster while she gave Austin's hand that was still wrapped up in hers another reassuring squeeze. "I think his mom would prefer it if I went with him."

"I think that sounds perfect," Maggie said. "Are you ready, Austin? Your teacher is excited to meet you. I think you're going to really like Mrs. Brewster."

"Is she nice?" Without him even realizing it, Austin released Amber's hand and started to follow his principal.

"She's *very* nice and there are a lot of little boys your age in your class that I think you're going to be very good friends with."

Amber trailed along behind them and listened as Austin peppered the principal with a new list of questions, his nervousness fading as his excitement grew.

She smiled to herself. Bringing him to school had been the right choice. She hadn't meant to steamroll Drew's wishes to have him at home. In fact, Amber felt badly about it. But it was easy to see that the real reason Drew hadn't wanted Austin to start school had nothing to do with the child himself and everything to do with her.

And that's why Amber was there, to help Drew get through these difficult few weeks, maybe months, and then she'd go back to—what?

"Ms. Monroe?"

Amber blinked hard as Maggie Foster came into view in front of her. She'd been daydreaming and not only had she not realized they'd arrived at the class, she also hadn't noticed as Austin had bravely gone inside. Without so much as a look backward.

"I don't think you need to worry about Austin at all," Maggie said. "He looks like he's settling in already." She gestured to the door and Amber peeked in. Sure enough, Austin looked fine. He sat in a circle on the floor with a group of children, a wide smile on his face.

Careful he didn't notice her, Amber whipped out her cell phone and took a picture of the scene to show Drew when she got home.

Satisfied, Amber left the boy in the capable hands of Mrs. Brewster and the class, and walked back to her car, where she sat behind the wheel and took a deep breath as she stared at the cell phone still in her hand. Not that she actually expected it to ring. There likely weren't any voicemails waiting for her either. And her email inbox would be just as empty.

The anxiety started to creep in around the edges again. She could feel the fingers of it wrapping slowly around her chest, squeezing until she struggled to take a breath. Amber closed her eyes and did the breathing exercises she'd learned. After a moment, the panic was gone again, but the emptiness wasn't.

Would she ever get used to it? The quiet? No one needing her or waiting for her to make a decision?

She didn't think so.

Amber pulled her shoulders back and took one more deep breath.

There may not be anything work-wise she needed to do, and the law firm might no longer need her, but there was plenty she could fill her day with. She started the car and pulled out of the parking lot, headed back to Drew's. Her best friend needed her, and she was the biggest project of all.

BY ELEVEN O'CLOCK, Amber had already done everything on her list for the day, which mostly included throwing in some laundry and running the vacuum in the living room. She was just putting the finishing touches on a salad for her and Drew to share for lunch when her friend finally appeared from her bedroom.

"Well, good morning." Amber tried to keep her voice light, but she was getting dangerously close to offering Drew some tough love, best friend style.

"Whatever," Drew mumbled before she slumped into a chair at the table and dropped her head into a hand. "I saw you this morning when you got Austin ready for school. Thank you, by the way."

"You don't need to thank me." Amber smiled as kindly as she could. It broke her heart to see her sweet friend so completely broken. She'd been strong throughout her husband Eric's cancer, handling everything in stride. It seemed to everyone that Drew had everything completely under control and was dealing with her husband's illness with more grace than anyone ever could have imagined.

The truth was, that despite the outward appearances she'd been working so hard to keep up, on the inside she was having a complete meltdown. In the days following Eric's passing and his memorial service, Drew started to struggle more and more.

Which was exactly what Amber had hoped wouldn't happen, but that she'd guessed would. She knew her best friend well enough to know that Drew would need her. And that's why she was there.

It's not the only reason.

Amber forced the thought from her head as she slid the plate of salad in front of her friend. "Seriously," she said. "You don't need to thank me. I'm happy to be here to help you guys. And you should have seen Austin. He was so brave about meeting the new kids. I think it's going to be really good for him. Look, I even took a picture for you." She passed Drew her cell phone with the picture of Austin in his new class.

Her friend stared at the picture, fresh tears pooling in her eyes. "I should have been there."

"It's fine. He hardly even noticed that *I* was there," Amber said kindly. "Eat something."

"Send me that picture, please." Drew handed the phone back and looked at her plate for the first time. "Salad again?" She picked up her fork and pushed the leaves around the plate. "Do you think I need to be on a diet or something?"

"Not at all." Amber slid into the seat across from her. "It's kind of all I know how to make. Besides shaking chicken fingers out of a bag and putting them in the oven, but I thought I'd save that for dinner." She grinned, but Drew didn't look impressed.

"Seriously? You don't cook?"

Amber shrugged. "When would I ever have learned how to cook? Dad always made dinner or brought home frozen dinners, and ever since then it's just been easier to order in."

"What about the lasagna and the shepherd's pie we had the other night?"

"Pretty much everything we've been eating has been thanks to the kindness of your family and friends," Amber explained. "They did a good job filling the freezer, but supplies are starting to get a little low."

"So, we get salad?" Drew lifted her fork and held a cucumber aloft.

"Don't forget the chicken fingers." Amber winked and stuffed a forkful into her mouth. "But if you don't like it," she said after a moment, "maybe you could cook something? What's Austin's favorite meal? It might be nice to surprise him with that on his first day of school, don't you think?"

The instant Amber suggested it, she regretted it. Drew's eyes filled up with tears and she dropped the fork and buried her face in her hands.

"What did I say? Drew?" Amber prodded gently.

"My spaghetti is Austin's favorite."

That didn't seem like a reason to burst into tears, but then again, Amber was definitely not an expert in grief. "That sounds good," she said. "Why don't we make that? I'll get the ingredients at the store and—"

"It was Eric's favorite, too."

Ahhh.

"Okay," she said cautiously. "How does chicken fingers sound?"

Drew lifted her head and even managed a small smile. "Perfect. Thank you."

Amber reached across the table and squeezed Drew's hand. "It's nothing."

Thankfully, they were able to finish lunch without any more tears and Amber even got Drew to smile again when she told her about all of Austin's questions before they went into the school. But despite her best efforts, she couldn't convince her friend to leave the house to pick up her son with her.

Baby steps, she reminded herself later that afternoon when she made her trip to Timber Trade to pick up the supplies for dinner, including a bag of frozen French fries and a pint of ice cream for dessert. It was his first day of school, after all; they should celebrate at least a little bit.

It had only been a few weeks since Eric died. Amber needed to remember that everyone went through the grieving process differently. She'd just turned thirteen when her mom died from breast cancer. It was a short-lived battle, as her mom had ignored all the signs and symptoms, pushing them off as "just feeling under the weather." By the time she saw the doctor, there wasn't much that could be done. And even though she'd only been a kid and everyone around her expected her and her father to fall apart, the opposite had happened. Amber only remembered seeing her dad cry the one time, the day he told her that her mother had passed in her sleep. After that, he'd been strong and stoic.

She herself *had* cried.

Secretly, in bed, after all the friends and relatives who meant well had gone home. It was important for her to keep her feelings in check, because if she lost control, if she let her hurt show through, even a little, her dad would start to worry about her. And he had enough to worry about. Everyone kept saying that. How much Joseph had to worry about now.

When they thought Amber wasn't listening, the adults

would huddle their heads together and talk about how much pressure was on his shoulders now to raise her all on his own and they didn't know how he was going to do it.

The last thing Amber needed to do was add more worry to his stress load. Which was why, after crying herself to sleep for the first few nights, the tears dried up and she vowed to keep the promise she'd once made to her mom.

She'd never lose her drive to be successful. No matter what, Amber was going to achieve all of her dreams. Not only for her, but for her mom.

And she had, too. Mostly. At least for a little while.

Would her mom be proud of her now? She was pretty sure she knew the answer to that question.

Amber shook her head and was about to do what she always did, which was make a mental list about what she could do to get back on track, when her phone chirped with an incoming text message.

It had once been such an ordinary sound in her daily life, almost like a soundtrack to her day, but that was before. Now the sound was jarring, snapping her back to her current situation, which was anything but ordinary.

She grabbed at her phone and clicked it open, eager to see who'd finally reached out.

HOW R U? *You missed the meeting again last night.*

THE SECOND SHE READ IT, guilt flooded through her. She should have known that Cody wouldn't let it slide that she'd missed her meeting yet again. That was the point of a sponsor. To hold her accountable and make sure she stayed on track. It didn't seem to matter that she *was* on track. There just weren't any meetings that she knew of in Timber Creek and even if there were, it's not as if she could go to them. It was a small town, and despite the fact that they were supposed to be anonymous, she wasn't stupid enough to actually believe that it wouldn't get out. And the last thing she needed was for anyone, especially her best friends or her father, who'd give her that *look*, to know that, despite the fact that she'd tried so hard to have it all, instead she'd ruined everything.

Chapter Two

THE NEXT DAY, Austin was awake before Amber, dressed and ready to go to school. He'd been so excited the night before when he'd come home, that instead of having trouble sleeping, he'd drifted off almost at once because the sooner he fell asleep, the sooner he could go back to school.

It was good to see the little boy excited about something normal. Beyond good. Amber only wished that Drew was witnessing it as well. But she didn't get up much before ten these days. Mostly because she didn't go to sleep until way after three or four in the morning.

When Amber first moved in, Drew had lied about her sleeping, but soon enough she hadn't bothered. Mostly because Amber caught her sitting in the yard, or in the living room, or just aimlessly pacing the halls of their small house too many times to believe that *something had woken her*.

It was a process—similar to her own—and this too would pass. Amber nodded to herself as she poured a cup of coffee and tuned into Austin's constant chatter about what was planned in Mrs. Brewster's class for that day. She listened to him all the way to school and into the playground before he tore away from her to join his new friends. She watched him for a minute, but she needn't have worried. He blended in with the other kids, and was laughing and smiling within seconds of catching up to them.

Friendly and popular, just like his parents had been in school. Austin would be just fine.

Once again, after dropping him off, Amber sat in her car and stared at her phone. Just like the day before, and the day before that, there were no missed calls, no voicemails, no emails waiting for her attention.

Nothing.

It was the hardest part of everything she'd been through for the last three months. Harder than the rehab, harder than detoxing her body after years of abuse, harder than keeping the secret from her friends and family. By far, the hardest part had been losing her job and everything she'd worked for her entire life. Going from being an *important* person—who was so necessary to close deals, to answer questions, to make decisions that were essential—to someone who might as well not even exist. She'd lost her entire identity.

It was more than hard. It was devastating.

Amber stared at her still quiet phone, willing it to ring with a question only she could answer.

But it wasn't going to and she knew that. Because there was no one to ask questions anymore. Not since she'd been fired mere weeks before finally making partner at the firm she'd devoted her life to. Not that she deserved anything less. She'd put the firm at risk with her irrational actions. And if it had been her decision, she would have made the same one.

But that didn't make it any easier to accept.

Amber had hoped that helping Drew out after Eric's passing would be a good distraction from her own life, and it had been. At first. But with Austin in school now, and Drew more or less happy to spend her nights walking the halls and her days sleeping, it was getting harder and harder for Amber to forget that her own life was in complete shambles.

She needed more.

With a sigh, she tucked her cell phone back into her purse and put the car in drive. Not that it would be any kind of substitute for a real job, but maybe paying a visit to her father would feel just enough like work so she wouldn't feel totally useless. Besides, she'd been back in town a few weeks now and she still hadn't gone to visit.

Not that he'd care whether she waited another month, but still. It was the right thing to do. And more than that, it was *something* to do.

AMBER COULD HAVE MADE the five-minute drive to the house she grew up in in her sleep. The sleepy little street hadn't changed, at least not on the surface. A few houses had seen some much-needed upgrades, and a few others were in need of some. The kids she'd grown up with were gone, but mostly there were new kids in their place. It made her smile to see the abandoned bikes, balls, and various toys scattered around the front lawns, waiting for their owners to return home from school and start playing with them again.

Her dad's house looked almost completely unchanged from the last time she'd been there, which had been earlier that year when she'd returned to Timber Creek for the big reunion party at the high school.

Two visits in less than a year. Must be some kind of record.

She left the car at the curb and without hesitating, marched up and rapped on the front door. While she waited, she straightened her skirt and blouse and tossed her long black hair behind her back. She knew she was overdressed, wearing the same designer clothes she would have worn to the office, but she couldn't seem to bring herself to put jeans on during the work week.

A few moments later, her dad opened the door. "You don't have to knock," he greeted her. "It's still your house."

That wasn't true and they both knew it. The house hadn't felt like her home since the day her mom died. It became cold and sad and empty. Maybe it wasn't fair to her father, but increasingly after her mom passed away, she'd spent more and more time with her friends Cam, Christy, and Drew and their families. Not that her dad seemed to mind.

It was probably easier for him, too, that she hadn't been around much.

"Hi, Dad." She didn't reach her arms out for a hug, and Joseph Monroe didn't ask for one. Instead, he turned and led the way through the house toward the kitchen. It was as much of a greeting as Amber expected.

"I heard you were back in town." Joseph pulled two mugs from the kitchen cupboard. "Sorry to hear about your friend."

"You heard about Eric?"

"I read the paper."

"Right." She nodded and accepted the cup of coffee he poured her. "Well, I thought I'd come back home for a bit and help Drew. I couldn't imagine what it would be like to lose a husband like that and with such a small child."

"No," Joseph said. "You couldn't."

Amber knew her father didn't mean anything by the comment, only exactly what he said that no, obviously she couldn't imagine what it would feel like considering she wasn't married and had no children of her own. But it still stung.

She took a sip of the strong coffee and avoided looking at him for a minute. It had always been this way. It wasn't that her dad was completely void of emotion; it just seemed that way. At least to Amber. But she'd gotten used to the lack of hugs, the constant criticism for marks that weren't perfect, the holidays that went uncelebrated, and always feeling like more of a nuisance than a daughter.

She'd *mostly* gotten used to it.

"How are you, Dad? Keeping busy?"

"I retired two years ago, Amber. You know that."

"I do, Dad." She nodded and forced a smile through her gritted teeth. Of course she knew he was retired. When the doctor finally told him he was going to work his way into an early grave if he didn't sell his insurance company, he'd kicked up such a fuss that the doctor had called Amber personally to see whether she could talk some sense into him. Ultimately, Joseph had sold his business and retired the way it had been suggested. At the time, Amber had hoped he'd get out of the house more, maybe make some friends and find some hobbies he enjoyed, but as far as she could tell, he still mostly kept to himself. "So what are you doing with your days now? I know you like to keep busy."

"I've got my pens," he said. "I just got a new wood I'm going to try out on the lathe next week." His face lit up a little bit when he spoke about the pens he'd started making. Amber had never paid much attention to his handicraft, but he did seem to enjoy turning the wood and assembling homemade pens to sell at the markets.

"That's good." She nodded and took another big sip of her coffee. "And did you sell a few this summer?"

"All of them," Joseph answered matter-of-factly.

"*All* of them?" She sat up straight. "How many did you make?"

"Fifty-five."

"*Fifty-five?*"

"Is there something wrong with your hearing, Amber?"

"No." She shook her head and put her cup on the table in front of her. "It just seems like a lot of pens. And you sold them all? That's great."

"It is." He nodded, his mood shifting again. "How's the firm? Have you made partner yet?" The subject changed quickly and not entirely unexpectedly. He never did like to talk about himself, but he always had a lot of opinions about what Amber was doing. "I expected to hear that you'd made partner already. You're not getting any younger, you know?"

"I know that, Dad." She shook her head and muttered under her breath, "Thanks for pointing that out."

"Pardon?"

She smiled as sweetly as she could. "I was just saying that I was aware of how old I was." At thirty-three, Amber was *very* aware that not only had she not made partner the way she'd planned, she never would now. She'd have to start over and the idea was more than a little daunting.

"I'm sure you are." He looked at her strangely, as if he couldn't understand why she would say such a thing, which he probably couldn't. Her sarcasm had always been lost on him. "So what cases are you working on? Still doing corporate law, aren't you?"

"It was always my focus," she answered as ambiguously as possible without outright lying to him. There was no way Amber was going to tell her dad that she was fired. It simply wasn't an option.

"Well," Joseph continued. "I don't know why it's taking so long for you to make partner then. If you work half as hard as you say you do, you should have been partner years ago."

Amber nodded. It was easier than trying to explain to him for the dozenth time that hard work didn't necessarily equal a partnership.

"How long are you in town for then? I'm sure you'll need to get back." Her father pushed his coffee mug back and forth between his hands, but didn't actually drink any, from what she could tell.

"I think I'll stay for a while," she answered honestly. "I had a lot of vacation time banked up, and I can't think of a better time to use it then to help a friend." Again, it was another *not quite* lie. But he didn't seem to notice.

"Well, we'll have to visit again before you go." Joseph pushed up from his chair unexpectedly and took his untouched coffee to the sink. "I have to get going if I'm going to make it on time."

"On time for what?" His abruptness took Amber off guard and it took her a moment to catch up. "You're working? Where? I thought the doctor told you if you didn't—"

"I'm not working, Amber." He clucked his tongue. "I'm volunteering. It's different. Except for the commitment—that's the same. When I say I'm going to be there at a certain time, I sure as hell will be."

"I get that, Dad." Amber took her mug to the sink. Her dad was always punctual. He considered tardiness a personality deficiency. "Where are you volunteering? Why didn't you tell me?"

"It didn't come up."

She refrained from pointing out that she'd asked him only a few minutes ago what was new and what he was doing with his time. "Right," she said instead. "Where are you volunteering?" she asked again.

"At the stables. There's a new program. It's been around a few months and I stumbled upon it one—"

"Stables? Like at the ranch? With horses?" She didn't bother to hide the surprise on her face. "But…you…*horses*?"

"Why not me and horses?"

Amber bit her tongue because she couldn't really think of a good reason why it didn't make sense. She could actually remember when she was a little girl and he would talk about being around horses when he was young. Somewhere along the line, he'd stopped talking about it, but…maybe it did make sense. Still, something seemed off. "What program were you talking about?"

"A young local man started it up. It's called equine therapy. And basically it's where people use horses to help them get over their problems."

"What?" Amber truly couldn't believe what was coming out of her father's mouth. This was a man who, for her entire life, had dismissed therapy as a useless waste of money. *"Why would you pay someone to talk to them?"* And not only did he think therapy was a gimmick, but the man Amber knew would have scoffed at the idea of using horses for therapy; he most definitely wouldn't be volunteering at such a facility. It didn't make any sense.

Stunned, it took her a minute to formulate the next question. "Horse therapy? Why?"

"Because it seemed like they could use the help out there and I needed something to do." Her dad gave her a look that instantly made her feel as if she were twelve again. "Besides, the doctor says it's good for my blood pressure."

"Blood pressure? What's wrong with your blood pressure? I can talk to Mark...I mean Doctor Thomas about—"

"So many questions." Her father shook his head in dismissal. "I don't have time to get into the details right now, Amber. The horses are—"

"The horses are *animals*, Dad. Not therapists. And they're definitely not doctors. If you have high blood pressure, you should be—"

"I just said that I didn't have time to have this discussion right now, Amber. Particularly if you insist on continuing to interrupt me." He plucked his car keys off the hook by the light switch and moved through the house with the expectation that Amber would follow him out.

Which she did.

"We'll visit again," Joseph turned and said to her when they reached the front step. "It was nice to see you."

He was gone a moment later, leaving her standing on the porch of her childhood home, staring after her father just the way she had so many times before.

Chapter Three

LOGAN MYERS RAN the brush over Peanut's back one more time before patting her gently on the side. "All done, sweetheart. How about a treat?"

The horse twitched her white head and her ears flickered, which meant she thought the idea of a treat was a good one. Logan chuckled at the animal's predictability and gave her an apple. He'd been working with her all morning and she'd more than earned it. Peanut was a calm, easy horse and was going to be absolutely perfect for the kids' group therapy program he wanted to start up.

There were a lot of programs he wanted to get up and running now that he was officially certified to offer equine therapy in the state of Washington. It was just a matter of the town accepting the idea and finding a few more clients for his new business, Taking the Reins. Logan planned to start small, which was a good thing because he currently only had two horses to work with and he didn't even have his own stables.

Logan left Peanut in her stall and moved to the pile of muck just outside the barn doors, setting himself to the task of shoveling it.

Ruby Blackstar was a third-generation rancher in the Timber Creek area and luckily for Logan, she had no heirs, was getting older and less interested in ranching, and was in the process of downsizing her operation. For Logan, that meant that he was able to lease the stables for a more than generous price, and she threw in the old rancher's cabin for free. Ruby allowed him to use the facilities to get his practice up and running. It was still in the infancy stages, to say the least, but he'd get there. It was just a matter of time before the word got out and he started building up his clientele.

Between his work at the ranch, trying to grow a business, and his volunteer commitments with the Timber Creek fire department, Logan barely had enough time to sleep, let alone to think about much else.

Almost anything else.

It had been almost four years since Tina died. Four years since he'd been alone. Four years since he'd even thought about another woman. Despite the constant physical ache that he carried with him where Tina's love used to be, in many ways, the last four years had been a quiet respite from the real world. He'd thrown himself into school and work and anything to distract himself from the reality of his loss. Which, for too long, meant he'd drowned his sadness in booze. But the bottle had never been deep enough, the drinks never strong enough to numb the pain.

Logan drove his shovel into the pile of muck and lifted the load into the wheelbarrow, driving out the thoughts of Tina and his past. He was a different person now than he was then. A very different person.

One day, he'd been staring mindlessly at the TV, the way he'd taken to spending most of his days, and he'd seen something about horses being used for therapy. There'd been a time, when he was a kid, when he'd loved horses. The idea intrigued him. He put down the bottle, mentioned it to his family, and started looking into it seriously. That was the day everything changed.

Everything about that time of his life was completely different and he liked it that way.

Mostly. There were days when he still missed Tina with a ferocity that continually threatened to bring him to his knees. Maybe if he wasn't so lonely, he—

"Logan!"

The voice calling him across the yard distracted him from his line of thought. Thankfully. It was dangerous to even entertain such thoughts. The distraction was more than welcome. Especially because when he looked up, he saw Joseph Monroe, the older gentleman who'd been coming around to help him out with the horses.

"Joseph." He waved a greeting, jabbed his shovel in the pile of muck and went across the yard to greet the man. "I didn't think you were coming in today." Logan tugged his leather gloves off and shoved them in his back pocket before shaking Joseph's hand. "I didn't expect you until tomorrow."

Joseph had been coming out to the ranch three times a week for the last month or so and despite never actually settling on a schedule, the older man was very predictable and obviously enjoyed a routine. Which was why it was strange to see him on a Tuesday.

"I just thought you might like a little help with mucking out the stalls today. I know you're on your own here and—"

"No explanation needed," Logan cut him off. "Your help is always welcome here."

Joseph was a man of few words, but it didn't take much for Logan to see that he was also a man with a lot of pent-up emotions, and a story he hadn't told Logan yet. The horses had quickly become important to Joseph, and even if he was only there to help out and volunteer his time, Logan wasn't blind. He saw the changes in the man over the last few weeks.

"In fact," Logan said, "if you just want to spend a little time with Peanut today, putting her through the motions, that would be a big help. I have a new client coming in next week, and I want to make sure she's ready."

It wasn't totally a lie. He did have a new client coming in. But he wasn't worried about Peanut. She was more than ready.

The older man nodded, giving the idea some thought. Logan knew he liked being with the horses; he'd caught him talking to them on more than one occasion. He could also see that something had Joseph wound up today. There was a reason he'd broken his routine to come out to the ranch. Even if he wouldn't tell Logan, there was a good chance he'd tell Peanut.

But a few minutes later, the older man did tell Logan. Maybe not exactly, but after fetching Peanut from the barn and leading her out to the ring, Logan couldn't help but overhear Joseph muttering to the horse.

"Don't know what she expects," he said to the horse as he led her by the reins. "Barely spoken in years and I'm supposed to drop everything when she pops in. Unannounced, too."

Logan tried not to listen, but at the same time, he couldn't help but be intensely proud of what was happening. Horses had a way of bringing out emotions and feelings that people didn't even know they had. Peanut was doing a perfect job of letting Joseph vent whatever was going on inside him, and it was entirely likely that the man himself didn't even realize it.

"She's probably going to leave again anyway. Back to work. She always goes back to work." Peanut stiffened and planted her feet in the ground, causing Joseph to stumble and misstep. "What the— Horse. Come on."

From the other side of the ring, Logan stopped shoveling and leaned on his shovel as he watched the scene unfold. Peanut had sensed Joseph's stress and whatever tension he was feeling and had dug in. How Joseph handled it would be the real magic of equine therapy.

Logan watched for a few minutes while the other man tugged on the reins, spoke sharply to the horse and grew more frustrated. Finally, when it seemed apparent that Peanut definitely didn't have plans to go anywhere anytime soon, Logan called out. "She senses your tension, Joseph. She won't go anywhere if you try to force her."

"I'm not forcing anything," he hollered back. "And what tension? I'm fine."

Logan tried not to smile. "Are you?"

"This is stupid." Joseph tossed the reins aside and stepped out of the ring toward Logan. "I'm happy to help out and I like to volunteer here, but I don't know what's wrong with that animal today. She's never been so stubborn with me before. If I wanted to deal with a stubborn female, I would have just stayed home with Amber."

Almost the moment the words were out of his mouth, Joseph's face reddened and he turned away.

"Who's Amber?"

Logan wasn't really sure what he expected considering he barely knew the other man, but maybe Joseph had a lady friend, or Amber was a sister or neighbor. For whatever reason, he hadn't considered the possibility of what he said next.

"My daughter." Joseph shook his head. "We're not close."

"A daughter? You have a daughter?"

"I don't know why that's so surprising." The older man glared at him and Logan almost laughed, because he didn't know either.

"I guess I just didn't picture you as much of a father type." Quickly, Logan held up his hand and tried to backpedal. "I didn't mean that the way it sounded. It's just that—"

"I'm not," he interrupted him. "Much of a father, I mean. Never have been. And I'm sure Amber would say the same."

Joseph turned in on himself, obviously reliving a memory that he didn't feel like sharing.

Logan wasn't going to push. He waited patiently while the other man worked through whatever he needed to and finally he spoke again.

"She left after high school." He gazed out over the ring to where Peanut stood patiently. "Never really found much reason to come home over the years. She's back for a visit, I guess. Can't imagine she'll want to see much of me, though."

There was so much hurt in Joseph's voice, a vulnerability that Logan had never witnessed with him before, that instantly Logan found himself becoming defensive of his new friend. What kind of daughter left an old man and never came to visit? A man who clearly loved her and was distressed by her absence, and she didn't care at all?

"I don't suppose you know her," Joseph said. "She's probably a few years older than you, not that it matters."

"No," Logan said. "I don't think I do."

Logan looked at his boots in the dirt and shook his head. He couldn't do much about a selfish woman he didn't even know, but he could help Joseph work through things. And that's just what he was going to do. "You know what?" he said after a moment. "I appreciate you coming out here a few times a week to help with the animals, but if you want to come more and spend a little more time with Peanut, well…I think you would probably both benefit from that."

AMBER ALMOST HAD Drew out of the house to help her do the grocery shopping, but at the last minute, something made her cry and she begged Amber to do it without her. Again.

Not that Amber minded. Not really. She needed something to fill her days, but she was pretty sure she could find something a little more productive than buying groceries. At least she *should* find something more productive to do. The question was…*what?*

Amber shrugged off the question as she pulled a shopping cart from the row at the front door of Timber Trade. It wasn't the first time she'd wondered about what the hell she was going to do with herself. In fact, it was a pretty constant question that looped through her mind. But instead of coming up with any actual solutions, she just shoved it off. It was easier that way because there was only one thing she knew how to do. Be a lawyer. It's not as if she couldn't keep being a lawyer. There were other law firms, other cities, and other opportunities. She knew that.

But if she went back to the only thing she knew, would the old habits return? She wasn't sure it was a risk she could take. At least not yet.

Besides, she had other things to focus on. Drew and Austin needed her and that would be her priority. She'd have lots of time to figure everything else out later.

Which was why grocery shopping seemed like the most important thing she could do. And she was going to do it well.

Before Amber could push her cart into the store, her cell phone rang. She moved out of the way and fished it out of her pocket.

"Cam? What's going on?"

"Hey, Amber." Her friend's voice came across the line. "I hope you're not in the middle of anything."

Amber looked to the brick building behind her and shrugged. "Not really. I was just going to pick up a few things for dinner."

Cam's sigh meant that she knew exactly what that meant. "Drew's still not leaving the house?"

"Not much," Amber responded. "And she really hates going to the store."

"I can see that."

"You can?" Amber was surprised, because she could never understand Drew's insistence that Amber do the shopping. "Why? It seems like a basic thing she could start doing with me."

"You see it that way," Cam said. "But for Drew it means running into everyone she knows and hearing their endless condolences. Never mind fielding questions about how she's doing and how Austin is handling things. It would be exhausting."

"It would." Amber nodded with new understanding. "I never thought of that. I feel like an ass for trying to convince her to come."

"Don't feel like an ass," Cam said kindly. "You've been amazing for her, and I know she appreciates having you around." There was a short silence before Cam asked, "How *is* she anyway? Is it any better yet?"

Amber shook her head despite the fact her friend couldn't see her. "No. But it's still early."

"It is. Why don't I grab Christy in the next few days and we can pop over to watch a movie? Something funny. Or maybe she'll agree to go to the park and get some fresh air?"

"I like that idea." Amber didn't bother telling Cam that watching movies could be tricky and so far hadn't gone very well. One night, she thought she'd start with the classic, *Sleepless in Seattle*. It wasn't her fault that Amber hadn't remembered that Tom Hanks's character in that movie was a widower. The next night, she convinced Drew to let her pick a different movie. That time she went with action, but how was she to know that *Iron Man* had been Eric's favorite Marvel movie? No, movies were a minefield of emotions. "I think it's best to go outside."

"Great," Cam said. "We'll set it up. I'll let you get to your shopping. But Amber?"

"Yes?"

"Make sure you let us know if you need anything, okay? Anything at all."

"Of course," she responded, although they both knew that Amber would never ask for help.

As soon as Amber set foot into the air-conditioned store, she pulled out the list that she'd carefully crafted before leaving the house. The first time Drew asked her to do the shopping, all she'd said to her was, "Get the essentials."

Considering the fact that not only did Amber have no idea that Drew's idea of an *essential* was very different than hers, but also that it had been an unreasonably long time since she'd done an actual grocery trip—for the last ten years or so, she'd primarily eaten out—Amber didn't think she'd done too badly a job. But apparently hummus, smoked salmon, and arugula weren't considered essentials in Drew's house.

Ever since that first trip, where she'd walked around the grocery store, picking up packages of pasta, trying to decipher the difference between spaghetti and capellini, she'd been developing a system for the groceries.

Before leaving the house, she'd take an inventory of what they had, what was getting low, and what they were going to have for meals for the coming days. Then she'd carefully list all of the items, being sure to cross-check them one more time with what was in the cupboard and refrigerator.

After the first time Amber spent almost two hours in the store crisscrossing the aisles and doubling back on herself, she took the time to sketch out a little map where she highlighted the places she needed to hit. She took the time to consider frozen items and perishables—no more melted ice cream—and had developed a strategy for getting all the items on her list in the least amount of time.

To say she was impressed with herself was an understatement. Apparently organizational skills were useful in more than just the courtroom.

With her list in hand, a pen ready to cross each item off, and her reusable shopping bags already lined up in the cart, Amber started to move through the store with efficiency. It was still mostly an act, because even after developing the system, she still didn't feel very comfortable with what she saw as a great responsibility. After all, she never wanted to make the mistake of buying the crunchy peanut butter instead of the smooth again. Having a little boy who'd already gone through so much in tears because of a *sandwich* was not high on her list of things to repeat.

Even with her list, shopping still wasn't easy. Amber took her time in every aisle, looking at all the options for pastas, sauces, what ketchup had less sugar. Despite all her careful selection, she was pretty sure she'd get it wrong and buy a different brand than Drew normally did, but she was getting less concerned about that all the time, considering Drew didn't seem to care. She didn't seem to care about much these days.

Amber had tried everything she could think of to get her friend to re-engage with the world, but so far her efforts had been met mostly with tears, indifference, and sadness. There'd been a few glimmers of hope, and it still hadn't been very long. She wouldn't push Drew—yet.

With her list almost complete, Amber steered her cart down the next aisle and stopped in front of the books and magazines. Her hand instinctively reached for the monthly selection of romance novels. She'd been buying them for so long, it was second nature for her to put the familiar covers in her cart. When she was in high school, Amber had been initially embarrassed about her romance novel habit. She'd hide the books in her textbooks and sneak them out only when she thought no one was looking.

Losing herself in the love stories with cowboys, firefighters, and real-life heroes had been the perfect way for her to relax and escape from her daily life. Especially because she'd never had a boyfriend of her own.

While her friends were all hooking up with the boys who would for the most part become the loves of their lives, Amber's only focus had been on school, running whatever committees she was currently in charge of, getting the top marks that would get her into the best schools and out of Timber Creek. She didn't have time for boys, or relationships, or love. She only had time for one thing—succeeding.

At any cost.

With the books still in her hands, Amber squeezed her eyes shut and for a moment she felt as if she were sixteen again. Standing in that very store, with those very same books in her hand. Only, when she was sixteen, she still had everything in front of her. All of her doors were open; success was hers for the taking. And she had taken it. It was at sixteen, in the eleventh grade, when she'd struggled for the first time to keep her marks up, hold down a job, and take part in the student's union. She was exhausted and despite all her efforts, she couldn't keep up. When she finally did lay down at night, she couldn't sleep for the nightmares of failing out of school and not getting into a good college, which meant—staying home in Timber Creek.

Desperate, she'd turned to caffeine pills at first, but when they lost their edge and she still needed more, she'd discovered that Tommy Jenkins had been prescribed medication for his ADHD. And for a price, he'd sell those pills to her. For an even higher price, he'd keep his mouth shut about it.

The drugs had the desired effect and had more than given her the boost she'd needed. The best part was, no one knew about it.

If only she'd known then what she knew now. Would it have changed anything if she'd thought that taking a few pills in high school to help her study would lead to a few more? And finally a dependency that would control her life through college and into her adulthood? Would she have made a different decision if she knew then that by taking those first few Adderall pills, she was signing up for an addiction that would cause her to lose everything she'd worked for? And almost her own life?

For a moment, Amber forgot herself and that she was standing in the middle of the grocery store with a cart full of food. With her eyes still squeezed shut, an icy trail of panic started to thread its way through her veins. The still unfamiliar and terrifying feeling of losing control started to take over. Her pulse was racing, her palms sweating, and, to her horror, there was nothing she could do about it.

She was about to have a full-fledged panic attack in the middle of the grocery store.

LOGAN TRIED his best to avoid the grocery store, not because he hated actually shopping for food, but mostly because he really didn't like to go into town. Even though Timber Creek was his home town, and he should feel comfortable and relaxed there, it was the exact opposite. Things had changed so much since he was a kid. He'd changed. Now, when he went into town and saw the familiar faces and the people who waved and tried to make small talk with him, all he felt was an uncomfortable itching under his collar, as if all of a sudden the room was too hot and his clothes were too small.

He knew people meant well, but either they didn't know how to talk to him after Tina's accident, or they tried too hard. Either way, Logan often thought it might be easier to go somewhere where no one knew him. But when it came right down to it, Timber Creek was home and something he couldn't quite describe held him there.

Logan powered his way through the aisles. He kept his head down and his mind set to his task. He just needed enough supplies to hold him for another week or so. He was so focused on getting what he needed and getting out of there, he didn't notice the woman with a full cart standing in the middle of the aisle until his cart almost smashed into hers.

"Oh." He stopped short. "Sorry. I didn't see—hey, are you okay?"

Even without the training he'd had, he would have been able to see that there was something wrong. Her eyes were squeezed tightly shut, her breath was coming fast and in short pants, and there was a bead of sweat along her forehead. Her hands were wrapped around a small stack of books and she was completely unaware that he was standing there.

"Hello," he said again. Logan reached out and, gently so as not to startle her, touched her hand. "Is everything okay?"

The woman's eyes flew open and she looked directly at him. There was a flicker of recognition. She looked vaguely familiar, but he couldn't quite place her. That wasn't completely unusual; they'd probably gone to school together. But it was something more, as if maybe he'd seen her recently, or…

"I'm fine," the woman said after a moment. She closed her eyes and took a few deep breaths. When she opened her eyes again, the panic he'd seen there a moment before had faded. "I was just…" She looked down at the books in her hands. "Trying to decide what book to read." She faked a smile and shrugged before putting all three books in her cart. "Sorry, were you trying to get by?" She maneuvered her cart out of the way and just like that, the distressed woman from a moment before was completely gone, replaced with a much more confident version that Logan suddenly remembered.

"Don't I know you?"

She blinked hard before a look of recognition crossed her

face as well. "Yes. The reunion. I remember now." She straightened her shoulders and beamed a smile at him.

It was the reunion where Logan remembered seeing the tall, striking brunette. She looked so polished and put together and so completely big city. She was the exact opposite of what Tina had been with her worn jeans and t-shirts, maybe a cute sundress when the occasion called for it. But Tina never would have been seen in a tailored suit or designer dress. Maybe that's what had caught his eye in the first place: that she was so completely different than the love of his life had been. And yet, still, he'd been somehow drawn to her.

"We went to school together?" he asked, trying to place her from days gone by.

She smiled and tucked her long hair behind her ear. "We did, but I was a few years ahead of you. Logan Myers, right?"

The fact that she knew his name pleased him in a way he couldn't have expected.

"Evan Anderson told me," she admitted. "I honestly didn't recognize you at all, Little Logan."

Despite the fact that he'd hated that nickname almost his entire life, he laughed. "That's me."

"Not so little anymore." She extended her hand. "I'm Amber."

Amber.

He'd definitely remembered seeing her at the reunion, but there was something else. *Where had he heard that name recently?*

He slipped his hand over hers, the softness of her skin registering in a place deep down inside.

"Amber Monroe."

Monroe?

That's where he'd heard the name before. She was Joseph Monroe's daughter. The very same one who had the old man worked up and upset. Logan's instinct was to say something to the woman and let her know the effect she'd had on her father, but the training he'd had as a therapy facilitator kicked in. It wasn't his place to get involved.

Besides, he didn't know the situation and he didn't know her very well. But something about her definitely made him want to change that.

"It's nice to meet you, Amber." He let his gaze linger on her face as he released her hand. "And yes, I've grown up a little bit."

"You certainly have." The moment the words came out of her mouth, she flushed a bright red. "I mean…well, I didn't mean…I just…"

Logan got the impression that Amber wasn't a woman who flustered very easily. Or very often, and he couldn't help but laugh.

"It's okay." He let her off the hook. "Are you in town for a visit? Or did you boomerang, too?" He certainly couldn't explain it, but something about this woman in only a few short minutes had lit up a part of him that had been in the dark a very long time. Despite all of the reasons he shouldn't have been, not the least of which was that she was Joseph's daughter, he was attracted to her. It was a part of him that he'd been so sure had died along with Tina. And the feeling left him unbalanced and shaken. But not enough to stop talking to her.

"Boomerang?" She laughed and the sound filled him. He wanted her to do it again. "That's an interesting way of putting it. But I guess I did boomerang." She looked pensive for a moment. "At least for a little while," she added. "I came home to help my best friend. Her husband just passed away. Eric Ross? He went to school at Timber Creek High, too. But he was a few years ahead of me."

Logan nodded. Eric had babysat him and Kyla, his little sister, when they were kids. Eric had been older than him by a few years, but he'd always been a sort of hero to Logan, and he'd looked up to him long after graduation. "I knew Eric,"

Logan said. "Cancer is such an asshole." He shook his head. "But it's good you can be here for Drew. It's so terrible."

"You know Drew?"

He shrugged. "Only in the sense that she is—or was—Eric's wife. I don't really know her, though. I was at the memorial service. It was…." He let his thought trail off. They didn't need to stand in the aisles of the grocery store discussing something so terrible. "Anyway, I bet Drew really appreciates you being here. How's she doing? I know that's a stupid question, but…"

"It is." Amber nodded. "But it's a caring question, too. She'll be okay."

"I believe that," Logan said with a kind smile. "How long are you planning on staying?" He surprised himself by asking the question. "Are you headed back to…" He realized he didn't know anything about her or where she was from. "Well, are you headed back in a bit?"

A shadow crossed her face and her control slipped a little, reminding Logan of the way he'd stumbled across her, looking as if she were on the verge of a panic attack.

"No," she said after a moment. "At least, not right away. I'll stay as long as she needs me and now it looks like I need to keep an eye out for my dad as well."

"Your dad?" Alarm bells went off in his head, warning Logan not to get involved, but he couldn't help it. "Is he okay?"

"He's fine. Well, I hope he is." She groaned and rolled her eyes. "It's a long story, but I think he might be being taken advantage of. He seems to have gotten involved in some sort of horse therapy thing. I'm not exactly sure what it's all about, but from the little I know, he's spending a lot of time *volunteering*. And hopefully he's not spending all his money, too. He's retired and while he's certainly not poor, I don't want to see him giving all his money away to some sort of circus operation, or hocus-pocus thing."

As she spoke, Logan could feel his blood pressure rising. She was ranting on and on about something she clearly knew nothing about.

Logan's feelings warred with each other. The need to defend his horses and what he was trying to do was strong, but he also didn't trust himself not to say something he would regret. Instead, he gritted his teeth and looked at the floor. If Amber noticed, she didn't say anything. Likely because she was too busy disparaging his life's work.

"I can't stand it when these types of places pray on elderly people because they don't know any better or they're lonely," she continued. "I mean, have you ever heard of anything so ridiculous? Horse therapy? What the hell is—"

"I think maybe you shouldn't talk about something you have no idea about," he interrupted, finally having enough. Logan did his best to control the anger in his voice, but he knew it was a losing battle. "I have, in fact, heard of equine therapy and I don't think it's ridiculous at all. Have you done any actual research into it, or are your thoughts on it all based on your totally inaccurate and uneducated opinions?"

Amber took a step back. Her mouth opened and closed, but it only took her a moment to regain her composure. "Who do you think you are, speaking to me like that?"

A number of replies came to mind, but instead of speaking them, Logan squeezed his lips together and shook his head. It wasn't worth it to get into an argument here in the middle of the store. Particularly with this woman, who obviously wasn't afraid of confrontation. It wouldn't end well and he had to be professional. No wonder Joseph was so worked up over his daughter. She was definitely a piece of work.

Without saying another word, he turned and walked away, leaving her no doubt fuming behind him.

Chapter Four

CHRISTY THOMAS HAD NEVER BEEN SO exhausted. Or so happy. It had only been about a month since she and her husband Mark had officially adopted their sweet little baby girl, but the moment she'd held Mya in her arms, Christy had felt a completeness that had been missing before.

Despite the stressful circumstances leading up to the adoption, Christy was adapting to motherhood with ease. But she could definitely do with more sleep. She'd put on two different shoes before leaving the house that morning and had to double-check and then triple-check the diaper bag to make sure she'd remembered to prepare a bottle for Mya because she couldn't seem to actually remember.

It felt like a miracle that Christy was able to get to the park on time to meet her friends for a Saturday morning catch-up.

"You made it," Amber called as she pushed the stroller toward the bench where she and Drew were sitting, watching Austin play on the slide. Amber got up to offer Christy her seat and peek into the baby seat at a sleeping Mya. "She's so sweet."

"She is so sweet," Christy agreed. "Especially when she's

sleeping." She smiled. "And what do you mean, I made it? Of course I made it."

"I was just teasing." Amber laughed. "You really are rocking motherhood like no one else."

"As if we're surprised." Drew spoke up. "You were born to be a mother. We always knew you'd handle it like a pro."

Christy smiled and accepted her friends' compliments. It had never been a secret that all Christy wanted was to be a mother. She'd been preparing her entire life to fill her house with the sound of little feet running around but a struggle with infertility had left her devastated, and the accompanying stress had almost fractured their marriage. *Almost.*

Now Mark and Christy were stronger than ever, and after a little bit of soul searching, they'd readjusted the way they thought their life would look, and were embracing this new version. And they'd never been happier.

"Thanks, ladies," Christy said after a moment. "It's certainly not easy." She tipped her head to Drew. "You must remember those early days with Austin."

Drew shook her head. "No way. I completely blocked them. Besides, Eric did a lot of the—" Tears sprang to her friend's eyes the moment she mentioned her deceased husband's name and Christy instantly felt terrible.

"I'm sorry, Drew. I—"

"No. It's fine." She nodded sharply. "I'm fine. Besides, soon it will be Cam's turn to remember late-night feedings. She obviously blocked it out, too, if she was willing to do it again after fifteen years."

As if mentioning her name had summoned her, a moment later Cam walked up to the bench, holding a tray of drinks. "Sorry I'm late. I brought tea and coffee. I should have known Daisy's Diner would be crazy on a Saturday. What will be my turn to remember?"

"Motherhood." Amber laughed, the only one of the group

who was not a mother and as far as Christy knew, never wanted to be.

Cam's free hand rested on her stomach that was just starting to swell. "I'm already a mother, remember?"

"That's just it," Drew said. "I was just saying that I'd blocked all of those late nights and days on end with no real sleep, and I thought maybe it had been awhile for you too, and you'd maybe blocked out what it was like to have a little one."

"Are you kidding?" Cam laughed. "Absolutely, I blocked it out. Otherwise I'd never have done it again." She was kidding; they all knew it. Cam had a beautiful, if not somewhat challenging teenage daughter from her first marriage, but after reconnecting with her high school sweetheart and the love of her life, Evan, they'd found themselves pregnant and couldn't be happier about the new addition, even if it did mean they were postponing their wedding.

The friends settled in to the park, taking turns holding baby Mya and pushing Austin on the swing. Christy couldn't remember a time she'd ever been happier. Finally having the baby she'd longed for, and having all her best friends back in town: everything was perfect.

The moment she allowed herself to think that, she felt a flash of guilt. Everything was *not* perfect. The reason all of her friends were back in Timber Creek was because something had gone wrong for each of them in their own lives. Cam had gone through a terrible divorce, Drew had returned so her husband could have his final few days surrounded by family and friends and she was now a tragically young widow, and Amber…well, besides Amber coming home to help Drew, Christy didn't know why she was back in town. Maybe that really was all there was to it, but Christy's instincts told her there was more to the story.

"She seems to be doing better," Christy said about Drew

when the woman got up to help Austin with the monkey bars. "It's good to see her out of the house."

"It is," Amber agreed. "I mean, I don't really know what to expect in these situations, but at least she's not spending all her days in bed anymore. She even took Austin to school yesterday. It was his first week."

"That's right," Cam said. "I'm glad she has you." She took a sip of her tea. "I'm glad they both have you."

"It really is great that you can be here for them," Christy said, seeing an opening to finally find out what was going on with Amber. "And even better that you managed to make the move so quickly."

That was an understatement. Amber had arrived in town for Eric's funeral and that same day had announced that she'd be moving back to Timber Creek and in with Drew without even going back to San Francisco to pack her things. Amber always did have a way of making things happen, but even for her, that was fast and she never had explained to anyone how she'd been able to make that happen with her high-powered job. There was definitely more to the story.

Amber was an expert at managing her emotions, but Christy was paying close attention and she didn't miss the way her friend's mouth turned down into a quick scowl for just a moment. She didn't answer right away, so Christy pushed. "I mean, you've never really said, Amber. Did you take a leave of absence from your job or…well…I guess I'm just wondering what happened in San Francisco? Was there a man?"

Amber almost spat out her coffee. "A man?"

It was a bit of a stretch, as Christy had never known her friend to have a boyfriend or a relationship at all. But she'd always held out hope that Amber would find someone and settle down.

"There was definitely not any man involved in me leaving San Francisco."

"Then what happened?" It was Cam who asked and Amber, who was clearly growing uncomfortable, shifted her gaze to her. "We've all been so wrapped up in our own lives, I can't believe we haven't talked about what's going on with yours."

"It's fine." Amber's lips pressed into a thin line and the narrowing of her eyes were a clear indicator to anyone paying attention that, despite what she was saying, it was definitely not *fine.*

"What's fine?" Drew returned and stared at each of the women in turn. Her eyes finally landed on Amber, her eyes wide in question. "What are you guys talking about?"

"Nothing," Amber said sharply. She shot Christy a look to make it clear the subject was closed.

But as far as Christy was concerned, the subject was *far* from closed.

"We're talking about Amber," Christy said definitely.

"No." Amber's voice was tightly controlled. "We're not because there's nothing to talk about." She stared at Christy. "Really," she said. "There's not."

"You do know that none of us believe that?" Cam tilted her head with the rhetorical question.

"It's true," Christy agreed. "You loved your job." She knew she was pushing too hard, but what kind of friend would she be if she didn't try to get to the bottom of whatever was going on? "If something is—"

"I just couldn't do it anymore, okay?" Amber jumped up from her seat and threw her coffee in the trash bin. "I needed a change. A break. And I'm taking it. I'm here and I don't know why that's so goddamn hard for everyone to accept."

It wasn't normal. That's why it was hard for them to accept it. Amber *never* needed a break. She excelled with a packed schedule. The more balls she had in the air, she faster she juggled. No, something wasn't right. But Christy didn't say any of that because Mya cried out from her baby seat, distracting them all from the conversation.

AMBER KNEW her friends meant well, but she didn't care how well-intentioned their questions were; she didn't want to answer them. There was no way she could explain to them that she hadn't quit her job—she'd been *asked to leave*, which was just a nice way of saying *fired.* There really was no way she could come clean to them about her drug abuse that had landed her in the hospital, which was why she hadn't been able to be there for Drew earlier when her friend was going through the terrible pain of watching her husband pass away.

No.

There was no way she could do any of that. Ever.

It would just have to be her shameful secret because carrying that around with her would be easier than admitting to her friends what she'd done. They'd never look at her the same way again.

Once Christy got the baby calmed down and the conversation shifted safely away from her, she was finally able to take a breath.

Christy and Cam were chatting away about Cam taking baby pictures for little Mya, and Drew had drifted back into her own world where Amber saw her go time and time again. She'd get quiet, and stare out into nothingness. It was heartbreaking to watch her friend go through the grieving process, but Amber wasn't going to push her too hard. Coming out to the park with the ladies on a Saturday was a good first step.

"Drew?" Her friend blinked and looked up to her. "Are you okay to take Austin home? I need to go check on something."

"For sure." Drew nodded and rubbed her hands together.

"I was going to stop by my parents' place anyway. Mom said she made some pies or something. Where are you going?"

Amber shrugged. Ever since hearing that her dad was spending time at a ranch with horses doing some kind of therapy, alarm bells had been going off in her head. The run-in with Logan Myers in the grocery store certainly hadn't helped either. He'd been so rude to her and then he'd stormed off before she even had a chance to challenge him on it.

Even so, she wasn't going to worry about Logan. Not when she had other things to take care of. Like her father. Maybe there was nothing sketchy going on with the ranch, but she'd seen similar situations in San Francisco and sadly, it was all too common for people to take advantage of the elderly. She was definitely not going to let that happen to her dad.

"I was just going to take a drive out to Blackstar," she finally answered.

"The ranch?" Christy turned, suddenly paying attention. "Looking for your very own cowboy?" She wiggled her eyebrows and to her horror, Amber blushed, which was something she never did. "You *are* looking for a cowboy?"

It was no secret that some of Amber's favorite tropes in her romance novels that she loved to devour were cowboys and firefighters, but she'd never actually dated one. She'd never actually dated anyone, unless you counted the occasional, super-brief relationships she'd had.

"I'm not looking for a cowboy."

"Then why did you blush?" Drew winked.

The truth was, she'd blushed because the instant Christy teased her, Amber's thoughts had gone to Logan and the way he'd made her feel in only a few short minutes in the grocery store. Of course, that was after he'd seen her almost have a full-fledged panic attack and before he'd become a total asshole defending the horse thing. But still, even if it was only for a few minutes, Amber had actually thought he was flirting with her. And more than that, she'd liked it.

"I don't know," she lied. "And I'm going to the ranch to check out something that my dad said he's been doing. I want to make sure it's not all bullshit and they're not trying to con him out of all his money. I'm sure it's nothing, but I can't help but check it out." She dusted her hands together and stuck them on her hips. "So I'll talk to you all later, okay?"

"Sounds good," Cam said. "And hey, I was hoping we could get a group together and go listen to Christy sing next weekend at the Log and Jam. I'll text you the details, okay?"

Amber nodded. She'd love to hear Christy sing. She didn't know how the woman still found the time to be in a band while taking care of a newborn, but she couldn't help but be impressed.

"Perfect," she said as she started to walk away. "I'll see you at home, Drew."

A few minutes later, she was in her car, driving through town to the highway that would lead out to Blackstar Ranch. Even as she drove, she couldn't shake the unsettled feeling that had crept over her. Usually being with her friends grounded her, calmed her. Being home in Timber Creek had always been a way for her to relax and center herself.

But it hadn't worked this time. At least not yet. Maybe she needed to settle in a bit more. Or maybe it was time for a new approach at life. After all, she'd always said, if you're not getting the results you want in life, try something new. The only problem was, Amber still didn't know what results she was looking for.

Chapter Five

BY THE TIME Logan had finished touring the ranch and the handful of horses he was using for therapy with Brent Baker, the psychologist from town he'd finally been able to convince to come out and see what he could offer, he was bursting with excitement. To his surprise, Brent had done his research before their meeting and asked all the right questions. He'd spent some time with Chester, Logan's other horse, in the ring and Logan was so confident that it was going well, he'd left Brent and Chester alone to *talk*.

He was dying to ask Brent what he thought about forming a partnership, but Logan forced himself to play it cool. Instead, when they arrived back to the parking lot, and Brent's SUV, he shook the man's hand. "Do you have any other questions I can answer for you before you leave? Or is there anything else you need to see?" The unasked question hung between them: *Do you think it will be a good addition to your practice?*

"I'm very impressed, Logan." Brent smiled and looked around again. "I've been out to Blackstar Ranch a time or two over the years, mostly on school trips if I'm being honest with you, but you've really done something here with these horses and Taking the Reins."

Logan straightened back his shoulders with pride. He'd worked hard to create a space that would be perfect for therapy of all kinds. "Thank you, Brent. I really believe in what we can do out here. Horses are powerful creatures and I'm sure you have some patients who could really benefit from this type of work."

Brent nodded thoughtfully. "I think you might be right."

Logan had to work hard to maintain a professional demeanor when all he really wanted to do was let out a whoop.

"I've really looked into it, and there definitely are some naysayers out there," Brent said. "And I'm sure in a town like Timber Creek, we'll have our fair share."

Logan's thoughts flashed to the run-in he'd had earlier in the week with Amber Monroe. She was certainly a *naysayer* and that was putting it mildly. It was too bad, too, because despite all the reasons he shouldn't have been, he'd been attracted to her striking good looks and cool confidence. But it had been the moment he'd found her vulnerable in the grocery store that really had attracted him to her. As confident and in control as she was, something lurked under the surface that softened her somehow.

It was too bad she turned out to be so damn annoying and confrontational. And that's probably the reason Logan couldn't seem to get her out of his head.

He shook his head and refocused because Brent was still talking and he could not afford to get distracted. Particularly by a woman who was clearly so against what he was trying to do.

"Let me go back to the office," Brent was saying. "I have a few patients I think could really benefit from this type of therapy. I'll reach out to them, and then touch base with you. They'll have to be okay with you acting as a facilitator…"

"Sure. But it's really the horse doing the work. I'd just be there on the sidelines."

Brent nodded and offered him another smile. "I think we might just—"

His voice was lost by the roaring of a vehicle coming up the road and sliding into the parking lot in a whirl of dust and gravel.

"What the—"

Logan turned to glare at the driver of the shiny black SUV who displayed such poor manners driving into the yard so rudely. But before he could say anything, the dust settled and he got a clear look at the driver.

Amber Monroe.

"Shit," he muttered under his breath.

"Pardon?"

Logan shook his head and turned quickly back to Brent. "It's nothing." He started to walk toward the door of Brent's vehicle and hoped he wasn't coming off as rude. But he needed to get the man out of there before he met one of Timber Creeks' biggest naysayers of equine therapy. Because he had no doubt that if Amber started spouting off the way she had the other day, it would not be a good thing for their tentative partnership. "How about you give me a call later once you have some potential clients lined up and we'll work out a schedule?"

If Brent thought he was being rushed out of there, he didn't show it. He shook Logan's hand once more, got into his vehicle and drove out of the yard.

Logan didn't even wait for Amber to get out of the car before he turned and walked back toward the barn in an effort to ignore her. He didn't know why she was there, but it couldn't be good. And if she was looking for a confrontation, he sure as hell wasn't going to have it right there in the parking lot.

"Hey!" He heard her voice behind her and kept walking.

He'd almost reached the fence where Peanut and Chester were grazing on the other side, when he heard her voice again. "Hey! I'm talking to you."

There wasn't much help for it. With a sigh, he turned around, leaned his arms back against the fence, and faced Amber Monroe.

AMBER HAD USED the short drive to Blackstar Ranch to get herself fired up once again at the idea that her dad was being swindled out of his retirement funds. Her resolve to confront the person in charge of the operation fluttered momentarily when she'd seen the back side of a cowboy walking away and toward the barn. She hated to admit it, but she'd always had a soft spot for cowboys. At least the romance novel, fantasy version of them.

When she lost herself between the pages of her beloved books, her heroes of choice were either cowboys or firefighters, because it just didn't get sexier than that. Of course, it had always been fantasy, but there was nothing wrong with that. Not really.

She was sure the man had seen her pull into the parking lot. How could he not have? But he'd turned and walked away before she could even get her car into park and open the door. Irritation flared through her. If this was indicative of everything else at Blackstar Ranch, her instincts had been spot-on.

"Hey!" she called out to the cowboy, but if he heard her, he didn't even slow down.

With a groan in frustration, Amber gritted her teeth and started off after him. It was a good thing it was Saturday and she'd opted for jeans, a blouse, and boots instead of her usual attire because even though her clothes were far from ideal for a ranch setting, at least she wouldn't sprain her ankle trying to get some answers.

"Hey!" she called again. "I'm talking to you."

This time she saw him pause; his broad back stiffened at the sound of her voice. Amber tried desperately not to notice the way the man's jeans hugged him, or the way his plaid shirt strained across his defined shoulders. She shook her head in an effort to clear it. *What was wrong with her?* She'd never before allowed herself to be distracted when she was on a case. And that's how she needed to look at this situation. Just another case she needed to win.

But when the man finally turned around, that thought went right out the window as her breath caught in her throat.

"Logan?"

Annoyingly, Amber was aware that her voice had squeaked and his name had sounded strangled and twisted.

She cleared her throat and tried again. "Logan Myers?"

He nodded and tipped his hat. "Afternoon, Amber."

Dammit if she didn't want to swoon, just a little bit. *How had she not known Logan was a cowboy?*

No. He wasn't a cowboy. He was arrogant, and rude *Little* Logan Myers who had confronted her in the grocery store earlier that week. There was *no* way she should be feeling anything except annoyance.

Period.

And she wasn't.

"What are you doing here?"

He winked and tipped his cowboy hat. "I run this hocus-pocus operation."

"What…you…you what?" Amber tripped over her words and was instantly annoyed with herself for it. It was so much harder to concentrate than it used to be. She squeezed her eyes and gave herself a moment before looking at him and trying again. "You run this? The ranch?"

"No." He shook his head. "The equine therapy program, Taking the Reins, that your father is volunteering and participating with. I lease the space from Ruby. At least for now."

Amber worked quickly to process what she was hearing. The last thing she'd expected was to see Logan there. Naturally, she hadn't known what to expect. But it most definitely was *not* Logan dressed like a cowboy who could have come straight off the cover of the novel she currently had stuffed under her pillow.

"Is there something I can help you with?"

Amber realized Logan had already asked her a question and instead of paying attention, she'd been standing there, letting herself think about him in a completely inappropriate way. She cleared her voice and tried to appear way more in control than she felt. "Yes. I came to see exactly what is going on here." She straightened and crossed her arms over her chest. "I want to make sure my father isn't being taken advantage of."

Logan shook his head and didn't bother to hide the grin as he did so. "I'd be happy to show you anything you'd like to see."

Was he trying to flirt with her in an effort to distract her? She wouldn't rise to the bait.

"Good." She pressed her lips into a line and waited for him to say more. *What was it about this man that threw her off-balance?* He stared at her for a long moment, his lips twitching into a smile. But still he didn't say anything. "Is now a good time?" she finally asked.

"Oh." He pretended to be surprised and Amber's annoyance grew stronger. "You wanted to check things out now?"

She tilted her head and glared at him.

"Okay, okay." He laughed and waved his hand in a gesture for her to follow. "Let's start in the barn."

LOGAN COULDN'T HELP IT. Amber was way too easy to get worked up. She'd struck him as being the completely-in-control type and as much as she'd irritated him the other day with her judgments and assumptions, he couldn't help but enjoy watching her get flustered.

Besides, she was cute when she was frustrated.

Not that he was paying attention to that.

She was also a giant pain in the ass who could make way too much trouble for him and his horses if she wanted to. And there was no way he was going to let that happen. Which was why he'd decided to play nice.

It might not have been the only reason, but it was the only one he'd admit to.

"Let's start in the barn."

"The barn?"

"It is a ranch, after all." He nodded and once again had to stifle a smile. "We do keep the horses in the barns."

He started walking in the direction of the open barn doors, knowing she'd follow. Sure enough, a moment later, she was next to him.

"I understand that horses are kept in barns, but that's not what I want to see. I want to see this—"

"Hocus-pocus?" Logan stopped walking and stared at her. "That is what you called it, isn't it?"

She had the decency to look embarrassed, but only for a minute. "Look." She crossed her arms again. "I'm not going to apologize for the other day in the grocery store."

"I didn't ask you to."

"Good."

"But I am going to ask you to keep an open mind now that you're here. You're welcome to form all the opinions you want after I've shown you what I'm trying to do here. Deal?"

For a second, Logan thought she was going to argue again. Instead, she nodded. "Deal."

"Good. Now," he said again. "Let's start in the barns."

HE GAVE her an abbreviated version of the tour he'd just given Brent Baker, and just like before, Logan wound up leaning on the fence rails of the ring where Peanut and Chester were waiting. "These are the two horses I'm using right now," he told Amber, who, had much to his surprise, listened with what seemed like an open mind throughout the tour. "I have a few more, but I don't need them quite yet."

"Okay." She stared out over to the animals for a moment. "I still don't understand. What do they do? I mean, what do you do with them?"

Logan beamed. "That's the beauty of the entire program. The horses just *are.*"

"They *are?*"

He nodded. "You see, horses are incredibly in-tune animals and they can pick up on the feelings and emotions of humans. Even when the person themselves may not understand what they're feeling. The horse picks up on it and reacts."

"That doesn't make sense."

"It does." He smiled. "For example, let's say someone is struggling with anger about something they've gone through or are going through. The horse will sense that anger and might become difficult themselves, or obstinate. Through dealing with the animal, the client can recognize what's going on within themselves. Their self-awareness actually grows and soon, they're able to find strategies to communicate more effectively. When the animal responds the way they want it to, they know they're on the right track."

"That sounds…"

Logan held a hand up. "I know…it sounds kind of crazy at first. But it really is one of those things. You need to experience it to really believe it."

Amber turned away from the horses and looked at him. "Did you experience it?"

The question was so blunt and straightforward, it took him off guard. "Excuse me?"

"Did you experience it? This *magic* with the horses? Is that how you got involved with it?"

He could have lied. He could have said that he'd read about it, or heard about it from a friend who'd tried it. But the question was so honest and nonjudgmental that he decided to answer it honestly. "I did." He nodded slowly. "A few years ago, I was in a very different place and I don't think it's too much to say that the horses saved my life."

Her eyes widened, but she didn't say anything for a moment. Instead, she nodded slowly. "Can I try it?"

Of all the questions he'd been expecting her to ask, that wasn't one of them.

"I mean…I—"

"Of course." He recovered from the unexpected question and moved quickly before he changed his mind. "Come on." Logan ducked through the rails and stood on the other side of the fence. When Amber didn't move right away, he held out his hand for her and guided her through as well.

"There's really nothing too it," he said as they approached Chester. "He's a good boy and loves to be patted. Start slow with him and maybe just talk to him for now."

They stopped in front of the horse, who nuzzled Logan's hand in greeting.

"What do I say?"

"Whatever you want." Logan smiled. "Chester here is a great listener. And don't worry about me. I'll be over there."

Logan pointed to the other side of the ring where Peanut was hanging out. "It's just the two of you."

Amber nodded and Logan couldn't help but notice how apprehensive she was. Gone was the tough-girl act. She actually seemed to be open to the *hocus-pocus,* even if it was fleeting. It was a very big step.

Just as he promised, Logan left her alone with the horse. He did his best to be unobtrusive as he talked to Peanut and moved her around the back half of the ring. But he couldn't help but notice Chester's mild noises of protests, and when he snuck a glance in their direction, the way both woman and horse stood stiffly, staring at each other. The horse was definitely picking up on something in Amber, and if he had to guess, it was a whole lot more than merely her skepticism. Logan had no idea what it was that Amber needed to work out, but it was clear that it was something big.

Chapter Six

IT WAS ALMOST a week after their play date in the park. Christy had changed her mind on which outfit baby Mya should wear for her photoshoot at least four times, so before Cam arrived with her camera, she simply laid out all her choices and waited for her friend to help her make the decision.

"Nothing," Cam said without even looking at Christy's carefully selected choices. "A newborn baby shoot is best done with just the birthday suit. Except for maybe that beautiful blanket your mom crocheted. And I have a few little accessories," she added.

"But Mya's already almost two months old. She's not totally a newborn. Will it still work the same way? I should have done it sooner." She rubbed her forehead. "Did I totally screw this up and miss an important milestone?"

"Oh my goodness, Christy. Not at all." Cam smiled and bent to put a soft kiss on the baby's forehead. "There aren't many new moms who can get organized enough in the first week or two of having a baby to get photos done. This is the perfect age and you are well within the time frame of newborn. She's perfect."

"She is pretty perfect, isn't she?" Christy glowed and focused on the baby, who never failed to make her heart flip. She'd waited so long for the dream of motherhood to come true. So long that she didn't think it actually would ever happen. And then it had, in the most unexpected way.

After so many years of it just being her and Mark, her high school sweetheart, their family was finally complete when one of Mark's patients, a teenage mother who was in way over her head, offered her baby girl up for adoption. The last few weeks had been a whirlwind and Christy was both exhausted and completely overwhelmed. She'd also never been happier.

"She's amazing," Cam agreed. "And she'll be a total star in her very first photo shoot. Are you ready to get started?"

"We better," Christy said. "Before she gets fussy."

As it turned out, Cam was right and Mya was a complete star for her first photo shoot. They moved her into a number of cute positions, each one more adorable than the next. And Mya didn't fuss one time. In fact, she finally fell asleep and Christy's heart almost completely melted as Cam caught the final few shots with her baby wrapped up tight in a cocoon with one perfect daisy lying next to her.

An hour later, with Cam's equipment tucked away, and Mya sleeping soundly in her bassinet, the two women sat at the kitchen table, sipping tea.

"I can't believe you're ready to do a gig tomorrow already," Cam said to her friend. "Have you even had time to rehearse since Mya's come along?"

Christy smiled. There was one thing she enjoyed talking about more than her little family and that was her brand-new singing career. "The guys have been great," she said. "I've been writing songs faster than I thought possible. I mean, there's a lot of time in the middle of the night when I'm up with Mya feeding her and rocking her back to sleep."

Cam laughed. "I never would have thought of that as productive time."

"It's not for much more than composing in my head," Christy agreed. "But maybe there's something about the middle of the night, for me. I don't know. But whatever it is, the words are just coming to me and as soon as I get the guys the songs, Josh puts it to music and they start rehearsing. I've only been able to join them a few times, but I think we're ready to showcase some of our new stuff. Besides, we're hoping to record a live demo that we can shop out to a few agents on the coast."

"Wow." Cam shook her head and took another sip of her tea. "You really do amaze me. And I, for one, cannot wait to hear you perform again. I think we're all going to be there."

"Even Drew?" Just like the others, Christy was worried about her friend. Not that anyone expected her to be able to bounce back from the devastation of losing her husband, so quickly. But Christy would be lying if she said she hadn't missed Drew's smile and the light that was normally so present in her eyes.

"She said she was coming," Cam said. "And I have a feeling that Amber will make it happen."

Christy laughed. Amber was a force to be sure, but her laughter died when she thought about her friend and how she, too, didn't seem to be quite right. "Have you noticed anything strange with Amber lately?"

Cam sipped her tea and didn't answer right away. "Besides the fact that she's not working?"

"You're right," Christy agreed. "That's strange enough. But there's something else. She hasn't been quite right since she was here for the reunion party, don't you think?"

Cam thought about it for a minute. "You might be right. I

guess I just thought it was because she wasn't working. I don't think Amber actually knows how to take a vacation. Do you think she's going to go back to work?"

Christy shrugged. "She hasn't said anything to me about it but then again, I haven't asked. I was actually going to see if she might help Mark and me put together a will." She glanced toward the sleeping baby. "I mean, now that we have Mya, if anything were to happen…"

"I totally get it." Cam nodded. "I've been meaning to get mine updated, too. Maybe I'll wait until…" Her hand rubbed her stomach, which was starting to bulge in the cutest way. Christy felt that old familiar pain of jealousy that she'd likely never carry her own child, but it was short-lived. Things changed. And so did the way she felt about them.

"Do you think she'll mind?" Christy asked. "I mean, I'll pay her. But I don't want to assume that…well, I don't want to assume anything. It's just so strange…" She let the thought trail off and shook her head to clear it.

"I totally get it," Cam agreed. "I mean, we've all changed a lot over the years, but I didn't think Amber would ever change so much that she'd leave her job. I mean, that's just not normal. It's almost like there's a—"

"Reason," Christy finished for her. "There has to be a reason."

The conversation changed and drifted away from their friend, but Christy couldn't shake it. It was no secret that she'd been wrapped up in her own life for the last little while, but that didn't mean that she planned to ignore what was going with Amber forever. There was definitely a reason Amber had left her job and moved back home. She had no idea what it could be, but she knew Amber, and that meant it had to be one very good reason.

And she was going to find out what it was.

THE NEXT NIGHT, the Log and Jam was packed by the time Amber and Drew walked through the front doors. Amber hadn't worried about getting there early to save seats because Christy had promised reserved seating right up front. She said it was because she wanted to make sure there were friendly faces in front of her in case her new songs tanked, but from what Amber heard, Timber Heart wouldn't have any problem with the crowd. In the short time they'd been performing together, they already had a small but loyal fan base. There wouldn't be any disappointed fans in the audience tonight, Amber was sure of it.

"I can't believe how busy it is in here." Drew twisted to the side to squeeze past a group of men. "Ben must be run off his feet tonight."

Ben Ross, the owner of the Log and Jam and an old classmate of theirs. He also happened to be Drew's brother-in-law, and unbeknownst to Drew, had held onto a fierce crush for her back in the day. But that was before Eric had asked her out and she'd started happily dating his older brother. To Amber's knowledge, Drew had never found out about Ben's crush. Not that it mattered anymore. That was an entire lifetime ago.

"There he is." Amber raised her arm in the air and waved to Ben at the bar. "Let's go say hi."

Drew nodded and led the way. "Hey. It's crazy in here." She had to yell to be heard.

"I know, right?" Ben shook his head, but he was in his element. The Log and Jam had been a huge success from the moment he opened. Ben had captured the right mixture of small-town charm with the decor of antiques and rustic wood finishing, combined with excellent food, delicious drinks, and even better service. "I wish I could take all the credit. But this town loves Timber Heart."

"This town loves you, too." Drew reached across the bar and squeezed Ben's hand. Amber didn't miss the sad smile he gave her in return, but she didn't seem to notice.

"I'm glad you got her out of the house," he said to Amber instead. "Drew needs something to smile about. And I think I can help by getting you lovely ladies some drinks."

"Nothing for me." Amber waved her hand. "I'll be happy with a soda water."

"Glass of white for me, please, Ben."

"I'll bring it out to you. Are you sure, Amber?"

She nodded. There had been a few comments on the fact that she wasn't drinking much lately, and it wasn't that she felt pressure to partake; it was more that she didn't want to have to explain her choices to her friends. How could she tell them that sometimes when she had a few glasses of wine, she felt the familiar tug in her brain to follow it up with an Adderall to clear the fuzziness? The uppers and downers had started to swim together for her at the end, and one or two glasses of wine wasn't worth risking any of the old feelings. Especially when she was already feeling anxious.

It had been a few days since she'd been out to Blackstar Ranch, where she'd been so determined to confront the people in charge. Instead, she'd met Logan and instead of confronting him, she'd surprised herself by letting him show her what he actually did there. More to her surprise, she'd *tried* it.

Amber had been out with the horse on her own for what felt like only a few minutes, but there was no denying that something had happened while she stood there with Chester. She felt something…shift. She couldn't even put it into words and it sounded so ridiculous to think that just talking to a horse had made her feel anything at all, especially to her black-and-white brain. But even so, the feeling had stayed with her all week. She couldn't stop thinking about it and it had left her a little unsettled.

"Amber?"

She blinked hard and Drew came back into focus.

"Are you ready to sit down?"

Amber nodded and made herself smile. If she was going to have a good time with her friends, she needed to stop thinking about her own troubles for a little bit and focus on them. Especially Drew. It was the first social outing she'd made since Eric died, and even though she didn't want to make a big deal out of it, Amber knew it was. "Of course," she said. "Let's go see who's here."

Without waiting for a response, Amber took Drew's hand and led her toward the front of the bar and the stage where the instruments had been set up and were ready for the band. The table in front held a reserved sign and Mark, Christy's husband, was already seated, front and center.

"Hey." He rose from his seat in greeting. "You made it."

"Of course we did." Amber squeezed Drew's hand. She wasn't going to say anything about how only an hour before, Drew had tried to change her mind about going out. "We wouldn't miss it." They took their seats across from Mark. "I've been looking forward to this since I heard Christy was singing again. Who's watching the baby?"

Mark launched into a story about how reluctant Christy had been to leave Mya with both grandmothers, who were doing double-duty. He smiled and laughed about how hard it had been for his wife to say good-bye for a few hours, but Amber could see the love radiating out of him.

What would it be like to have that too?

The thought hit her so unexpectedly, it took her off guard for a moment. But instead of completely dismissing the idea the way she had her entire life, she let it linger in her mind for a moment. It might not be too bad at all to have someone look at her the way Mark looked at Christy. To have a real man's arms around her at night instead of just her steamy books to keep her company.

No, the thought wasn't half bad. Not at all.

"Hey." Drew snapped her fingers in front of Amber's face. "I thought I was supposed to be the one who's all out of it tonight?"

Guilt immediately flashed through Amber but she recovered quickly. "Well, A…you're not supposed to be out of it at all tonight. You're supposed to have a good time with your friends and that's just what you're going to do."

"And B?"

Amber blinked hard. "And B…well, B is that I was just wondering where everyone was."

Drew gave her a look that made it clear that she didn't believe her at all. Fortunately, before she could press, Mark spoke up.

"Cam and Evan should be here any minute. And Aaron and my running partner, Alicia, should be here soon, too."

"That sounds like a setup?" Amber wiggled her eyebrows and Mark laughed.

"I'm pretty sure that Christy did all the setting up on that one. But we'll see. I'm not sure what's going on there."

"It looks like we have more seats than that." Drew pointed to the big table. "Are you expecting anyone else?"

Mark shrugged. "You never know, right? I put out the invite to a bunch of people, so I thought it best to keep a few extra spots just in case. I'm just so proud of her, you know? I couldn't stop inviting people."

Drew laughed. "We're all so proud of her. I can't blame you at all."

After a few minutes, Ben arrived with their drinks, and when Cam and Evan showed up, followed closely by Aaron and Alicia—who Amber couldn't help but notice sat next to each other—the conversations around them exploded in a cloud of noise.

But one person wasn't joining in the chatter. "Hey." Amber leaned close to Drew's ear and squeezed her arm. "You okay?"

Drew nodded and blinked hard. "I just don't know…I mean, how am I supposed to act?"

Amber's heart broke a little bit more for her friend. "You just act however you want to," she said. "You're surrounded by people who love you and loved Eric. Life goes on, Drew. Eric knew that too. He'd want you to be here having fun and enjoying yourself. You know that. So you feel whatever it is you need to feel, but sweetie…try not to feel bad, okay? You're not doing anything wrong."

Drew nodded and pressed her lips up into a smile, but Amber saw the glimmer of tears in her eyes. She squeezed her friend's arm one more time as the band struck up and Christy's voice came over the speakers.

Chapter Seven

IT HAD BEEN a long day and Logan was exhausted. He'd been called out with the volunteer fire department to respond to a car accident fire west of town, and although it only took a few hours to control the situation and get it cleaned up, it was hard work and the adrenaline rush, compounded after a day of working on the ranch, had left Logan ready for an early night.

But after he showered and was settled into the couch, scrolling through Netflix looking for something mindless he could lose himself in for a few hours, Logan just couldn't settle his thoughts. Memories of Tina and her own accident on the highway outside of town flooded his mind.

It had been years since he'd replayed that night like a bad movie he couldn't forget. Somehow time had lessened the vividness of it all, but after seeing the accident today, where thankfully everyone was okay and walked away, something had triggered for Logan.

If he'd gone with her that day on her trip to Seattle instead of begging off to spend a lazy day with his friends fishing, she wouldn't have been driving alone on the highway late at night, rushing to get home to him instead of spending the night in the city the way she should have. Together, they would have gotten a hotel and she would have been cuddled in his arms instead of driving on that stretch of dark, lonely highway when she fell asleep at the wheel and drove her car into a tree. He should have been fast asleep next to her instead of answering the call on his cell phone that there'd been an accident.

Logan squeezed his head and jumped up from the couch. He couldn't stay there. He was too tired to do anything else, but if he stayed home alone for one more minute, he was going to drive himself crazy with the memories and the guilt.

Normally, the last thing he would want to do was subject himself to a busy bar full of people, but Mark had invited him to the band's performance when he'd run into him in town the other day. And it sure as hell beat the alternative of sitting home alone with nothing to keep him company but Tina's ghost.

Fifteen minutes later, he walked into the Log and Jam and was instantly glad he'd made the choice he had. The music of Timber Heart filled him, with their catchy beats and happy lyrics, and he found himself smiling as he ordered a beer from Ben at the bar.

"Mark has a table up front," Ben told him. "There are a few seats left."

Logan thanked him and pressed through the crowd, some of whom were dancing in the open spaces, until he found the group of people he mostly knew. They hadn't gone to school together, but more and more they were becoming his friends. They were good people.

He spied an open seat. "Is this seat taken?" He slid the chair out.

"I don't think—Logan?"

He blinked and for the first time noticed in the dim lighting that it was Amber Monroe who occupied the seat next to him. "Hi." He smiled and gestured to the seat, doing his best to ignore the way his body reacted to the sight of her. He shouldn't feel anything for her. After all, she did nothing but annoy him and aggravate him. *Mostly*.

"Go ahead." Amber turned her attention back to the band, which gave him the opportunity to watch her. Her fingers bounced along the table in time to the music and her body swayed just slightly, as if she wasn't willing to completely give herself over to the beat. She was mesmerizing, and Logan was so lost in watching her he hardly noticed when the song ended.

It wasn't until Amber cleared her throat that he realized she'd caught him staring at her. "Hi."

"You said that already."

"It never hurts to say it again." He smiled and to his surprise, she smiled back. He hadn't been sure how she would react to him after being at the ranch. After her time with Chester in the ring, she'd been quieter and way less opposed to the idea of equine therapy. In fact, she hadn't said one word about *hocus-pocus* or voodoo or whatever else she thought about what he did with the horses. She hadn't said much at all, really. But he could tell she'd been impacted by her time with Chester. "I'm glad I ran into you, actually."

Her face changed; the smile faded and her lips pressed into a thin line. It had been the wrong thing to say.

She turned away as the band struck up a new song and he didn't push the conversation. This time while Timber Heart was playing, Amber didn't bounce to the music. Her fingers didn't tap on the table. Instead, she held herself stiffly, as if she knew he was watching her.

"Aren't they great?" The moment the band signed off to take a break, Mark turned to face the table and share his enthusiasm for his wife's performance. "They're recording for a demo tonight. Hey, Logan. I didn't see you come in."

Logan waved his hand in greeting. "I snuck in during the last set," he said. "And they are awesome. I'm glad I came." He turned to look at Amber as he spoke, but she wasn't looking at him; she'd excused herself from the table and was moving quickly away from him into the crowd.

Without saying a word to anyone at the table, he got up and started after her. He couldn't be sure she was avoiding him, but he was definitely going to find out. "Hey." He reached out and grabbed her arm before she could disappear into the crowd again. She spun around, her eyes narrowed, but he didn't let go of her arm. "Can I talk to you?"

She didn't respond, but she stiffened under his hand.

"I swear, I don't bite." He held up his free hand in surrender, but was unwilling to release her completely. "I just wanted to talk to you."

THERE WAS no good reason for her to keep running away from Logan. At least not one that she could say out loud without sounding like a complete idiot.

Or coming clean.

Either way, it wasn't an appealing choice.

She stared at him for a moment, assessing him and trying to ignore the heat that his hand on her skin was sending through her. Finally, she nodded. "Okay."

His smile was so disarming that she almost forgot herself. Almost.

"You left so quickly the other day I never got to ask you what you thought about Chester?"

She blinked.

"The horse," he clarified, as if she didn't know exactly what he was talking about. "You didn't tell me what you thought about the whole thing."

What she felt about it? She'd felt a lot of things talking to the horse. Mostly she'd felt relief and an unburdening in a way she never could have imagined. She hadn't intended to say the things she'd said either, but after a few minutes, the words just came out.

More importantly, the horse hadn't judged her when she'd told him about her pills and her addiction. He hadn't turned away from her when she told him about how she'd lost her job because she'd let her addiction get out of hand. Or how it had almost killed her. Talking to the horse, she'd felt better than she had in a very long time and all week she'd been trying to figure out how she could get out to Blackstar Ranch again and spend time with Chester without coming off like a total and complete hypocrite.

But she couldn't tell Logan any of that.

Could she?

"Can we talk outside?" She surprised herself when the question popped out of her mouth. And she was even more surprised when she took Logan's hand and led him through the crowded room to the cool fall air outside.

The minute she breathed in the crisp mountain air that already felt like winter was on the way, she felt emboldened. Before she could chicken out or let her pride get in the way, Amber turned to him. "I'd like to see Chester again."

"You would?"

"Don't make me beg."

"I wouldn't." He shook his head quickly and the smirk that had appeared, disappeared. "Not at all. I'm just surprised is all. I thought you—"

"Look." She held up a hand. "I know what you thought I thought. But I don't think that anymore. At least, I don't know if I do. I don't think I do." She closed her eyes for a moment and tried again. "It's been a hard year." Her voice dropped. "And I understand if you say no. After all, I wasn't very supportive of my dad helping out and…I know I said some things…"

"It's okay."

She continued as if she hadn't heard him. "I still don't know if I believe in what you're doing, but maybe I just need a little more time to make up my mind."

"You can have all the time you need." He was so calm, so nonjudgmental, and so understanding—all of which was completely the opposite of the reaction she'd expected from him—that Amber was totally thrown off guard.

She scanned his face for any hints that he might be messing with her but there was nothing but openness and kindness there.

"Really?"

Logan reached out and took her hands, which should have felt a little too forward, but for whatever reason, felt like the most natural thing in the world. "Amber, I'm not going to pretend to know why you need to talk to Chester, but I could see from the few minutes you had the other day that it was helpful. And that's all I'm trying to do with Taking the Reins. Help. You don't have to tell me anything more."

His presence was so unexpectedly calming that Amber felt if she could just hold his hands forever, everything might be okay. The fact that her opinion had changed so completely about Logan and his horses in only a few days wasn't lost on her. As much as everything in her personality and experience up until now told her to be skeptical about this man and his *therapy*, her heart told her something very different. And maybe it was time she started listening to her heart a little more.

"Thank you," she said after a moment.

"It's nothing." He squeezed her hands and smiled before letting them go. "I'm not a bad person, Amber. And I promise you that I'm not trying to swindle your dad, or you for that matter. I'm just trying to do a little good in a world that could use it. Equine therapy helped me once and I saw an opportunity to do the same for others."

"How did it—"

"You guys are going to miss the show!" Amber's question was lost as Mark opened the door to the pub, and the noise and music from inside spilled out. "Sorry." Mark smiled. "I didn't mean to interrupt—"

"You didn't interrupt anything." Amber pulled back and turned away from Logan. "We were just getting a bit of air."

"Well, hurry up. The second set is about to start." Mark grinned and disappeared back inside.

Amber couldn't help but laugh at his enthusiasm.

"He's pretty excited," Logan said, reading her thoughts. "It's cute."

"It is." Amber moved toward the door. "You coming?"

Logan shook his head, and disappointment flooded through her. "You know what? I think I'll call it a night. It's been a long day."

"Oh yeah?" To her surprise once again that night, Amber was genuinely interested. "The horses keep you running?"

"Cute." He laughed and then shook his head. "But no. It was just a long day. At any rate, I'm beat. I probably should already be in bed. But you make sure you get back out to the ranch, okay?"

She nodded. "I will. And I promise not to be so judgey this time."

"Oh," he added. "Your dad usually comes by on Mondays and Wednesdays. And the occasional Friday, if that matters."

"Okay, but it doesn't matter."

He winked, seeing straight through her lie. Either way, it got a smile out of him before he said goodnight, waved, and walked away, leaving her standing outside the bar and wondering what the hell had just happened.

Chapter Eight

IT TOOK Amber two days to work up the courage to drive back out to Blackstar Ranch again. But the moment she stepped into the ring with Chester and took hold of his reins, the anxiety she'd felt about talking to the horse again melted away.

At first, she just walked with him, gently leading the horse around in a circle. She checked over her shoulder and saw Logan watching her from a distance. He'd promised he'd stay close in case she needed him and to help facilitate things, whatever that meant, but that he wouldn't be able to overhear anything she said to Chester.

It felt different than it had the first time she was there. Now that she knew the very little that she knew, Amber found herself feeling self-conscious saying anything at all.

As if Logan knew what she was struggling with, he called out to her. "Go ahead and talk to him. Chester is a great listener."

The horse neighed and nudged her with his head and Amber laughed. "Okay, okay," she said to the horse. "I'll talk. Is that what you want?"

Chester snorted, which Amber took as an affirmative.

"I don't really know where to start," she said. "I feel kind of stupid talking to you about it all since you probably don't even understand. Well, I know you don't understand what it's like to have a lot of pressure on you." She rubbed the horse's flank and kept walking in a long, slow circle. "For as long as I can remember, there were these expectations on me to be a certain way, to get the right grades, get into the best schools and do something great with my life. And I know what you're going to say," she continued, as if Chester were having an actual conversation with her. "But it wasn't like that with my friends and their parents. Sure, they all had certain expectations on them too. But for me it was different. My mom was dead and I needed to be *someone.*"

As Amber started talking, the words came out in a flood. So quickly she hardly had time to process what she was saying.

"Sometimes when you have that kind of pressure on you, you need a little edge." She swallowed hard. "I guess that's how it all started. I'd read somewhere that ADHD medication was legal and safe and would give me the ability to concentrate and focus like I never had before. So I tried it. And you know what? It was amazing."

Amber remembered those early years when she would buy Tommy's Adderall pills from him in the parking lot behind the football field. Every time she took a pill, she had laser-like focus and could accomplish more in one night than she could in an entire week. She could study longer and harder. Her papers were better, she aced all her exams, and she still had time to head up whatever committee she'd committed to at the time.

They were miracle pills.

"In college, the pills were way easier to get and I even managed to convince the campus doctor that I had ADHD and couldn't focus in class." She stopped walking and turned to stand in front of the horse. "I didn't even think I'd done anything wrong," she told Chester. "I lied to the doctor and instead of feeling bad, I felt like I'd won. And I guess in a way, I had. I graduated with a perfect GPA and had more job offers after school than any of my classmates. Things were pretty perfect."

And they had been perfect. She'd had it all. At least she thought she had. If a high-powered career, expensive apartment, designer clothes, and a fat savings account was having it all, she had it.

Until the day it all crashed down.

"I woke up that morning and I knew something wasn't right," Amber told the horse. Chester whinnied and took a step backward, but Amber pulled him toward her again and kept talking. "My heart was racing and I couldn't stop sweating. But I had an important meeting with a client we'd been trying to lock down for months. I couldn't miss it and I needed to focus. So I took my pills. By then, I needed more than one. Sometimes a few a day. Sometimes more. That day the pills didn't work the way they usually did and I couldn't calm down. I was shaking and my thoughts were so scattered, I could barely form a sentence. And then, in the middle of the meeting…"

Her words drifted away as the horse blurred in her vision. The ground tilted and she looked for something to grab onto. Amber pulled away and the horse stamped his foot. She dropped the horse's reins and started to back away from him. Chester brayed in protest but Amber only barely heard him.

It was happening again. The cold sweats, the increased heart rate, the feeling that she wasn't connected to the earth. Her vision clouded; she couldn't focus on anything. The world started to spin around her. She reached blindly behind her, but the fence rail wasn't there.

Vaguely, she felt herself slipping…falling…

"Whoa. I got you." Strong arms wrapped around her and held her tight. "It's okay, Amber. You're okay. Just breathe."

She did as she was told. One breath. And then another.

She focused on taking one deep breath after another until finally the world around her came back into view. Slowly, she was able to make out the fence, the grass, and the horse standing a few feet away. She blinked hard and looked up at Logan, who still had a tight grip on her.

"Are you okay?"

She pressed her hand over her heart and felt the solid beat in her chest. *It was just a panic attack. That's all it was.*

She nodded. "I'm okay."

"Does that happen often?"

She should have been embarrassed and not that long ago, she would have been. But at that moment, she no longer had the energy to keep pretending.

Amber nodded. "Yes. At least, it used to."

Logan led her to a bench nearby and they sat, but he didn't release her hand. She kept her free hand pressed to her chest and the reassuring steady thump of her heart.

"I'm glad you were here," she said. "Thank you."

"Chester alerted me."

Amber stared at Logan and then at the horse who lingered nearby. "He did?"

"The horses are very in tune. He sensed something was going on. You didn't notice?"

She shook her head.

"Do you want to talk about what happened?"

Amber took another deep breath and gazed out at the field. "Yes." She did want to talk about it. More than that, the *need* to talk surprised her with its intensity. "I was telling Chester everything. It felt good to let it out, to tell someone. You're right—he is a good listener."

"He really is."

Amber managed a smile but it faded when Logan asked, "What was it specifically that triggered you, do you think?"

"I was remembering," she said simply. "It's been easier to block it all out and pretend that nothing happened."

"But something did happen."

It wasn't a question, but she nodded.

"It was in the middle of the most important meeting of my career," she started. "We'd been working on this company for months to sign us on as their corporate legal team. I had them. I was so sure of it. It was going to be the deal that would finally make me partner at the firm."

"And you had a panic attack?"

"Yes." She snort-laughed and shook her head. "Only not really. I've been having these attacks or episodes every once in a while, since college, but this one was different." She looked up and straight into his brown eyes. "They called the ambulance…the doctors called it a *cardiac event*." Question and concern crossed Logan's face. "Caused by drug use and abuse."

THE MINUTE she said the words out loud, Amber felt a mixture of panic and relief. She'd never before told anyone about her Adderall use. Not even her best friends. It wasn't until she was lying in the hospital bed thinking that she might die that she came clean to the doctors.

It felt good to finally let her secret out, but more than the relief, it was terrifying.

What had she done?

"You won't tell anyone, will you?" She jerked up on the bench and stiffened her back. He shook his head, but she hardly noticed as she scanned the horse ring and the yard. "My father? He's not…" Her head turned and her eyes locked on his again. "He's not here, is he?"

"No," Logan said. "He's not here. He hasn't been coming as much lately."

Amber felt a twinge of guilt because that probably had something to do with her.

"And you—"

"No." Logan shook his head. "I won't tell anyone."

Amber searched Logan's face for any kind of indication that he was lying to her or judging her in any way. There was nothing reflected back in his expression but caring, earnest concern, but she also knew it was his job to stay calm.

"Drug abuse?" he asked after a moment.

She nodded slowly.

"What kind of drugs?"

"Adderall." She should just stop talking. She might still be able to walk away without having to tell him too much. "For almost eighteen years."

Why was she still talking?

"I don't understand," Logan said. "Isn't that a medication for—"

"Attention deficit hyperactivity disorder?" She nodded. "Yup. But it's pretty much like legalized speed. By the time I realized that, it didn't matter. I didn't care. I liked the high too much." She shook her head. "No. I *needed* the high."

He opened his mouth but didn't say anything, which was just as well. Amber couldn't seem to stop herself despite knowing that telling her secrets couldn't possibly be a good idea.

"Pretty soon one pill wasn't enough so I needed two, then three, and then I was balancing the high with sleeping pills or alcohol. It was a constant balancing act."

A sob caught in her throat as she remembered the way it felt to be trapped in the web of addiction. The panic that she didn't know how to stop. That she *couldn't* stop. Every single day of her life, she'd been backed into a corner with no way out. Until the day she'd been given a way out.

More like *forced* out.

Would she still be using if she hadn't ended up in the hospital? Would she still be living the same insane life, trying to prove that she could do it all and have it all?

The fact that she didn't really need to ask the question in order to know the answer scared the hell out of her. Especially considering even now that she was back in Timber Creek, she still felt the pull to take one of her little pills. Not every day, but more often than not. Even knowing they could kill her, the desire not to let anyone down was intense.

Despite everything that had happened, she was still trapped.

Tears spilled from her eyes and for once Amber didn't try to wipe them away or stop their flow. She didn't have the energy to keep pretending everything was fine.

"Hey." Logan still held her hand in his and the slight squeeze brought her back to the conversation.

"It's fine." She shook her head and shrugged. "I mean, I didn't die, right?"

"But you did have a heart attack."

"A *cardiac event*," she corrected him with a wry smile. "But yes. As it turns out, taking excessive amounts of what in essence is speed, for almost two decades, isn't good for your heart."

"You don't say?"

Amber laughed.

"It's true. And, something else I learned…apparently having a drug addict on the payroll isn't really what the firm was looking for in a partner, so…"

"They fired you?"

"They suggested I take a leave of absence, but yes. They fired me." Amber let out a long sigh. That had been the hardest part of the whole thing. Not only had she ended up in the hospital, she'd lost the job she'd been working her entire life for. The irony was that she'd taken the pills to get the job and they'd been the reason she'd lost it all.

No. She self-corrected. *She* was the reason she'd lost it all. Her poor decisions. The choice to use was hers and hers alone. She only had herself to blame.

"Anyway…" Amber pulled her hand free of his and immediately missed the steady presence his touch had given her. She ran her hands through her hair and stood. "This was just one of those pesky panic attacks and not a heart thing, so that's good. I guess I was hoping that they would all stop now that I'm not taking the pills. The doctors told me that's a side effect of abusing Adderall. And here I thought I was just panicky." She tried to make a joke, but Logan didn't laugh.

"So, you're not still taking the pills?"

Amber spun to face him. "No. I'm not taking them anymore."

He held up his hands in defense. "I'm not trying to say anything. I was just—"

"Do you really think after almost dying, I'd still be taking them?"

He shrugged. "I've dealt with addicts before."

Anger flared through her veins. "I'm not an addict."

Logan stood so he faced her, but didn't say anything.

"I'm not."

Why was she defending herself? Especially considering she knew that was exactly what she was.

"I'm not like one of the drug addicts you work with out here." She spat the words at him. The anger came hot and fast. On one level, she knew he didn't deserve her vitriol, but she couldn't stop herself. "I'm sure you think that just because you have a few horses and you can get people to talk to them that you think you're a big expert in all of this. Well, you're not."

He shook his head and took a step toward her. "I didn't say I was—"

She held up a hand to ward him off and stepped away. "I don't need this," she said. "I don't need to be here. I don't know why I told you anything at all. It was just…" She closed her eyes and looked down at her feet. "It was a mistake," she said when she looked up again. "It was just a big mistake. All of it. I shouldn't have come here."

"Amber, don't say that."

"No." She shook her head again. The need to get out of there and away from Logan was intense. The need to run and hide was overwhelming her. What was she thinking, coming out to the ranch and talking to a *horse*? "I shouldn't be here." She turned and started to walk back to her car, but Logan's voice stopped her one more time.

"Amber."

She turned.

"Stay." His arms were down by his sides. Unassuming. Unthreatening. *Safe.*

It would be easy to stay there and talk to him. Spill even more of her secrets and finally unload the burden she'd been carrying around for too long.

It would also be incredibly hard.

Too hard.

She looked at him for a long moment. Another tear escaped down her cheek but this time she swiped it away. Without another word, she turned and walked away.

LOGAN DIDN'T THINK she'd actually leave.

It had been hours since the incident with Amber out in Chester's pen and he still couldn't figure out what had happened.

It seemed to him that she'd had a breakthrough with the horse and had finally been able to release some of the pain and hurt she'd been holding onto for so long.

But then…she'd closed right up again.

He'd been over it a hundred times, and he still didn't know what had shifted.

It was late, and he should be asleep. The entire day had been exhausting and the next would be more of the same. He should have been in bed hours ago. Instead, he sat on the old rocker in the corner of his porch and looked out over the ranch. Ruby had let him stay in the old rancher's quarters in exchange for him cleaning it out and putting a fresh coat of paint on the walls. It wasn't much. Barely more than one main room and a small bedroom. But it was his and it left him close to the horses, where he could keep an eye on things.

More importantly, it got him out of town and away from people, where he'd have to make conversation and fend off personal questions about his life.

But that wasn't as big of a problem anymore as it used to be. There'd been a time, shortly after Tina died, when he'd done his best to hide from life and anyone who challenged him to live it. Which was pretty much everyone. But lately, he found himself actually accepting a few invitations, like the one he'd accepted a few nights earlier to go to the Log and Jam. He should probably be thankful that his friends hadn't entirely given up on him.

Logan closed his eyes and let the peace and quiet of the country night air surround him in an effort to clear his thoughts.

Moments later, as if she could read his mind from thousands of miles away, the phone rang, shattering his peace, and there was only one person it could be.

He left his chair outside and snatched up his cell phone on the table just inside the door. Sure enough, his little sister's name and face flashed on the screen. He couldn't help the smile that crossed his face as he took the call.

"Good evening, Kyla," he said into the phone. "Or should I say good morning?"

"I didn't wake you, did I?"

"Nope. I'm just sitting here contemplating life's greatest mysteries."

Her laughter carried across the line and filled his heart. It was almost as good as having her right there in front of him instead of on the other side of the globe. "And did you come up with any solutions, big brother?"

"Not one. But that's okay, that's what keeps things interesting."

"Truth."

"I hope you're calling to tell me you're finally coming home." Logan pushed the screen door and made his way back onto the porch. He already knew what his little sister's answer would be, but it didn't stop him from asking every time he spoke with her. It had already been almost two years since she'd gone backpacking in New Zealand during a summer break from college. Two years since she'd discovered that living in a beach town, and putting all the mechanic skills she'd learned from all those summers working at Junky's, their father's auto shop, was preferable to sitting in a classroom working on the engineering degree their father wanted her to get.

"You know I'm not doing that," she said with a trace of sadness in her voice. "I miss you, though. Have you changed your mind about coming to visit?"

"It's not that I don't want to, sis. But now's not a good time."

"It's never a good time," she moaned. "I'm beginning to think that's just an excuse."

Logan felt a twinge of guilt. "It's not this time," he said. "I promise. Remember when I told you about the ranch and the horses and the business I was starting?"

"Taking the Reins," she said. "I think it's awesome. Are you helping tons of people already? I always knew my big brother could change the world, one troubled soul at a time."

He laughed and shook his head. "I appreciate your faith in me, but it's not quite like that. At least not yet." For the next few minutes, he told her all about his meeting with Brent Baker and how he expected to have more clients any day now.

"I knew you'd make a go of this," Kyla said. "Have you had any actual clients yet? Or are you still waiting?"

He hesitated, unsure of how much he should say about Amber. "Well…I mean, sort of…"

Once again, Kyla's laughter filled the silence. "What's her name?"

"What are you talking about?" There was no way his sister, from all the way on the other side of the world, could have any idea that he had any kind of feelings for Amber. Especially considering he didn't even fully understand them himself. Or for that matter, even recognize them as feelings in that way.

"Is she a client?"

"Not technically." Logan rubbed his temple. He knew exactly how it was going to sound to his sister. "But it's complicated. She's kind of an old school mate and she was coming to check things out because of her father and…well…one thing led to another…not like that…but she spent some time with Chester, and I think it was actually a really good thing. She made a lot of progress. I mean, there's still some work to be done but I think I can—"

"You need to take a step back, brother."

The serious edge in his sister's voice took him off guard. "What are you talking about?"

"You need to remember that you can't fix everyone. That's not your job, Logan. You're a facilitator, right?"

He nodded even though she couldn't see him.

"And you can't get involved with your clients."

"She's not a client." *Was she?* No. Amber was definitely not a client. She was…what *was* she?

"Well, I'm not going to tell you how to live your life."

"Good."

She laughed. "And I'm glad that there's a woman in your life again."

"It's not like that." He jumped up from his chair.

"Okay."

"It's not," Logan insisted. "It's really not."

"Isn't it?"

Damn. Sometimes he hated that his sister knew him so well. They'd always been close, but after Tina died, Kyla had been his rock. Maybe too much. Sometimes he thought that's why she'd moved away, to force him to stand on his own. She was way too smart for her own good sometimes.

"I don't know how it is," he finally admitted. "This woman aggravates the hell out of me, but…"

"You like her."

"I do," he admitted. "There's something about her. Maybe even more so now that I know she's not as hard and cold as she tries to pretend she is."

"Careful."

Logan shook off his sister's warning. "I don't know how to explain it, Kyla, but there's a lot going on with this woman and I think I can—"

"There it is."

"What?" Logan moved to the far end of the porch and looked up at the stars overhead. This far out of town, it was dark enough that they really popped on the night sky. His eyes landed on the Big Dipper. "There *what* is?"

"That's your thing," she said. "You want to fix everything. But you don't have to fix whatever is going on with this—"

"That's not…what the hell are you talking about?"

"Logan, I'm not trying to be a jerk." Her voice was smooth and soft, but it didn't take the sting out of her words. "After Tina died, you…"

"I what?" He already knew what she was going to say.

"You started looking for a way to make things better. And I don't think that's a bad thing, Logan. Not at all. I think what you're doing with the horses is amazing. It really is."

"Then what?"

"I just don't want you to lose yourself. Not now when you're just finding yourself again and starting this new adventure."

He shook his head. "I wouldn't—"

"You would," she interrupted him. "That's just who you are. You care too much. You pretend you don't, but you do." She chuckled and Logan couldn't help but offer up a small smile to the dark night. She was right. He cared way too much, which was why it was safer for him to keep that part buried. "I don't want you to get hurt, Logan. It's not your job to fix anyone. It's your job to *help* them along the path to see their own way. Okay?"

"I hear ya, sis. And don't worry. I have training. I'm not going to get personally involved in a situation with a client." Even as he spoke, he could feel the lie settling inside him. But it wasn't really a lie, was it? Amber wasn't a client. Not really. Besides that, he wasn't personally involved with her.

Not yet.

He pushed that feeling aside for the moment because whatever it was that was going on with Amber was clearly more complicated than he even knew.

"Okay." Kyla sighed. "I won't go there. Not now. Just be careful, okay, Logan? You do know there are women in the world who don't need any actual fixing, right? Like you can have a relationship with a woman who already has it all together. That's a real thing."

He laughed. "But what fun would that be?"

Logan finished his conversation with Kyla, moving on to safer topics, like their dad, who was known in town as Junky, and operated the local auto shop. Kyla had been trying to get him to go and visit her, but neither of them actually believed he would. After their mother left Junky really settled into Timber Creek. He was more of a homebody than anyone else Logan knew.

They talked about a few other things, like yes, she still loved New Zealand, and no, she wasn't dating anyone serious. When he finally ended the call, he didn't feel the usual sense of stillness he got after talking to his sister.

He knew Kyla meant well and he knew she only came from a place of care and concern, but that didn't make her words hurt any less. But maybe she was right. Maybe he was getting too involved with Amber. He could tell himself all he wanted that it was only out of a professional concern, but he knew it was bullshit. As a professional, his job was to facilitate her progress with the horses so she could allow herself to heal.

But as a man, there was more than that going on. A lot more. The need to wrap his arms around her and hold her and tell her everything was going to be okay was almost overwhelming.

But early, she'd run from him. And maybe that was for the best. Maybe Kyla was right; he should stay away. He couldn't take on her hurt as his own. That wasn't healthy for anyone.

Maybe distance was the best thing.

Chapter Nine

IT WAS easy for Amber to convince herself why she was too busy to get out to Blackstar Ranch to see Logan and the horses. At first it was because Austin needed help with schoolwork, and then it was helping Drew go through Eric's things and donate them to charity.

One day turned into the next and finally it was easier for Amber to ignore any of the feelings she'd had both at the ranch with Chester and the other, equally unnerving feelings she'd experienced for Logan than actually deal with any of them. After all, she'd had years of practice not dealing with anything at all. It was definitely more comfortable to ignore what was going on.

But it didn't mean she hadn't thought about it. She had. A lot. The days got shorter and the leaves started to change colors, but she couldn't forget the way Logan had stood there, asking her to stay. Amber couldn't forget the way she'd told him everything and he hadn't judged her or been disappointed in her or thought less of her. Instead, he'd encouraged her to keep talking, to work through the demons that chased her.

But she hadn't.

She ran.

Maybe it was for the best.

Autumn settled into Timber Creek and over the course of only a few weeks, the entire town had undergone a transformation. Pumpkins sat on every porch and decorations of skeletons, spiders and witch hats adorned the houses and storefronts as people prepared for the Halloween festivities that would take over the streets of Timber Creek in only a few days.

Drew and Amber had spent the majority of the day before decorating their little house with a mixture of store-bought decorations Drew's parents had dropped off for them, and a collection of crafts that Austin had made at school. Despite the fact that Amber had never paid much attention to Halloween, she was starting to get into the spirit.

"Do you have a costume for Austin yet?" she asked Drew as she flipped through her phone. "Because I was thinking maybe we could go as a group costume."

Drew looked up, her mouth hanging open. "A group costume? Does that mean you'll be participating in Halloween this year?"

"Why wouldn't I?" Amber pretended to be offended. "It's Halloween and the whole town will be out. Why shouldn't I go, too? It'll be fun."

"Will it?" Drew rolled her eyes.

"It will. Besides. I thought you liked Halloween."

"I used to like a lot of things." Her friend sounded so sad and defeated that Amber wasn't sure how to respond. "It's different now."

"Maybe so," Amber conceded. "But it doesn't have to be bad different." Drew's head popped up from the crossword puzzle she was doing. "It doesn't," Amber said quickly before she lost her again. "It just has to be different. But it doesn't mean that the fun should stop for Austin, right?"

Drew nodded slowly. "You're right. And I know I need to

think about him first and I do." Amber smiled, because she knew it was true. "But some days I just don't have it in me, ya know? I just don't know how I'm going to be able to wake up day after day without Eric here and still be able to be a good mom and give him everything he needs. I just don't know." Tears streamed down her friend's face but instead of rushing over to hug her, Amber simply slid Drew the box of tissues. She took them with a look of thanks. She didn't like Amber to bring attention to her tears.

They sat quietly for a few moments before Drew finally slapped her hand down on the table. "You know what? You're right. We do need costumes."

Amber grinned as Austin walked into the room. "Hey, buddy." She pulled him in for a hug. "Have you thought about what you want to be for Halloween?"

"Totally." He wiggled out of Amber's arms. "A superhero!" He crouched into a stance with his arms out. "Just like Dad."

"Like Dad?"

Amber looked at Drew out of the corner of her eye.

"Yeah," Austin said, his excitement growing. "Uncle Ben said that Dad was his hero because of what a good guy he was and how hard he fought the cancer bugs. And even though he didn't win, he was still his hero."

Amber felt her own tears threatening to spill over. She blinked hard.

"Uncle Ben said all that?"

"He did." Austin jumped up and down with the enthusiasm only a child could have. "I wanna be a superhero just like Dad."

Amber lost the battle of her tears and they fell down her face. She didn't have to look at Drew to see the same thing was happening with her.

But it was Drew who regained her composure first. "I think it's a great idea," she said to Austin. "We should all be superheroes for Halloween. Do you think Uncle Ben would like to come, too?"

THE DAY BEFORE HALLOWEEN, Amber found herself with a box of leftover decorations on the car seat next to her as she drove down the familiar streets to her father's house. She'd only visited him once since the first time, and it hadn't gone much better.

"What's all this?" he said when he opened his door to her.

"Hi, Dad." She held the box up. "I thought you might be able to use some decorations. Halloween is tomorrow."

"I don't decorate."

He didn't make a move to let her in, but Amber didn't let that deter her. Her breakthrough with Chester hadn't been a complete waste. Because, at the very least, she'd realized one thing quite clearly: all of her first opinions about equine therapy had been wrong. She might not be tripping over herself to go back there, but that wasn't because she didn't believe it worked. It was because she was afraid it *did.*

It wasn't hocus-pocus. Which meant she owed her dad an apology.

"Let me put a few decorations up, Dad. I promise you won't even notice but the kids in town will."

His mouth turned down into a scowl, but he nodded and stepped aside. "Okay. But just a few. I'll make coffee."

That was as good of a welcome as she was going to get. And she'd take it.

Amber spent the next few minutes hanging a ghost wreath on the door and sticking some pumpkin decals on the front window. She finished up by hanging a skeleton from the tree in the yard before joining her dad in the kitchen, where they sat across from each other with cups of steaming coffee in front of them.

"Have you been busy, Dad?"

He nodded. "Been making lots of pens. I tried a new wood. Cherry. Turned out well."

"I bet it did." She held the mug in her hand, absorbing the warmth from it. "And have you been out to Blackstar lately?"

His eyes narrowed, as he prepared no doubt to defend himself against his opinionated daughter, but he nodded. "Down to once a week now. I usually get there on Wednesdays. My knees get achy in the cold. Imagine I won't be able to keep it up much when the snow falls. You'll be happy to hear that."

Guilt seared through Amber and she shook her head. "It was never my intention to make you feel badly about volunteering at the ranch, Dad."

"Wasn't it?"

She sat back sharply, unaccustomed to his forthright attitude. "No," she began and then corrected herself. "Well, maybe it was," Amber admitted. "But that was before I understood what Logan was doing at the ranch."

Her dad watched her warily. "And now?"

She could say something sharp or clever, but what was the point? Amber was exhausted. She'd done a good job pretending that she was still the same, cutthroat, sharp-tongued, overachieving woman she always was. But ever since coming clean with Logan weeks earlier, it had been harder and harder to pretend that everything was okay and nothing had changed. More than that, she didn't want to anymore. There'd been a shift and with more than her thoughts. She hadn't had a panic attack since that day at the ranch. Maybe being truthful about her life was more therapeutic than she could have expected.

"I'm sorry if I said anything negative about the ranch and the horses." Amber looked up from her coffee and straight into her father's eyes, which clouded with confusion as she spoke. Clearly he'd expected something different from her as well. "I shouldn't have said anything until I knew what it was all about."

"And now?" he asked again.

"Now I know," she said simply. "I went to check it out."

Her father tilted his head, waiting for her to say more, and for the first time, Amber noticed how old he looked. Her dad had always seemed to her to be an indestructible force that never aged. But now, looking at him, she could see the deep lines around his eyes, the subtle softening of his skin, and the thick head of hair that was definitely more gray now than it was brown.

"I think Logan's doing good work out there." She spoke truthfully. "And I think it's really good that you're doing some volunteering. I know you used to like horses when you were a kid."

His eyes shone with surprise that she would even know something so personal about him, let alone remember it. But she did. There was a time when Amber was a little girl before her mother died, when things were simple and her dad used to tell her stories of when he was a little boy growing up on a small farm. She'd never forgotten the way he'd get excited when he spoke of the horses and how it felt to sit up on their backs. The memories of those stories had faded over the years, but it made perfect sense as to why he wanted to volunteer at the ranch. She should have seen that right away.

And maybe she would have, too, if she hadn't been so wrapped up in her own messed-up life.

"I didn't realize you…"

"I did." Emotion was hard for him; she didn't need him to finish his thoughts. "I hope your knees don't bother you too much and you can get out there and help Logan out. If you like, I can see about making you an appointment with Mark

Thomas. Maybe he can prescribe something for the aches? And it would be good to get your blood pressure checked, too."

They spoke for a few more minutes, with her dad refusing—as usual—to make a visit to his doctor. Finally, Amber decided to speak to Mark privately before pressing the issue of the appointment. She knew if the pain finally got to be too much, he'd relent. Amber finished her coffee and, satisfied with the visit, prepared to leave.

"Thanks for the coffee, Dad. I should get—"

"You've done well."

She froze. *Had he just paid her a compliment? For what?*

"Pardon?"

"I said…" He looked as if he might say more, maybe elaborate on what he was talking about. She waited a beat and finally he grunted and said, "For the decorations. They look good."

The decorations?

Amber paused before pushing up from the table and waited.

She stared at him for a minute, trying to process what he'd just said. When she was chosen as the valedictorian for her graduating class, or walked across the stage to receive her diploma, Amber had wanted nothing more than to hear those words from him. When she graduated from law school at the top of her class and received multiple job offers from reputable firms, once again, she'd waited in vain to hear those words.

But they never came.

And now…for *decorations*? They both knew it was more than that and that's what broke Amber's heart.

The irony that it was only now that she'd given him every reason to be ashamed of her that he finally said those words she'd so desperately wanted to hear was a sharp knife to her heart.

Somehow Amber managed to say her good-byes to her dad

without completely falling apart in front of him and telling him everything so that he could take it all back. She hadn't done well at all. It wasn't until she was sitting in the front seat of her car, taking deep gulps of breath, that she let herself cry.

She'd ruined everything. And she had no idea how to fix it.

Chapter Ten

LOGAN COULD HAVE SAID NO. In fact, after the last few weeks that he'd had, being all but run off his feet between the clients Brent Baker sent to him and the mounting chores at the ranch, he probably should have said no. Joseph hadn't been coming around as much lately due to the cooler weather and Logan hadn't realized just how much he'd come to depend on the man's visits. Either way, Logan was exhausted and no doubt no one would have blamed him if he'd begged off Halloween duty.

The Timber Creek fire department made it a tradition to volunteer at the annual town Halloween party. It was definitely one of the perks of being a volunteer firefighter, as far as Logan was concerned. He'd always loved Halloween.

What was not to love? Between the costumes and the candy and the fact that everyone in town participated and had a great time, it was one of the highlights of the year. The streets were shut down, there were portable fire pits, and kids ran all over the place.

Which was where the fire department came in. The local police and fire department teamed up to provide a security presence, control traffic, and just generally make sure everyone had a good time.

Logan didn't even mind that it meant he couldn't dress up in a costume of his own, opting instead for his official fire department jacket. This year, however, he had a bit of a surprise lined up for later on. Which was just one more reason why it didn't matter how tired Logan was; there was no way he was going to miss the annual town Halloween party.

He grabbed a quick shower, made himself an easy sandwich, and headed into town. He'd been assigned the early shift, which mostly meant he spent a few hours setting up blockades before walking down the streets to inspect the fire pits many of the residents had put out on driveways and front lawns.

"Hey." A voice grabbed his attention as he walked down the Main Street. He turned to see a woman he vaguely recognized. "You're Logan," the woman said. "Logan Myers, right?"

"I am." He nodded and took a step toward the woman. "Do I know you?"

"Not really." The woman nodded shyly. "I'm Kalen's mom. He's been coming out to your ranch. Doctor Baker suggested it." She sounded tentative, as if she wasn't sure but as she spoke, Logan realized where he'd seen the woman before: in the parking lot of Blackstar Ranch when she dropped her son off. She hung around the barns a little bit, but never actually went near the horses where Kalen was.

"Yes." Logan smiled warmly. "I recognize you now. You know, you are welcome to come over to the barns or the fences and—"

"Oh no," she cut him off. "I wouldn't want to interrupt what Kalen's doing. And you, too," she added quickly. "I mean, I wouldn't want to get in the way."

"You wouldn't."

She shrugged uncertainly but Logan could see he wasn't going to change her mind. "I just wanted to say thank you," she said. "I wasn't sure about the horses and when Doctor Baker suggested equine therapy for Kalen, well, I didn't know what to expect but I guess I thought we didn't have anything to lose, so..." She shrugged again and fell silent for a moment. "Anyway, I've been really surprised. I don't know exactly what's happening or how, but Kalen finally seems to be a little bit more himself again lately and I think I have you to thank for it."

Excitement bloomed through him, but he did his best to stay calm and professional. Brent Baker had sent a handful of patients out to the ranch and although it was too soon for Logan to tell whether any of the equine therapy had been helping, he'd been hopeful. But maybe it wasn't too soon to tell? *Maybe…just maybe…* "I'm so glad to hear that it's helping," Logan said. "Can I ask what kind of difference you're seeing?"

The woman's face lit up. "He's smiling again," she said. "And talking. I can't tell you how long it's been since I've seen that smile and now, in the last few weeks..." Unshed tears shone in her eyes. "Well, it's just..." Spontaneously, she reached out and grabbed his hand. "Thank you. I know we still have a long way to go. He's been sad for such a long time. But the horses have helped in a way that therapy never could. It's like I can finally see an end to all of this. That maybe, I just might get my little boy back."

It shouldn't have surprised him. After all, Logan knew first-hand the impact equine therapy could have. The horses had allowed him to have the breakthrough that ultimately let him make his way back into the land of the living. But even though it shouldn't have surprised him to hear that his horses were making a difference, it did. In all the best ways.

He could feel a swell of emotion build inside him. "I'm so happy to hear that, Mrs...."

"Harmon," she said. "Peggy Harmon. I don't mean to keep you. I'm sure you're busy tonight. I just saw you and thought…well, I just wanted to let you know that what you're doing with those horses." A tear slipped down her cheek. "It's amazing. Thank you."

The woman gave him one more smile before turning and walking down the street. She left Logan standing in the middle of the street, staring after her and feeling for the first time that all the late nights, long hours, and stress were finally all going to be worth it.

KIDS WERE RUNNING all over the place and Amber could hardly keep up to Austin as he scurried from one house to the next, trick-or-treating. Thankfully there was a group of them and Amber wasn't solely responsible for the boy, who was way too hopped up on sugar and the excitement of the night for one person to handle alone.

Their little group made an awesome sight walking up and down the streets of Timber Creek. Drew, dressed as Mrs. Incredible, had come out for the night, a small thing that Amber was grateful for because sometimes it was just the littlest things that meant progress for her friend. True to his word, Ben had shown up earlier that night, dressed as a super authentic Batman. He'd spent most of his night running at Austin's speed from door to door while the women hung back in the street and carried the extra candy bags as Austin continually filled them with his loot.

Amber had opted for a Wonder Woman costume, which, judging from all the little girls in red capes who'd been running past her all night, seemed to be one of the more popular costumes of the year. She was just happy that as a group, they were able to fulfill Austin's superhero request. He himself had chosen Captain America, which he said reminded him the most of his dad. He'd jumped around the house with his plastic shield all afternoon before it was time to finally leave. Drew had been holding it since about the third house, but they'd managed to get some good pictures before he'd ditched his prop completely.

"This is nice," Amber said as they moved farther down the street to keep up with the guys. "He's having fun."

"He's having a great time." Drew nodded. "Eric would have loved it."

"Don't be sad." Amber spun around to face her friend. Aware that she really shouldn't be telling her friend how to feel, she kept her voice light. "Not tonight. You know Eric wouldn't want you to be sad on Halloween."

"I'm not," Drew lied. "Okay, well, I'm not as sad as I thought I'd be." Amber gave her a look. "Honestly," she insisted. "I thought I'd be a total mess. But this is actually… well, it's kind of nice. Don't you think?"

"I totally think so. And it's so great that Ben could be here, too."

Drew's face changed and she smiled. "He's been so great. I know they weren't as close after high school as Eric would have liked, but it's so incredible to see Ben step in and give Austin that male influence he's going to need."

"We've all got your back." Amber gave her a quick hug. "We're here for you. For both of you. No matter what."

"About that." Drew took a step back and her face grew serious beneath her Incredibles mask. "I've been meaning to talk to you about—"

"I hear this is where the superheroes are hanging out."

Amber spun around at the familiar voice and her stomach flipped when she saw Logan standing behind them, wearing an official Timber Creek firefighters jacket.

"Is that your costume?" Amber sounded ruder than she'd meant to. "I mean, I believe that firefighters are absolutely real-life heroes. But if you're going to go for it, shouldn't you have the full coat and hat and—"

"It's not my costume," Logan interrupted. "I'm on duty tonight, volunteering for the Timber Creek fire department."

Amber's face flared with embarrassment and she was glad for the darkness of the night. "I didn't realize," she said. "A cowboy *and* a firefighter. That's quite the combination." She didn't add that they were her two favorite tropes to read about in her romance novels. Somehow that didn't seem appropriate, but her brain absolutely went to that place.

"I'm a man of many surprises." He winked at her and turned to Drew. "But I'm not on duty anymore. I took the early set-up shift, so now I'm all about the festivities. Where's the little man?"

Right on cue, Ben and Austin appeared to offload their latest candy haul.

"Hey, man," Ben greeted him. "Glad you could join us."

Austin waved shyly. "My dad said firefighters and police officers were the real superheroes. So you're just like my dad," he said in a strong, clear voice.

Amber didn't have to look to see that Drew would likely be fighting back tears.

"I don't think I'll ever be as brave as your dad." Logan had crouched down to look Austin in the eyes. "But he was right. Firefighters and police officers are real-life heroes. But you know what?" He stood and winked at Austin, who was watching intently as he unzipped his jacket. "Sometimes there's a little bit of a superhero hiding in all of us." Logan gripped both ends of his jacket and pulled them apart, revealing what was underneath.

Austin squealed and laughed as the giant *S* came into view, revealing the Superman costume Logan wore beneath his coat.

"You're a real-life hero *and* a superhero?" Ben joked.

"There's no hope for the rest of us normal superheroes, then, is there?"

"Hey." Logan shrugged. "I don't make the rules."

Ben gave him a friendly punch in the arm and looked back at Austin. "Are you ready to hit more houses?"

"Duh."

"Austin," Drew chastised him, but she was laughing, too.

"Logan?"

He shook his head. "This superhero needs to rest for a few minutes," he said. "I think I'll keep the ladies company and join you guys in a bit."

"Suit yourself." Austin and Ben took off running, headed to the next house at full speed.

"I think I'm going to find Christy and Cam," Drew announced. "Cam just texted and said they were in front of Daisy's. I could really use a coffee. Are you good to hold down the fort here for a few minutes?"

"For sure," Amber said.

"I'll see if I can bring back something a little stronger than coffee to get us through the rest of the night. You want anything, Logan?"

"I'm good. Thanks. I loaded up on caffeine earlier."

As soon as Drew left, Amber felt the shift in the air between her and Logan. Charged somehow. "I don't really drink," she said to him, feeling the need to explain herself. After all, he did know all her secrets. Would he judge her for having an occasional drink because she was recovering from an addiction?

Did it matter?

Somehow it did.

"Hey." He held up his hands. "I'm not judging you. You're a big girl."

"I am."

He winked at her and she laughed, the tension broken.

"Aren't we supposed to walk along with them?" Logan gestured to Ben and Austin, who'd gotten ahead of them.

"Right." They walked a few steps in silence. "I really like your Superman. That was clever."

"I like that it complements your Wonder Woman," he said in response and heat rushed through her body all the way to her fingertips. "You look great, by the way."

"Thanks. I didn't mean to—"

"I've missed you at—"

They spoke at the same time, but it was Logan who recovered first.

"Sorry." He waved his hand in her direction. "Go ahead."

"I was just going to say that…" She had been just about to tell him why she hadn't been back out to the ranch. But now, standing next to him, she knew he'd see it for what it was. An excuse. She swallowed hard. "I was just going to apologize to you," she said instead.

"What for?" He stopped walking and turned to look at her. "You don't owe me an apology for anything."

"Don't I?" Looking at him, standing so close to him, made her feel vulnerable in a way she'd never experienced before. Was it because he knew everything? *Or was it more than that?*

"Not at all, Amber," he said. "I was just about to tell you that I've missed you out at the ranch. I was really hoping you'd come back."

"You were?"

He laughed then. "Of course I was." When he took her hand in his, it wasn't entirely unexpected, but the thrill of his touch on her cool skin heated her through. "I get that it's hard for you." He spoke softly, although no one around them was listening. "But I don't think it has to be as hard as you're making it."

She thought about that for a moment but finally shook her head. "I don't know what you mean."

"Will you come out to the ranch again? Soon? I think that might be a better place to talk about this."

She wanted to go back. She also wanted to stay as far away as possible. They were conflicting emotions that had warred within her from the moment she'd driven away the last time. After spilling her secrets to first the horse and then Logan, Amber had felt a weight lift from her. A weight she didn't even know she was carrying. But also something else.

A crippling, overwhelming fear.

She never intended for anyone to know her shame. After all, what would they think? How could her friends and family possibly look at her the same way after they knew the truth about who she was?

They wouldn't.

The relief and the fear had paralyzed her into not doing anything but hiding.

But here was a chance…maybe she should—

"Okay," she said before she realized she'd made her decision. "I'll come back."

HE WASN'T sure she'd say yes. In fact, if Logan were a betting man, he might have bet against the fact that Amber would take him up on his offer to come out to the ranch again.

More than anything, though, he wanted her to. He hadn't even realized how much he wanted her to come back, visit with the horses and heal herself, until he'd seen her on the street with the others, dressed as the sexiest, strongest-looking Wonder Woman he'd ever seen.

It was the perfect costume for her, even if it wasn't entirely weather appropriate, and the more that Logan got to know about Amber, the more he realized how perfect it was for her. Even if she didn't know it herself yet.

"Okay?" he clarified. "You'll come out?"

She nodded and he pulled her into a spontaneous hug. Her body stiffened in response, but a second later, softened a little as she let him hug her. "I'm glad," he said into her ear and she shivered in response.

Or maybe it was just because she was freezing. Because she was.

"Why don't we go find one of those fires and warm you up?" He reluctantly released her from the embrace. "I think the snow will hold off for the trick or treaters, but you can absolutely feel it in the air." She only stood a foot away, but he already missed the spicy scent of her hair. *Cinnamon, maybe? With something sweeter mixed in that he couldn't quite place.* "You are freezing."

She laughed. "I *am* freezing." Amber pulled her cape around her. "I guess I didn't really think the costume thing through. I don't know what I was thinking. Halloween in the mountains is definitely cooler than in San Francisco."

"Well, I don't know," he said. "I think it's pretty perfect. But you're right…probably not very warm. Come on." He took her hand again and began to lead her down the street.

A moment later, Ben and Austin joined them. "Where are you guys headed?"

"Somewhere so Wonder Woman can warm up," Logan told Ben. "Are you guys ready for a break?"

"No way!" They all laughed because Austin didn't show any signs of slowing down at all. "Come on, Uncle Ben, let's go."

"Hold your horses, buddy. How about we go warm up for a minute? Amber's cold."

The little boy looked to Amber and appeared to think for a moment. "I know what will warm you up, Auntie."

"What's that?"

"Come run with me to get some candy. It's really fun. I promise."

Logan was about to protest so he could take Amber to the fire she so clearly needed, but Amber spoke up before he could.

"Definitely," she answered the boy, who jumped up and down in response. "That sounds like fun."

"It is!"

Ben laughed. "It is pretty fun." He turned to his nephew. "But go easy on Auntie Amber. She's not as conditioned to trick or treating as I am."

"Hey." She playfully smacked Ben's arm. "It's true I'm a bit more of a grown up than your Uncle Ben," she told Austin. "But I'm an equally awesome trick or treater." She winked at Logan, took the bag from Ben's hand and a second later, she and Austin were running down the road, hand-in-hand, to the next house.

Logan watched her red boots flash in the streetlights, her cape flapping behind her, affording him glimpses of her long, lean legs.

"She's been so fantastic," Ben said.

"She certainly is." Logan hadn't even realized he'd spoken until Ben laughed. "I mean, yes. Amber's been fantastic with Austin and being there for Drew."

"And she's pretty fantastic on her own, too."

Ben was setting him up and he knew it. Logan shot him a look.

"Something going on with you two?" he asked after a moment. They'd started walking in an effort to keep up with the trick or treaters. "I mean, you don't have to tell me anything," Ben added. "I just thought maybe…"

"No, it's okay," Logan said. "And…I don't really know," he answered truthfully. "Amber's kind of a mystery."

Ben laughed again. "Isn't that the truth? I remember when

we were kids, she was always hard to nail down. I don't think she ever dated anyone, but there were always a few who tried."

"Oh yeah?" Logan was a few years younger than them, and enough grades behind that he barely knew Amber and Ben when they were in school. Of course because he knew Eric, he knew Ben, but not the same way. Eric had become more than a babysitter to Logan over the years. Even after they didn't need a babysitter anymore, Eric always kind of looked out for Logan and mentored him a little bit. Logan credited Eric for the fact that he'd finally stopped screwing around so much in the ninth grade and actually started earning the marks he'd need to make something out of his life. He wondered, not for the first time, if Eric ever knew before he died what an impact he'd had on Logan. "So she never had a…I probably shouldn't be asking you this stuff." He let the question trail off.

Ben waved away his protest. "Don't worry about it. And no, I don't think she ever dated anyone at all. Maybe not even in college. I mean, we weren't as close as she was with the girls, obviously. But I don't remember ever hearing of anyone. But then again, I'm not really surprised."

Logan stared at him. "You're not?"

"Nope." Ben shook his head. "Amber was always way too driven. She's a force. Whatever she wants, she gets. I've never seen anything like it. She's pretty incredible."

"She is." Logan nodded. He watched her as she ran with Austin, collecting even more candy. Amber absolutely was incredible. Even now that he knew the truth about how she managed to accomplish all of the things she had that impressed her friends so much, his opinion hadn't changed.

At least not for the worse. If anything, Logan felt nothing but admiration for her. It couldn't have been easy to have so much pressure on you that you felt like the only way to succeed was to use drugs.

She'd done what she thought she had to do. Even at the expense of her own well-being.

And now…the drugs were gone, but she was still harming herself. Only it seemed that the mental way she was beating herself up about the secrets she hung onto was worse than anything she could have put in her body.

Amber must have sensed him watching her because at that moment, she turned. Her long, dark hair flipped around her face and when she brushed it away, Logan could see her smile. In that moment, she looked so carefree, so happy, and so completely unencumbered by everything that had been weighing her down.

She was gorgeous.

He offered her a little wave before she turned around again to chase after Austin with a laugh.

Amber was incredible. Now if only he could make her believe that, too.

Chapter Eleven

"WAIT UNTIL YOU SEE THESE." A few days later, Cam danced into Daisy's Diner, holding her laptop against her chest, and slipped into the seat next to Christy. "They are absolute perfection." She flipped open the top of her computer. "You're going to die."

Christy laughed. "I'm sure I'm not going to die. Unless you don't show me the pictures already." She gave her friend a look. "It's been torture waiting so long."

Cam immediately looked apologetic. "I really am sorry, Christy. It's been crazy busy lately and I could really use this morning sickness to go away. Seriously. I can't remember it ever being so bad when I was pregnant with Morgan. Do you think that means it's a boy?"

Her friend's eyes lit up and as much as Christy would have loved to sit there and guess on the sex of her unborn baby, she was going to lose her mind if she didn't get to see the product of the photo session they'd had weeks ago.

She waved her hand in the air and jabbed her finger at the laptop, which only made Cam laugh.

"Right," she said. "I'm sorry. Here." She tapped a few

buttons and turned the computer to face Christy, who immediately put her hand to her mouth.

"Oh my God." She blinked and shook her head slightly before pushing Cam's hand away so she could scroll through the pictures on her own.

With each image that flashed across the screen, Christy's eyes grew blurry. Cam had somehow managed to capture all of the innocence and pure beauty that was her little girl in every single shot.

"Are you okay?" Cam looked over to her friend who, despite her question, didn't look concerned at all but instead wore a huge smile. "Because you look like you don't like them."

"Stop it." Christy smacked Cam's arm lovingly. "It's not nice to make fun."

Cam laughed openly. "Sure it is. And you have every right to be caught up in the emotion. I can't even imagine what this means…I mean, I *know* what it means to you. But it's different for you guys. I get that."

It *was* different for them. But only in the way that every new parent felt. There were no two situations the same, and that was true for her and Mark, too. She shook her head. "It's just…I never actually thought this moment would ever really come."

She let the tears flow freely down her cheeks. There'd been a time, not all that long ago, where Christy had given up hope completely that they'd ever be parents and here she was, looking at her daughter's newborn pictures. It was still very surreal.

"I'm glad you like them," Cam said after a moment.

"I *love* all of them." Christy laughed and wiped at her tears. "But now I have a whole new problem."

"What's that?"

"Which ones am I going to choose to frame?" They

laughed together. "Every bit of my walls is going to be covered in baby pictures."

"There's nothing wrong with that. Especially when the subject is so gorgeous."

Christy gazed at the screen again. "She really is, isn't she?"

Cam smiled. "Where is the little princess today? Getting some quality daddy time?"

"She is." Christy was more than willing to bring Mya to her coffee date with Cam, but Mark had insisted that they wanted to have a daddy/daughter day. Every single day, it melted her heart a little bit more to watch him with Mya. Mark had slipped so easily into the role of a dad that there was no doubt he'd been born for the job.

"You look so happy." Cam was watching her and Christy hadn't even realized she'd drifted off into her own thoughts for a moment. "I mean, in a different way than before. You just look so…content."

"I really am. Life is so good."

"I hear ya, sister!" Cam raised the mug of tea Christy had ordered her and they toasted with their drinks. "Now if only all of us could be so happy."

Christy knew exactly what she was talking about. It seemed that she and Cam both had everything they'd ever wanted while their two other best friends were suffering. It hurt her heart to see her friends unhappy.

"What do you think is going on with Amber?" Christy got right to the point. Obviously they knew what was happening with Drew, but so far, Amber had still been hard to pin down. "I mean, besides not working. I spoke with her about doing up a will for us and she seemed to be receptive to the idea, but I still feel like there's something she's not telling us."

"I agree." Cam took a long sip of her tea. "But you know Amber. We're never going to get her to just tell us."

"You think we're going to have to trick her into talking?"

"You know she's smarter than both of us combined." Cam laughed but then grew serious again. "But I do think she'll tell us when she's ready. I really do. And…I don't want to gossip, but…"

It was Christy's turn to laugh. "I know exactly what you're going to say."

"You do?"

Christy nodded. "You were going to tell me about the way Amber was hanging out with Logan on Halloween."

Cam slapped her palm on the tabletop. "How did you know?"

"I know everything." Christy wiggled her eyebrows. "Seriously, I saw them. They looked like they were having a good night."

They *had* looked like they were having fun. Christy and Mark had wheeled Mya around in the stroller for a little bit and had tried to join up with Drew and Austin, but never quite could catch up with the rest of the group. They were on their way home when they saw a tall, striking Wonder Woman from the back laughing with a fireman. Amber and Logan. It was the first time Christy had seen Amber with a man and although she knew better, they weren't on a date... If she *hadn't* have known better, that might have been exactly what she thought.

"Do you think it's something?"

"Your guess is as good as mine." Christy shrugged. "But I kind of hope so. I mean…don't you think it's time that Amber met someone?"

It was Cam's turn to shrug. "I don't know. Do you think you *have* to have someone to be fulfilled? I mean, Amber always made it clear that she was choosing herself over a relationship. Her career instead of a man. That was a choice and I don't think she's been unhappy because of it."

"I guess you're right." Christy thought about it. It *was*

Amber's choice. It always had been. She never could understand what the rest of them were doing, wasting their time with boys when they could be out building their futures on their own.

"Drew seems to be doing okay," she said after a moment, changing the subject. "I mean, I guess as well as can be expected."

Cam nodded and looked down at her tea.

"But with the holidays coming up, it worries me," Christy continued. "I actually don't know if the best approach is to keep her really busy so she can't think about the fact that Eric isn't here, or maybe do something special to honor him this year. But I don't know if drawing attention to it is the right way to go either."

"I don't think it matters what we do—there will definitely be attention drawn to it." Cam thought for a minute and nodded. "But you're right. I think she'll be okay." She fiddled with her mug. "Besides…I think maybe there might be enough distraction around then anyway."

Something in her friend's voice caught Christy's attention. She narrowed her eyes and studied Cam. "What do you mean?"

"Evan and I have decided to get married." She said the words so quickly that Christy wasn't sure that she'd heard properly.

"What?"

"We're getting married."

"You were always getting married, weren't you?" She pointed to Cam's left hand and the ring Evan had put there months earlier. "But with the baby…"

"I know. But we decided to do it before the baby comes." She laughed. "It means I'll be a big, fat bride, but I don't care."

"You'll be beautiful," Christy said honestly. "That's so exciting. A Christmas wedding?"

Cam nodded. "I know it's fast but yes. Christmas Eve. Do you think that's crazy?"

"I think it's amazing."

IT WAS ONLY a few days after Halloween, but Logan had been right. Snow was definitely in the air. The clouds were heavy and gray, and although it wasn't winter quite yet, that didn't seem to matter to Mother Nature. Snow would be falling later that day. He was sure of it. Logan pulled his jacket over his flannel shirt and tugged his gloves on before heading out of the barn.

And he was ready for it, too. Logan never minded the changing of the seasons, and winter was one of his favorites. There was nothing better than going for a ride with the snow crunching under the horse's hooves, or heading out to a frozen lake to fish and huddle around a fire.

Maybe this year he could show Amber just how hot an ice fishing hut could be?

He tried to shake the thought loose, but there was no point. If he managed to push that one away, there'd just be another one on its heels. If he thought he'd been consumed by thoughts of Amber before Halloween, ever since their fun night as superheroes, he couldn't get her off his mind.

He smiled, thinking of how cute she'd looked in her costume. How vulnerable she'd been when she shivered a little and how he'd held her hand when he'd finally insisted they find some warmth at the end of the night. When Austin finally tired of trick-or-treating and Drew had dragged him—protesting the whole way—home, Logan had suggested they warm up at the Log and Jam before heading home and to his pleasant surprise, Amber had agreed.

The pub had been packed, but Logan found a few extra

chairs in a corner and had created a table for them out of a large portable speaker that probably belonged to the band. They tucked into the corner, drinking coffee. Even though it hadn't lasted long, the night had kind of felt like a date.

But if it had been a date, he would have kissed her. And he hadn't. No matter how much he'd wanted to.

Damn it. Logan kicked a clump of dirt as he walked through the yard.

He should have kissed her.

But he *had* managed to get her to agree on a date to come back and see him. He turned at the sound of a car and smiled when he recognized it as hers.

She'd kept her promise.

"Hey." He waved and made his way over to her as she got out of the car. She was dressed in a bright-blue puffy jacket that looked more suited to the ski hill than a ranch. But it was warm…and cute. "I'm glad you came." He stopped short of greeting her with a kiss and settled for a quick hug instead.

The spicy scent of her hair filled his senses. The woman was definitely getting to him.

"I told you I'd come." She shifted from foot to foot, a move that was subtle, but he noticed. She was nervous.

"No cape today?"

That made her laugh. He loved her laugh because nothing about it was halfway. Amber laughed the way he suspected she lived: full on. "I thought maybe I'd opt for something a little warmer today." She patted her jacket. "Besides, I wouldn't want to get my cape dirty."

He chuckled. "Definitely not." He reached out for her hand in a move that felt completely natural. When she accepted it and slid her gloved hand into his, even through the fabric, there was a heat between them. "Are you ready to do this again?"

"Honestly?"

"Obviously."

"I *am* ready." She smiled at him as they walked. "I wasn't sure I would be, but I actually think that the time away from… well, from all of it was a good thing. And then seeing you the other night…I'm rambling." She shook her head and looked away.

"No." Logan stopped walking and turned to her. "I think I get it. But it doesn't matter. What matters is that you came back and before you go talk to Chester again, I just wanted to tell you something."

"What's that?"

"I think it's incredibly brave what you're doing." He hadn't been sure he was going to say anything at all, but the more he thought about it, the more he realized she needed to hear what he had to say. "It takes a lot of courage to face your demons and make a change. And even more courage to talk about it."

"With a horse?" She tried to make a joke, but he could see the seriousness in her eyes.

"Especially with a horse, because you have to be completely honest."

She seemed to think about what he said for a moment before nodding. "Thank you."

"For what?"

Amber looked straight into his eyes. "For doing this for me," she said. "Or with me, or whatever. I know you don't have to. In fact, I guess I don't even understand *why* you're doing this. I mean, I was a total bitch to you."

He chuckled. "It's true. But I was also an asshole to you. Besides," he continued, the laughter gone, "none of that matters. I'm not helping you do anything. You're doing it all yourself and you're doing a great job."

Her lips twitched up into a smile but she didn't say anything more.

Logan squeezed her hand and gestured to the ring with his

head. "I think someone is ready to see you." Chester had spotted them and had made his way to the rail. "Are you ready?"

"I am." She let go of Logan's hand. "I have a few things to talk through with Chester here."

He didn't walk with her, but instead stood and waited for her to approach the ring and the horse. She patted his nose before ducking and climbing through the fence rails.

She was a natural as she took the horse's reins and started walking slowly around the ring, talking the entire time.

Logan was so caught up in watching Amber and the horse that he hadn't heard the footsteps approaching from behind.

"What you're doing here is very special." It was Ruby Blackstar who'd come to stand beside him. "When I took over this ranch from my daddy, I never would have thought we'd have the horses giving therapy."

Logan turned and smiled at the elderly woman. She still wore her cowboy boots and ranching jeans every day although it had been awhile since he'd seen her around the barns. Logan knew she still liked to ride, although he hadn't seen her up on a horse in a long time. He'd have to ask her about it.

"I know it's a little unorthodox," he said. "And it might seem a little strange."

"Not at all." Ruby shook her head. "Ever since I was a little girl, I've known that horses are special animals. Not like people at all. Horses listen. They understand."

Logan couldn't agree more and he told her so and then said, "I really need to thank you, Ruby. We're making a difference for people." He remembered Kalen's mother, who'd teared up talking about the changes in her son. But it was Amber he gestured to.

Ruby followed his gaze and smiled. "I'm glad to hear it, Logan. I really am. But I came to find you today to give you some news."

She looked him straight in the eyes, and Logan knew before she even said anything that he wasn't going to like what she said.

"I think it's time for me to move on, Logan. The ranch is getting to be too much."

He swallowed hard. He'd been afraid that something like this would happen. Even with him taking on a lot of the daily chores, it was obvious Ruby was winding down her operations and it wouldn't be long before the ranch was more than she could handle. Or *want* to handle. "You're selling Blackstar?"

She nodded. "It wasn't an easy decision. Blackstar has been my entire life and in my family for generations, but I'm not getting any younger and…well, I think it's time." She placed a hand on his arm. "I'm sorry."

"It's okay, Ruby." Logan put his hand on top of hers and patted it. "I understand." He tried to smile, but judging by Ruby's reaction, it hadn't quite reached his eyes.

"I'll make sure the buyer understands what you're doing here, Logan. I'll try to make a deal that takes into account your business and the leasing arrangements—"

"It's okay. You don't have to worry about me. I'll be okay."

"And the therapy?" Ruby was a tough old woman, but standing in front of him at that moment, she looked like she just might cry. "I'm so sorry, Logan. If there were any other way…"

"Don't worry about it, Ruby. Please. I mean it. We'll be fine and I'll figure something out. I can't tell you how much I've appreciated your generosity. Please don't give it another thought."

They stood in silence for a few minutes watching Amber, but Logan's mind was no longer on the complicated beauty before him.

AMBER WALKED around the ring with Chester at least a dozen times. Each time around, she found herself relaxing a little more. It was different than the first time, and maybe that was because she knew what to expect from both the horse and herself. Or maybe it was just because she was feeling that much better about herself and everything she'd been through.

It was nice talking to Chester. He neighed occasionally, a sound Amber found oddly comforting, and from time to time, he'd nuzzle his head toward her.

She vaguely noticed Logan watching her, and then another woman standing next to the ring talking to him, but she didn't allow herself to focus on anything except her and the horse. She was there for a reason, and although she still wasn't one hundred percent sure of what that was, Amber knew that the horse next to her was definitely responsible for the peace she was beginning to feel inside.

As was the man who stood close by. But that was more complicated.

"How was it?" Logan asked when she led the horse toward the edge of the fence line. "You look different this time."

Amber laughed. "Is that because I'm not crying and in the middle of a panic attack?"

"That might be it." He smiled and took the reins from her. "But seriously." He turned to her. "You look calmer, more…"

"Settled?"

"That might be it." They started walking side-by-side toward the barn, Logan leading the horse, who walked a few paces behind him. "How do you feel?"

"Honestly? I feel fantastic." She felt a little silly saying it out loud, but she knew Logan would understand. "After my...*incident*, the doctors referred me to an addiction counselor and I had to do some sessions with her. It wasn't rehab so much…but it was like rehab lite, I guess." Logan chuckled. "She wanted me to talk about why I was using the pills and why I felt I couldn't survive without them. She asked a lot of questions, and I think I was expected to…I don't know…open up and have some sort of breakthrough or something."

"But you didn't." It wasn't a question, but Amber shook her head anyway.

"Not at all." Together, they walked into the barn and toward Chester's stall. Amber leaned up against a pole while Logan tucked the horse in and gave him fresh hay and water. "In fact," she spoke while he worked, "I think it had the opposite effect than she intended. She'd sit there and ask me question after question, and all I could think of was how stupid it was. I mean, I used the pills because it was all I'd ever known. I couldn't understand why she couldn't see that. Why did I have to explain it? *How* could I explain it?"

"And now?"

She shrugged. "Now I at least feel better about why I did what I did. I mean, I don't *feel* better about it. But I think I might understand why I did it. At least at first."

Amber had the realization on her second lap around the ring with Chester, not that she should have been surprised by it. If she was really honest with herself, she'd already known why she'd turned to the pills when she was a teenager, and more importantly, why she'd continued to take them. In fact, she'd always known. But walking and talking to the horse allowed her to finally admit it out loud. And something about speaking the words made it crystal-clear.

"I had a lot of expectations put upon me by my father," she said. "And…more impactful, my mother before she died. They always wanted the best for me, and that included doing my best. I think because I was an only child, the pressure was more intense, but maybe it wouldn't have been." She kept talking as Logan finished up with the horse and they started walking outside again. "And maybe it's not fair to put it on my parents," she said. "Because I think I wanted it just as much as they did.

Maybe more. When I was young and got straight As, it was easy. And it felt good to get all the attention. I liked it."

"Of course you did. That's normal."

"But then it got harder, and it wasn't only the grades. Not only did I need to be involved in everything, I needed to *run* it all, work a part-time job, be awesome. And…I couldn't do it."

"Why did you have to?"

She shrugged again, but she knew exactly why. "Because that's what everyone expected of me. And most importantly, it was what *I* expected of me."

"The weight of expectations can crush you."

"They almost did."

They stood in silence for a moment. While they were inside, the clouds that had been building darkened and grew heavy. A few flakes started to fall around them and Logan turned to her. "I'm really glad you gave Chester a chance." He took a step toward her, closing the distance between them. The air was charged, but instead of scaring her, it excited her. "And me."

"You?"

He nodded and reached for her. "I'm really glad you gave me a chance." Before she even knew it was happening, his lips pressed to hers and the electricity in the air flowed through their bodies. His hand cupped her cheek, while his other hand wrapped around her and pulled her in to him. She slipped her arms around him and deepened the kiss, because all at the same time, kissing Logan was the most exciting, terrifying, and perfect thing.

Chapter Twelve

"THANK you for coming shopping with me," Cam called out from the changing room next to Amber at Dress Up. "It's been too long since we've all hung out together."

"I agree," Christy said. "Drew, I just found the cutest dress. You *have* to try it on. It will look perfect on you."

"I don't need a dress."

Drew had come along begrudgingly, but she'd made it clear to everyone that she had no interest in buying any new clothes and she definitely wasn't going to try any on.

"I told you I'd sit and offer opinions," she said. "Besides, you promised me lunch. That's why I'm here."

Amber laughed and opened the door to the dressing room to reveal her outfit. Tight black jeans with a bright-red button-down blouse. She'd jumped at the chance to do some shopping with the girls. She obviously was planning on staying in Timber Creek for a while and considering the majority of her wardrobe had been purchased for her past life in San Francisco, she was in desperate need for some new items.

Besides, it wouldn't hurt to have a date outfit or two. The

smile that crossed her face when she thought of Logan and their kiss a few days earlier didn't go unnoticed.

"I like it." Cam popped out of her own changing room. "And you clearly do. Look at that smile."

"I don't think it's the clothes that are making her smile," Drew commented. "Because if some skinny jeans and a new top could put that kind of smile on your face, I would have bought some months ago."

Amber shot her friend a look, but Drew shrugged. She hadn't confided in Drew about the kiss, but she had mentioned that she'd gone out to the ranch to see Logan. Her friend wasn't stupid.

"I love the top," Christy said. "And the smile," she added. "You must really like the outfit. Or…maybe you want to tell us why you're smiling so wide?"

Amber looked between her friends, all of whom were grinning as if they knew a secret she didn't.

"Why are you looking at me like that?"

"No reason." Drew winked. She stood from her bench and crossed the floor toward Amber. "But maybe if you're going to buy this as a date outfit, you should try…" She reached out and deftly unbuttoned the top button of her blouse, revealing a bit more cleavage. "There." She dusted her hands together and did a little dance back to her seat. "Now you're ready for a date."

"I don't know what you're talking about." Amber tried to play dumb, but clearly there was no hiding anything from her friends.

"You might as well just spill it," Christy said. "Otherwise we're going to make up our own story and you know how that can go."

"That could be fun," Cam jumped in. "Let's see…" She tapped a finger on her chin and grinned. "I think that maybe Amber and Logan are having a secret—"

"Okay, okay." She laughed. There was no doubt her friends would make up a story far more interesting than she was about to tell them. Besides, there was no reason she shouldn't just come out with the truth. "Logan and I…well, we're…I actually don't know what we're doing."

"Are you dating?" Drew asked.

Amber shook her head. "I don't think I could say that."

"Has he asked you out?"

She shook her head again.

"Have you kissed?" It was Christy who asked, but they all turned to stare at her for a moment, until everyone's head swung toward Amber when she didn't answer right away.

"Well?" Christy prompted. "*Have* you?"

Amber nodded.

She'd done nothing but relive the kiss in her head since it had happened two days earlier. It wasn't that Amber didn't have any experience with men. She just didn't have a lot. And the experience she did have was far from romantic. The few men she'd dated had never been anything serious. Just a minor distraction, and she certainly hadn't felt anything real for them. Everything about the kiss with Logan had been different. So, very different.

"You *did?*" Drew jumped to her feet. "How could you not tell me?"

"I just…I don't…I don't really know." But she did know. Amber had wanted to keep it to herself. Just for a little bit. Just long enough to savor the memory, because despite how amazing the kiss had been, she had no idea what it meant. What if after she said something to her friends, there was nothing left to say? What if the kiss was all there ever was or was going to be between her and Logan? At least if she didn't say anything, she could keep the moment for herself.

"You don't know if you kissed him?" Cam jumped in. "Or

you don't know if...well, I don't know what you might not know. Ya know?"

Christy laughed. "I think we do know." She turned to Amber. "Do you know?"

It was all so ridiculous, Amber covered her hands and laughed along with her. "I wish I did," she said after a minute. "But yes, I did kiss him. Or maybe he kissed me." She shook her head and finally settled on, "*We* kissed."

There was a schoolgirl squeal but Amber wasn't sure who it came from before Drew grabbed her hands and led her to the bench she'd been sitting on. "Tell me everything. I mean, *us.* Tell *us* everything."

"There's not much to tell." She shrugged because it was the truth. After their kiss, they'd been interrupted by another car driving into the parking lot, Logan's next client, and Amber had made her leave. There hadn't been any promises to see each other again, and as far as Amber knew, Logan didn't even have her phone number. The kiss had been amazing, but... "I'm not putting any pressure on it," she said more to satisfy herself than her eagerly awaiting friends. "We'll see what happens."

"Well, I think it's fantastic," Christy declared. "It's about time you settled down and found someone." She stopped and shook her head. "No. It's *way* past time. You deserve to have a good man in your life."

"You're getting totally ahead of yourself." Amber jumped up. "Remember a second ago when I said I'm not putting any pressure on it?"

Christy waved her hand, ignoring her protests. "Besides, maybe you can bring him as a date to Cam's wedding."

The second the words were out, a hand flew up to her mouth and her eyes widened before she turned to stare at Cam. Drew and Amber also turned, open-mouthed, to their friend.

"Cam's wedding?" Amber asked Cam directly.

Cam nodded. "I'm sorry I didn't tell you all sooner, but it was kind of a last-minute decision and I wasn't sure...well... we're getting married on December 24." She looked at Drew as she spoke, obviously worried how she'd handle the news.

She needn't have worried, though, because Drew smiled and even to Amber's surprise, looked genuinely happy. "I think a Christmas wedding sounds perfect," she said.

"You do?"

Drew nodded, but they all noticed the tear that came to her eye. "I can't expect you to put your life on hold because of me." She wiped at the tear before it could fall. "And I'm so happy for you and Evan. I think it's a perfect idea. Really."

Cam crossed the little changing room and pulled Drew into a hug. "Thank you," she whispered to her friend.

They embraced for a moment longer before Drew pulled away and looked straight at Amber. "Besides," she said. "I'm looking forward to seeing Amber with a date."

GROWING UP IN THE MOUNTAINS, Logan had always loved the snow. There was something refreshing about a crisp, fresh blanket of the white stuff that never failed to leave everything looking new and bright.

It was a little different now that he had to shovel mountains of it away from the barn, but despite the extra work the snow brought, he still couldn't bring himself to curse it like so many others did. Besides, he liked the physical exertion. It was a good outlet for his stress and it gave him time to think.

Not that he'd come up with any answers in the four hours since dawn that he'd been out working. If anything, he was more frustrated than ever. No matter how many times he ran it around his head, Logan couldn't think of any solution to keeping Taking the Reins open if Ruby sold the ranch.

"Hey there." A familiar gruff voice caught his attention. Logan turned, wiped the sweat off his brow, and leaned on the shovel as Joseph Monroe made his way across the newly shoveled pathway toward him. "Thought you could use some help after the snowfall we had last night."

The gesture was genuine and despite the fact that Logan would never ask an elderly man to help him shovel so much heavy snow, he very much appreciated the offer.

"I think I have most of the heavy lifting done." He leaned the shovel up against the side of the barn. "But I could use some help getting the horses fresh water."

Joseph nodded. "I'll get right to it."

"And maybe, they'd enjoy a little attention and a brush out," Logan added with a grin. He knew the real reason the old man had shown up at Blackstar. He definitely liked to help out, but more than that, he enjoyed spending time with the horses. And Logan was happy to oblige.

As they worked, they made small talk, commenting on the weather and how the forecasts were predicting more snow than usual this season. Logan listened while Joseph chattered with the horses and brushed down their coats. It never failed to amaze him how a man who appeared so gruff on the outside could be so soft and gentle when he was with the horses.

There was no doubt that people would disagree with him, but Logan could see the magical effect horses could have on people. It truly was amazing.

"It's nice to see you here again, Joseph." Logan handed the man an apple to feed to the horse. "It's been awhile. I thought maybe you'd forgotten about us out here. You know I like to have you out here."

"I know," he grunted. "Been busy," he said before he turned to the horse and said, "I wouldn't forget about you."

Logan tried to hide his chuckle but wasn't very successful.

"And you, obviously," Joseph added. "Truth is, it's hard to get out here in the cold. These old joints don't like the weather much. Everything gets creaky and sore."

"Well, I sure do appreciate your help when you can get out here. I'm glad it's nothing else keeping you away." He knew he shouldn't say anything, and he was probably stepping over a line, but Logan couldn't help but ask, "Your daughter isn't giving you a hard time about coming to the ranch anymore, is she?"

His hand still on the horse, Joseph turned and grunted again. "Not anymore. Said it was a good thing, actually. You talk to her?"

Logan couldn't lie, but he also didn't want to overstep what he should share about his relationship—or whatever it was—with the other man's daughter. "I did," he said after a moment. "It turns out we have some friends in common." It was as much of an explanation as Logan wanted to give, but Joseph didn't seem to mind.

The older man nodded and rubbed Peanut's nose.

"I hope you've been keeping busy, though." Logan changed the subject. He'd always liked the old man, despite his gruff demeanor. Maybe because of it. But now that he'd gotten to know Amber and liked her—a lot—he felt a different connection to her father. He didn't want to get carried away, but if things kept going so well with Amber, well…no.

He was *not* going to get ahead of himself.

"I have," Joseph said. "Been making pens and even got a few stores that asked to stock them."

"Pens? No kidding?"

"All hand turned wood," Joseph said proudly. "Put the finishing on myself. Turned out pretty nice, too."

"I bet they do. Where can I get one?"

"Timber Trade stocks them, and one of those fancy tourist shops in Seattle."

Logan was suitably impressed. "Is that right?"

"No reason to lie."

He didn't bother to hide his chuckle this time. "I had no idea you were so handy, Mr. Monroe." He shook his head and grinned. "Amber's never mentioned anything about it."

"Amber?" The man's hand stilled on Peanut's nose and he turned to look at Logan. "How did you say you knew Amber again?"

"We went to school together," Logan answered cautiously. "She was a few years ahead of me, but we have some friends in common. It's been nice to get to know her better now that she's back in town."

Joseph made a grunting noise. "At least someone is."

Logan tipped his head and considered asking him what he meant by that comment, but ultimately, he was saved from saying anything further at all by another voice bellowing into the barn. "Logan, you in there?"

"Is it noon already?" Logan asked the rhetorical question out loud. Because if Brent Baker was there for their meeting, then it was definitely noon. He turned to Joseph. "You good here? I have a meeting for a few minutes."

Joseph nodded but Logan heard him grumble something about young people always losing track of time as he walked away to meet Brent Baker at the barn doors.

"I'M sorry I haven't called you in a while." Even though Amber knew she was alone, she still glanced around and surveyed Riverside Park, where she'd retreated to make her phone call. After the snowfall the night before, the park was largely deserted besides a few hardcore joggers making use of the freshly plowed trail. Amber stuck to the edge of the path and walked slowly as she made her call to Cody.

Cody had been her sponsor ever since she went to her first addictions meeting back in San Francisco. The doctor in the hospital had recommended it, and even though she'd insisted she didn't need a support group of any kind, the partners at the firm had insisted. Not that it mattered. They obviously had no plans to promote her after the incident anyway.

Or keep her at all.

At any rate, she'd gone to the meeting and met Cody. He was about five years older than her and had been clean for two. He didn't pressure her and he wasn't too pushy, but he did seem to understand what she was going through, even if she didn't, and somehow she'd relented and accepted his offer to be her sponsor.

She'd gone to at least five meetings after that before returning to Timber Creek and, as far as Cody knew, vanishing without a trace. The fact that she hadn't returned any of his phone calls and only very infrequently responded to his text messages hadn't deterred him at all.

Cody clearly took his responsibility as a sponsor seriously and Amber did feel bad that she'd brushed him off. But she hadn't been ready to talk to him.

Until today.

"I'm glad you called," he said. "Are you okay?" He got straight to the point.

She nodded. "I am."

"You haven't used?"

"No. Only the occasional drink, but nothing stronger than wine."

"And you feel okay?"

She took a deep breath and answered him. "I feel great." It was an honest answer. Amber couldn't remember the last time she felt so in control of her life. Sure, there were parts that weren't perfect and there were definitely areas she still needed to work on, but all in all, she felt good.

"I'm really glad to hear it, Amber." She really could hear the relief in his voice. "I was worried."

"I didn't mean to worry you."

"Well, when you don't come to meetings or answer phone calls, it's kind of hard not to."

Guilt washed over her. "I really am sorry, Cody." She meant it. "It wasn't that I didn't want to tell you where I was going. I was just…"

She couldn't finish the thought because it seemed wrong to say it out loud.

"You were afraid?" He guessed. "That I would tell you to come to a meeting? Or give you a hard time for disappearing? Kind of like I'm doing now?"

"No." It was an honest answer. "I was afraid that I would chicken out." She gazed out at the river that still hadn't frozen. Steam came from the water, which, for the time being, was still warmer than the air surrounding it. She'd always thought the river was at its most beautiful right before it froze. It was almost magical. One day it would be open, with the water rushing past and the next day, a crust of ice would seal it shut, and you couldn't seem to predict when it would happen. No matter how much you tried.

"What would you chicken out of? Did you go back to work?"

She almost laughed. "As if they'd have me. No." She shook her head. "I came home. And I think maybe if I'd told you that's where I was going, I wouldn't have come."

"And once you got there?"

She could almost see him on the other end of the phone. He probably had a pen in his hand that he was tapping thoughtfully against his teeth while he waited for her answer. Cody had been in finance. He'd gotten his shot on the trading floor before he turned twenty-five and the frenetic pace caused him to turn to Adderall early on in his career.

He'd burnt out less than ten years later and did a stint in rehab after his family found out about his drug habit. Amber never could imagine him as a day trader, or really, anything that involved a fast pace of life. Cody was about the chillest person she'd ever met. He did yoga daily, cycled to his job as a music teacher, and spent his evenings volunteering.

"It's been okay."

"Just okay?"

"I haven't been tempted to go back if that's what you're asking."

"It is," he said. "And I'm glad to hear it. But why is it just okay?"

"It's different." There was a reason she'd called Cody, but even though she knew it was past time to check in with him, she was still reluctant to face the truth and she knew exactly what Cody would say about that.

"I'm sure it's different," he said kindly. "The last time you were there, *you* were different. How do your family and friends feel about the change in you?"

"They don't know." She shook her head and rubbed her hand over the cool skin on her face. "I haven't told them. I don't know if I can."

"You know what I'm going to say."

She did. Maybe that was the real reason she'd called him.

"You're going to tell me that they'll love me no matter what's happened, and secrets breed lies, and lies breed distrust, and you can't have any real relationship based on distrust."

He chuckled. "You have been listening."

"Just because I don't follow your advice doesn't mean I haven't been listening." She smiled.

"Are you ready to tell them now? It's been awhile."

"I know." From the beginning, Cody had encouraged her

to tell the truth. Although the addictions recovery group they were part of didn't have any particular rules or steps, there were still guidelines and being honest with your loved ones was a big one. Cody had subtly and at times, not so subtly, tried to encourage her to do just that.

But he didn't understand.

They were silent for a few minutes before finally Cody asked, "Why did you call, Amber?"

She swallowed hard. "I'm not sure. I think because I'm finally starting to be okay with things."

"Okay with what happened or your habit?"

"All of it." She pushed her foot through the snow, letting her boot be covered before shaking it off. "I don't know if I can explain it, but I don't feel so bad about it anymore." She didn't bother telling him about the horses or Logan, or that she'd finally admitted things out loud to herself that even in the group setting, she'd swallowed back. "I'm not ready yet, but I'm getting there and I guess I just…well, I just wanted you to know."

She could practically hear him smile on the other end of the line. "I'm so happy to hear that, Amber. I really am."

"Thank you, Cody. And I'm really sorry I was ignoring you. I just—"

"It's okay. We all have our process. I'm really glad you reached out."

"Thank you. I mean it."

"Anytime," he said. "And *I* mean that. Don't be a stranger, okay? I'm still your sponsor, whether you like it or not. Got it?"

She laughed out loud in earnest then. "I got it. We'll talk soon, I promise."

Amber hung up the phone and tucked it into her pocket. It was cold, and despite the big dump of snow they'd had the night before, it felt like it might snow again. She'd never liked winter in Timber Creek when she was a kid. Maybe it was because unlike her friends, she'd never participated in any outdoor sports. She'd been too busy to take up cross-country skiing or snowshoeing. The idea of spending her day in an ice fishing hut, waiting for a bite on the line, seemed like a massive waste of time and her father insisted that downhill skiing, the sport she might have the most interest in, was just a huge money grab and they had better ways to spend a hundred dollars than strap boards on her feet and slide down a mountain.

But walking through the crisp winter air, feeling the sting of the cold on her face, Amber found herself enjoying the nip in the air and the way she felt alive. Maybe it was the season? Maybe it was being back in her hometown? But maybe it was just that after so many years of hiding under her own expectations, she was finally coming alive on her own?

Whatever it was, she liked it.

She also knew she liked Logan. A lot. And even though her friends had given her a hard time, she wasn't upset or weirded out by it the way she would have been in high school. Things had changed. Including the way she felt about making the next move.

Amber pulled her cell phone out of her pocket again, and scrolled through her contacts until she found his number.

She opened up a new text message and typed.

Are you free tonight?

She didn't expect him to text back. Not right away. But to her delight, her phone chirped almost at once.

After seven. Dinner? I'm cooking.

Her face lit up in a smile.

What can I bring?

Just you.

"I'VE SAID IT BEFORE, Logan, and I'll say it again. What you're doing here is pretty special."

With the lack of a real office, Logan had invited Brent Baker up to his little cabin after their quick walk around the barns. The other man looked overdressed in the rustic space, but a hot coffee was exactly what each of them needed after being outside on the chilly winter morning.

"I'm glad to hear it, Brent. And I really hope your patients think so, too."

So far, Brent had sent up a total of five patients to participate in Taking the Reins, including young Kalen whose mother had stopped him on Halloween. Logan wasn't delusional; he knew that not all of them were responding as quickly as the teenager, but he was still hopeful it had been complementary to Brent's practice.

"I think most of them would absolutely agree," Brent said. "And I can tell you that I've noticed a real change in all of them. Even if they don't all agree." He winked at Logan. "But seriously. I see the biggest difference in those who have had a hard time opening up to anyone else about what they're thinking and feeling. The progress over the last few weeks has been incredible. After they come out here to be with your horses, they come back into my office and it's like something has shifted. They *want* to talk. And not only that, it's like they have some sort of deeper understanding about what they're going through."

Pride flowed through Logan, as if it had been him who'd made all the difference to those people and not his four-legged partners who were currently in the barn, happily munching hay.

"If I'm not careful, you and your horses are going to put me out of business completely."

Logan chuckled, but just as quickly the laughter died as he remembered there may not even be a program soon. "I don't think that's going to happen, Brent. In fact, that's part of the reason I wanted to talk to you today."

"What's going on?"

Logan told him all about how Ruby was going to sell the ranch, and how as much as she'd like to find buyers who would keep the equine therapy program going, she couldn't guarantee it. And then he told Brent about the idea he'd had just the night before. It was a long shot, but it was one he was willing to take.

"I think you should invest in the ranch," he said quickly. "As an addition to your practice."

Realization crossed Brent's face, followed quickly by a shake of the head. "Oh no." He waved his hand and Logan felt the tiny glimmer of hope he'd been holding on to fade. "There's no way I have that kind of capital."

"You just said yourself how helpful the horses have been. It could—"

"It doesn't change the fact that I don't have the capital." Brent shook his head apologetically. "I'm sorry, Logan. I just don't have it. Between you and me, there just isn't much left after student loans, business expenses, and a mortgage. And don't get me started about how expensive kids are." He smiled ruefully. "I'm sorry, Logan. I really am. Is there no other way? You're sure Ruby is selling?"

Logan nodded and sank back into his chair. "She is. And I don't blame her either. It's just…" He shook his head in frustration. "Even if the buyers allow me to keep running the business, there's no way they'll agree to the low lease that Ruby did. I'm not sure there's…." He didn't bother finishing the sentence because there was nothing else to say. Everything he'd worked to build, everything he'd dreamed about, would be gone in a matter of months. "It's okay, Brent. You understand that I had to ask."

"I would have thought less of you if you hadn't." The

other man smiled, and Logan could see why his patients opened up to him. He had such an easy-going manner that instantly made you feel at ease. "How's everything else going, Logan? I hope you're not working too much. I see it too often. Young men who put their career first and then…well, then something happens."

"It's okay," Logan assured him. "I'm good. I've been seeing —" He hesitated before completing the sentence.

Had he been seeing Amber? It wasn't official, but…it sure felt like that's what they were doing. Is that what Amber thought?

It was almost impossible to know what Amber thought. And maybe it wasn't a great time for her. After all, she did have a lot going on.

"Can I ask you a question?" He changed tracks, but Brent only nodded, going along with him. "In your professional opinion, do you think it's healthy for someone to hang onto a secret about themselves that has been life-changing? Or should they come clean to their loved ones?"

Brent considered the question for a moment. "Are friends and family at risk or impacted by what the truth might be?"

Logan shook his head. "No. It's more that the person holding the secret is also holding onto incredible guilt and self-hatred because of the secret." For a moment, he felt badly about talking about Amber when she wasn't there, but he hoped he was being obscure enough to keep her privacy. Besides, he truly was concerned about her. "Do you think it's better for the person emotionally if they can be honest with everyone?"

The other man was silent for a moment, but he finally nodded. "Without knowing the whole story, I'd say that in most situations it's always better to be upfront about things and not to keep secrets. Even if they're potentially harmless ones. When people hold things in, they tend to eat away at them and affect all parts of their lives. Often these things can fester and manifest as entirely new problems." He took a sip of his coffee. "If you're talking about yourself..." Logan shook his head. "Okay then, a friend?" Logan nodded. "If he or she doesn't want to consider talking to a professional, which I'd encourage by the way—"

"Naturally."

Brent winked. "I'd maybe gently suggest that they come clean. Particularly if it's solely for their benefit and no one will be negatively affected."

Logan thought about his words and thought about Amber. He was absolutely certain she'd feel better if she told her friends and family the truth. For a moment, he considered Joseph Monroe, who was likely still out in the barns with the horses.

There was no doubt that he loved his daughter, and Logan was positive that her friends would be nothing but supportive to Amber.

There was only good that could come from Amber opening up. He was sure of it.

Now he just needed to convince her of that.

And a few hours later, when she sent him a text, and he invited her over for dinner, Logan saw his opportunity to do just that.

Chapter Thirteen

IT WASN'T EVEN Thanksgiving yet, but that didn't mean anything as far as the weather in Timber Creek was concerned. Things were unpredictable in the mountains, so Logan wasn't surprised when the chilly, clear day once again clouded over. There was a good chance they'd get another dump of snow before dawn. But that was fine with him, because he expected Amber to knock on his door any moment and he couldn't think of much that would be more enjoyable than cuddling up in the cabin with her.

He'd already set a fire in the stone fireplace and he was certain they'd be perfectly cozy inside his cabin. With any luck, they'd be *very* cozy.

Before heading back out into the living room, Logan took another quick look in the mirror in the bathroom. He'd chosen a button-up shirt that was slightly dressier than his usual selection, as well as a brand-new pair of dark jeans. It was their first real date, even if it wasn't at a restaurant, and Logan was aware that Amber was probably used to men dressed in sharp suits. He'd never be one of those guys, but he did clean up pretty nicely.

He returned to the kitchen and checked on the roast chicken he'd tucked into the oven earlier. It wasn't fancy, but he knew his chicken and roast vegetable dinner was delicious, and it never failed to impress. He'd run into town and grabbed a fresh loaf of bread from the bakery and a bottle of wine, too.

Neither of them drank much, but a crisp white paired nicely with the chicken. And it *was* a date, after all.

Moments after he put the chicken back into the oven to finish up, there was a knock on the door and his stomach flipped the way it used to when he saw Tina.

Logan quickly banished the thought. He was not going to think of Tina. Not tonight. She was the past, from a different time of his life. Hell, a completely different life.

He opened the door and again his stomach flipped, only this time it was accompanied by a distinct reaction lower in his gut. *Damn. Even in a parka, Amber looked amazing.*

"Hey."

"Hey yourself." Logan shook his head, breaking the trance her presence had thrust him into. "Come on in." He held the door to the side so she could enter the warm, little cabin.

When she was inside, she handed him a bottle of wine and shrugged. "I know you don't really drink much…well…I mean…I didn't know what else to bring."

He laughed and took it from her. "I told you only to bring yourself."

"It didn't seem adequate."

He helped her out of her jacket. "It's more than adequate." Logan turned to hang her parka on the hook by the door and when he looked back at her, his breath momentarily caught in his throat. "You look gorgeous," he said after a moment.

Amber blushed a little, which had the effect of matching the skin that dipped down to her cleavage to the tight red blouse she was wearing. "You clean up pretty nicely yourself."

They stood staring awkwardly at each other for a moment

too long. Whatever else happened, Logan was not going to let their first date be awkward in any way and there was only one way to guarantee it wasn't. He took a step forward, threaded his fingers through her silky black hair, and cupped the back of her head. "I've been wanting to do this since the last time." He pressed his lips to hers. Gently enough not to startle her, but with enough pressure to make it perfectly clear about exactly how badly he'd been wanting to do it again.

She kissed him back, and a tiny moan escaped her lips as they deepened the kiss. Logan held himself in check, and before things went too far, he took a step back and put a little distance between them.

"That's better." He grinned.

Her fingers went to her lips. It was both a sweet sight and an incredibly sexy one. "What's that?"

"Like I said, I've been wanting to do that for days. And now that I have it out of my system, I think we can have a nice dinner."

She laughed. It really was a sound he didn't think he'd ever get tired of hearing, which was good because he was hearing it more and more. As far as Logan was concerned, that only meant she was relaxing and becoming more and more comfortable with him. And he liked it.

"Dinner smells delicious." She walked through the little living room into the attached kitchen and made a show of inhaling deeply. "I had no idea you could cook, too."

"There's still a lot you don't know about me." He winked and almost wanted to pinch himself. How they'd gone from almost enemies to this easy back-and-forth flirtation in only a couple months was beyond him, but he was certainly glad they had. "And it's almost ready. Maybe I could get you to open the bottle of wine in the fridge."

She looked at him sideways.

"Hey." He held up his hands in surrender. "I picked up a bottle, too, and white will go better with dinner."

"But I thought…"

"I didn't say I didn't drink at all." He answered her unasked question. "Just not a lot. And if you're okay with it…"

She nodded at the unasked question. "I am."

"I'm glad," he said. "Because tonight's a special occasion."

She took the corkscrew he offered her and got to work on the bottle. "Is it?"

"You know it is."

AMBER HAD no idea what to expect when it came to Logan's home, but she was pleasantly surprised at his cozy cabin. It was neat and tidy, and although it wasn't very big, it had all the comforts she would expect. There wasn't much in the way of decorations on the walls—a few pictures of horses and landscapes that looked as if they probably predated Logan. The living room had an overstuffed couch and a big easy chair she could imagine herself tucked up in, reading one of her romance novels in front of the fire.

The thought of making herself so comfortable in Logan's cabin didn't shock her or take her by surprise the way it might have a few months ago. For some reason as she stood there and watched him tidy up the last of the dishes from the delicious meal he'd prepared, it seemed completely natural to imagine they might have a future.

And why couldn't they?

"Tell me something," she said as she watched him wash a plate.

"What do you mean?" He laughed. "What kind of something?"

"You said before that there was a lot I didn't know about you." She shrugged. "So tell me something. Like, how come you're still single?"

His smile dimmed momentarily as he turned to put the plate on the counter and she wondered whether maybe she'd asked the wrong question, which, in her experience as a lawyer, meant it was exactly the *right* question.

"You really want to know?"

"Are you really asking me that?" She moved toward him, snatched the towel from where it hung on the stove and started to dry.

"Okay," he conceded. "I wasn't always single. I mean, I assume from what you've told me that you always put your career first."

That was an understatement and they both knew it, but she nodded.

"It wasn't like that for me." He started to scrub another plate. "I was in love once before, about four years ago."

Despite the fact that she'd asked to hear it, the knowledge still stung somewhere inside her chest but she kept listening.

"Her name was Tina. You probably wouldn't know her. She moved to Timber Creek after graduation to work at the ski hill for a season. You would have been gone by then."

Amber nodded.

"We started dating and when spring came, she took a job waitressing at Riverside Grill and…well, I thought she was the one." He smiled a little and handed her the next clean plate to dry. "You don't have to do that," he added as she took it from him.

"I want to," Amber said. "If she was the one, what happened?"

Logan's smile faded. "There was an accident."

The word hit her unexpectedly. She'd just assumed they'd

had a fight or maybe she'd met someone else, or something a little less…tragic.

"An accident?"

Logan focused his attention on the pan he was scrubbing for a few moments before speaking. "Tina was coming home from Seattle," he said. "I was supposed to have gone with her. We were going to get a hotel room and have a romantic evening." Amber pushed down the twinge of unreasonable jealousy. "But at the last minute, I decided to stay and hang out with my friends instead." He shook his head as he recounted the story. "She decided not to bother with the hotel room if I wasn't there, so she drove home." He took a deep breath. "She fell asleep at the wheel and hit a tree."

Amber's hand flew to her mouth. "Logan, that's so—"

"For a long time, I blamed myself," he continued, as if she hadn't spoken. "I couldn't handle it. I started drinking. A lot. One day, I saw something on television about equine therapy and something inside me just clicked."

"Just like that?"

"Just like that." He shrugged. "I started looking into it, and when I mentioned it to my dad and little sister, they thought it was a great idea, too. They helped me find a program outside of Spokane. I guess you could say the horses saved me."

"And that's why you decided to start Taking the Reins."

He nodded.

Amber shook her head slowly. "I can't believe I didn't know any of this."

Logan smiled slowly and pulled the drain on the sink. "Like I said, we still have a lot to learn about each other. And we will." He took the plate from her and put it on the counter before turning around and taking both her hands in his. "That was a long time ago," he said. "And I want you to know that I don't blame myself anymore." She nodded, glad to hear it.

"And...as important as Tina was to me, that part of my life is over. I've moved on."

He looked directly into her eyes while he spoke, and she believed every word he said.

"Come sit." Logan squeezed her hands before releasing them to grab the bottle of wine they hadn't quite finished, as well as their glasses. They walked through the living room, where Logan gestured to the couch. Amber happily joined him.

"Thank you for telling me that story," she said.

"I'm glad I told you." He poured her some more wine. "I feel like I know about some of your past. I don't want to keep anything from you."

"I appreciate that." She had never felt so comfortable with anyone the way she did with Logan. Not except her best friends, and that was different because she wasn't also very attracted to any of them. "I'm really glad we did this," she blurted a moment later. "I…well…" There was no harm in telling him exactly how she felt. "I'm really comfortable with you," she said before she could change her mind. "I think you're pretty great and I like spending time with you." She finished what she needed to say and laughed. "I've never had a problem saying exactly how I feel before."

"It didn't seem like you had much trouble just then either." Logan laughed, but then grew serious. "I feel the same way with you, Amber. And I have to say, I'm pretty glad I didn't go on my first judgment with you."

"Oh yeah?" She turned on the couch and tucked a leg up under her. "And what was that?" She already knew the answer, but she really wanted to see him squirm while he answered it.

As it turned out, Logan didn't squirm at all. "I thought you were an overbearing, know-it-all city girl."

She sat back and squeezed her lips shut because it was an entirely accurate assessment of who she *had* been.

"But now I know there is *so* much more to you. You do know how fabulous you are, right?"

There was a time she would have answered that question with a quick-witted answer about how she knew how great she was, and it might have been true, too. But now things were different. She still didn't have a self-esteem problem, not really; she was just slowly discovering that there was a lot more to her than the sharp-tongued, laser-focused, highly driven, get-it-done-at-all-costs woman she used to be.

In fact, that had never even been her. Not really.

"I know that I'm a work in progress," she said after a moment. "And I really think a lot of that is thanks to you. Well, maybe thanks to Chester," she added with a grin.

"You know I didn't do anything." Logan slid his hand along the couch between them and reached for her hand. "And neither did Chester. That was all you."

Amber took a deep breath and let it out slowly. "Maybe you're right, but I never could have done it if it hadn't been for you and your horses. You're doing such a great thing out here, Logan." His face changed, and his hands stiffened over hers. "Did I say something wrong?"

"No." He squeezed his eyes shut and when he opened them again, they were softer, the tension gone. "I wasn't going to say anything, not tonight. I didn't want to ruin our evening. But…"

"You're worrying me."

"It's nothing for you to worry about," he said quickly. "And I'm sure it will all be fine, but recently Ruby told me that she's going to be selling the ranch. She's hoping the new buyer will allow me to continue my work, and maybe lease the barn to me for the same rate, but it's a bit of a long shot. I'm not hopeful that will happen. Besides, it will take capital I don't know if I can raise."

A cross between fear, which was silly, and intense sadness came over her as he spoke. Her first instinct was to set up a fundraiser, start a petition, and make some noise about Logan and Taking the Reins. Her mind instinctually kicked into overdrive and she started to mentally make preparations, including potential legal action if that's what it took to keep Logan's operation going. But then she took a breath. And another and realized that was the old Amber. And as driven as she no doubt could still be, she also needed to be reasonable.

"Logan, that's terrible." She flipped his hand over and squeezed it in hers. "Is there anything I can do? Anything at all?"

"Do you have a million dollars?" He chuckled, but it wasn't a funny sound. "Because I think that's what it's going to take to save this. Otherwise, I'm looking at starting over somewhere and finding somewhere to put the horses and…I guess I'll need to find a new place to live, too." He looked around his tiny cabin. "It's all part of the ranch."

She let him have a moment before closing the distance between them and pulling him into a tight embrace. He melted into her, and she used the opportunity to soothe him. She'd never been a naturally comforting person, but the last couple of months with Drew and Austin had taught her a few things, and being with Logan made it seem natural.

Amber rubbed his back and her fingers found the nape of his neck, where she traced gentle circles on the sensitive skin there.

"That feels nice," he murmured into her ear.

She smiled, the satisfaction of the moment pleasing her more than she thought possible. "That's the idea."

He lifted his head from her shoulder so he could look into her eyes. "Is that the entire idea?"

The question was loaded, but Amber was more than ready to pull the trigger. "Not even close." She leaned forward and pressed her lips to his. Each kiss they shared was better than the one that came before, but this one held more than the possibility of what could happen.

It held the promise of what was *exactly* about to happen.

If she could let herself go.

The mental roadblock popped up so quickly, it took her off guard.

She'd never been so comfortable with a man before. Never so attracted.

And that was the problem.

Something inside her wanted to stop, pull back, and put distance between them. Not because she didn't want whatever was about to happen to happen. But because she *did.*

Never in her life had she cared about a man the way she was starting to care about Logan. Never had a man made her feel the way she was feeling now. And without a doubt, there had absolutely never been *anyone* who knew everything there was to know about her, and still wanted to be with her.

Logan liked her for who she was.

And that scared the hell out of her.

"HEY." Logan felt her pulling back. He'd felt the change in her, maybe before even she had. But whatever it was that was going on with her, there was no way he was going to let it happen. He leaned back, but only a little. He touched his finger to her lips in place of his own. "What's going on in that beautiful head of yours?"

Her eyes flashed as though she might actually tell him, but then she shook her head. "I should go." Amber hopped up from the couch before he could stop her and crossed the room quickly to the door.

Logan was up and behind her as she reached for the door handle.

The rush of windy, snowy frigid air hit them at the same time. "What the—"

"I thought it might snow," Logan said as he slipped between her and the door. He peered out into the dark night, the porch lights illuminating the heavily falling snow and the inch-deep layer of white stuff that had already accumulated on the railing in the time they'd been inside. "But I don't think I expected this much. There's no way you're driving in this."

Logan turned back to her and shut the door behind him before leaning against it. "Besides," he added. "I don't want you to go."

"You don't?"

He couldn't help it; he chuckled. "I would have thought that was pretty obvious."

There was a flicker of a smile on her face before she moved to the window and looked out to what was quickly becoming a blizzard outside. "I just…I'm not…"

Logan stayed quiet because it was easy enough to see there was an internal battle going on inside her, and he wasn't sure who was going to win the war.

Finally, after what seemed like forever, Amber turned around. "I've never done anything like this before and you…"

"I'm what?" He took a step closer to her, but still gave her the space she obviously needed.

"You're…" She dropped her head for a minute, before looking up into his eyes. "You're different in all the right ways."

He couldn't help it then; he had to touch her. With one hand, he reached out and threaded his fingers through hers. "I am," he said slowly. "And I'm not going to pretend to know everything there is about you, yet. Including your past relationships. But I can tell you with complete certainty that I *am* different than anybody else you've ever dated." She opened her mouth to say something, but he wasn't done. "And I like you, Amber. Really like you. Don't run from this. Not now."

She closed her mouth again and pressed her lips together. It took intense self-control for Logan not to kiss her again, but he waited. He could be patient. When she didn't say anything right away, he spoke again. "I mean it, Amber. Don't run." He took his free hand and tucked a piece of long, dark hair behind her ear. When she leaned into his touch, he felt that familiar tug low in his gut.

Damn, but he was falling for this woman.

"Okay." Her voice was soft at first, but whatever confusion and doubt she'd had appeared to be gone. She lowered her eyelids and the corners of her pouty, sexy lips turned up into a sure smile. "Okay," she said again. This time stronger and more sure. "I'll stay."

"Yeah, you will."

Her tongue flicked out and licked her bottom lip, leaving behind a completely kissable sheen in its place. He closed the remainder of the distance between them, wrapped one arm behind her back and, using his other hand to brace the impact, pushed her up against the log wall and kissed her.

Whatever doubt she had left about staying was sure to be completely eradicated with that kiss, and judging by the moan that slipped out of her lips, he was sure it was mission accomplished. Not letting his lips leave hers, he moved his hands down her sides, so he could feel all of her luscious curves before his hands found hers. With one in each of his, he raised them up, above her head, and pinned them to the wall.

She let out a gasp, and it was only then that he released her from the kiss and trailed his mouth down her smooth neck, licking, nibbling, and sucking as he went. Her body moved against his, but he kept her pressed tight against the wall.

Another moan slipped from her lips and he lifted his head so he could look into her heavily lidded eyes.

"I'm glad I decided to stay," she whispered.

It was Logan's turn to grin. "I think it's cute that you thought you had a choice."

She opened her mouth, no doubt to argue with him again, but he silenced her with a quick, hard kiss before scooping her up in his arms and carrying her through the tiny cottage to his bedroom.

THE SCENT of freshly brewed coffee wove its way through her unconsciousness and finally nudged Amber awake the next morning. Once her eyes fluttered open, it took her a few moments to realize where she was but the moment the memory of the night before came back, her entire body remembered it. Despite herself, her face split into a wide smile.

"Now that's a sight I could get used to seeing first thing in the morning."

At the sound of Logan's voice, Amber sat up quickly, realizing a moment too late to grab the blanket that had been covering her.

"I was wrong." He smiled. "*That* is a sight I could get used to seeing."

Amber laughed and took her time pulling the blanket back up. After all, what was the point in modesty after the night before?

"Did you sleep well?" Logan sat next to her on the mattress and handed her the cup of coffee he was holding. "I wasn't sure how you took it, but I guessed."

"Black?" She inhaled deeply, letting the smell fill her.

"I was right."

"Maybe I'm just too predictable." She took a tentative sip, testing the temperature. "Thank you. This is perfect."

"You're welcome." He brushed a strand of her long hair,

tangled from sleep, off her face. "And you are anything but predictable. I'm really glad you stayed."

So was she. *So* glad. Because the truth was, she was absolutely falling for this man. The night before she'd almost made a terrible mistake by running away from those feelings. The old Amber would have run. But she hadn't. Did that make her a *new* Amber? It must because the old Amber would *never* have spent the night with a man after the first date. But she didn't feel bad or remorseful about it at all because it didn't feel like a first date and with Logan it was just…so very different.

"Me too," she finally said. "But it turns out I didn't have much of a choice." She grinned over the lip of her coffee mug. Whether it was Logan or the storm that took her choice away, it didn't matter. "It's like something out of one of my romance novels, snowed into a mountain cabin. Oh, what should we do?" She batted her eyelashes in exaggeration and laughed.

Logan traced his finger across her bare shoulder and dipped it down into her cleavage. "I can think of a few things."

"I'm sure you can." She swatted his hand away. "But I'm starving, and I don't want to jinx it, but do I smell…"

"Bacon?" He leaned forward and kissed her quick. "You sure do. Breakfast is almost ready. I was hoping you'd wake up soon."

"What time is it? I never sleep in."

"Ten."

"Ten?" Amber almost spat out her coffee. She couldn't remember the last time she'd slept past seven and it must have been at least twenty years since she'd slept as long as ten. And that was when she'd been terribly sick with the flu. "I need to get up." She tried to move past him on the bed, but he held her in place.

"You absolutely do *not* need to get up. You have nowhere to be today. Mostly because you can't go anywhere. The plow will get here this afternoon to dig out the drive. So until then…"

Once upon a time, not so long ago, the thought that she was stranded in a tiny cabin with no way out would have caused her a huge deal of panic. But with Logan sitting in front of her, the smile on his face and the affection in his eyes, that was the very last thing on her mind.

LOGAN WAS RIGHT.

She wasn't going anywhere. Once Amber—dressed in only one of Logan's t-shirts—made it out to the main room and saw the piles of snow for herself, there was no doubt in her mind that her car wouldn't be getting out anytime soon. At least not until the road was plowed.

"It's kind of early in the season for so much snow, don't you think?"

Logan shrugged and put a plate of eggs, bacon, and toast in front of her. "Who knows? Every year it's different, right? Besides, it might still melt and we could have a warm Thanksgiving."

They both laughed because that wasn't likely to happen.

"Speaking of Thanksgiving…" he said after a moment. "I was thinking about something, and I don't want you to get upset or anything."

She froze, a piece of bacon halfway to her mouth. *Upset?* Was he going to ask her to have Thanksgiving with him? Was it too early in their relationship to celebrate a major holiday together? Certainly not. But maybe he wanted to introduce her to his family.

Amber dropped the bacon to her plate.

It was *way* too early to meet family or to declare anything or…it was just too early. *Right?* She shook her head.

"You haven't even heard what I was going to say."

"I don't care. I don't think it's a good idea." She squeezed her eyes shut like a child. "I don't think I should meet your family."

"I think you should tell your friends everything."

They spoke at the same time, so Amber wasn't sure she'd heard him properly. "Pardon me?"

"I could ask you the same thing." He tilted his head and looked at her, clearly questioning what it was that she'd said and why. Thankfully, Logan focused on what he'd needed to say. "I've been thinking about it and I know it's not my place, but in the time since I've met you, well...you've changed. You've..." He swallowed, obviously struggling to find the words. "Well, this sounds stupid, but I think you've grown a lot and you seem happier and more at ease since you started talking to Chester."

Amber nodded slowly. She couldn't argue with that. It was all absolutely true.

"And maybe," Logan continued, "if you told your friends and family everything you told Chester and me, you might feel even better?" She opened her mouth, but shut it again when he added, "And maybe you'd finally be okay with everything and be able to really forgive yourself."

"Forgive myself?" The words hit her hard. "I don't—"

"I'm not trying to upset you." He was out of his chair and crouching on the floor next to her. "In fact, I really care about you, Amber, and I just really think that—"

"Okay."

She spoke the word so quickly, she hadn't even realized she'd said it for a moment.

"Okay?"

Amber nodded.

"You'll tell them?"

"Okay."

Maybe it was time she came clean. Maybe she would feel

better about everything. Maybe it *would* be a load off. There was only one way to find out.

It might have been the cozy cabin with the fire in the stone fireplace. It might have been Logan, his support and obvious care for her. It might have been the afterglow of a special night or maybe it was just that Amber was sick of the secrets. Whatever it was, in that moment, she couldn't think of a reason *not* to tell the truth.

What could it hurt?

Chapter Fourteen

"ARE you really not going to tell me what happened?" Drew abandoned the pancakes she was flipping at the stove and plopped herself down at the table in front of Amber.

It had been almost a full twenty-four hours since the plows finally made it up to Logan's cabin at the ranch and she was able to go home. Somehow Amber had managed to avoid the interrogation that she knew Drew was dying to give her.

Until that morning.

"I spent the night," Amber said as innocently as she could manage without laughing. "I already told you that. In fact, I texted you to tell you that was exactly what I was doing. We were snowed in all day, but the plows showed up and dug us out, and here I am."

"You know that's not what I'm talking about." Drew looked pointedly at her. "What happened while you were *there*?"

Amber gestured toward the stove with her head. "Your pancakes are burning."

Drew spun around before jumping up from her chair. "Damn it." She flipped the charred breakfast into the sink and started again with more batter. "If I'm going to burn your breakfast, you might as well tell me what the hell happened." She turned to face Amber and pointed the spatula in her direction. "I'm your best friend. Now spill. Lord knows I need a little good news in my life."

"Ouch." Amber pressed her hand to her chest and pretended to look affronted. "Are you seriously going to play the woe-is-me card?"

Drew grinned. "Whatever it takes. Besides, we tell each other *everything*." A knife of guilt stabbed Amber in the gut at her friend's choice of words, and the knife was twisted when she added, "Best friends don't keep secrets from each other."

Right. Amber swallowed hard. *Best friends don't keep secrets.* Except the giant, mega, King Kong secret that she'd been keeping from all of her best friends for her entire life.

"Now tell me all I need to know before I burn round two."

Amber was brought back to the conversation at hand and forced a smile. There may be some things she still wasn't sure about coming clean to her friends about, despite her promise to Logan, but there were somethings she *could* tell them. "I'm not one to kiss and tell, but…he made me a delicious dinner, we talked, and…"

"And?"

"You know it's not my style to go into details." She wiggled her eyebrows and Drew squealed.

"Okay, okay. I'll accept that. But just tell me, did you…"

Amber nodded and Drew squealed again. "I knew it!" She ran to her and threw her arms around her. "I'm so happy for you. It's about time."

"Wait." Amber managed to wiggle out of her friend's embrace. "About time for what?" She assessed her friend, who'd turned away, back to the stove and the pancakes. "What are you talking about? It's not like I've never been with a man before."

If Drew thought that just because she'd been a workaholic

most of her life and focused on her own goals that didn't involve men, that she was a virgin, she didn't know her as well as she thought she did.

Drew burst out laughing. Despite the fact that Amber knew she was laughing at her, it was nice to see her best friend so happy, no matter what the reason. "I know *that.*" She wiped at her face, leaving a streak of batter behind.

"Then what are you talking about?" Amber couldn't help but laugh at Drew's response. "It's about time for what exactly?"

"For you to have a relationship, silly."

"A what?" The laughter died on her lips as she stared at her friend with an open mouth. "You think that's what it is?"

"Yes." Drew deftly flipped a pancake. "Because isn't that exactly what it is?"

Amber was going to open her mouth to object because that most certainly was *not* what it was. At least she thought it wasn't. Relationships were all dinner dates, and making plans for Friday night, and texting throughout the day, and—shit.

"Am I wrong?" Drew asked. But it was a rhetorical question because she kept talking. "Besides, I think it's awesome. You know, it's never too late to have a second chance."

"A second chance?" Amber shook her head. "What do you mean? I never had a first chance with Logan. This isn't really—"

"I mean at *life.* It's like all those years ago you made a choice to go down one path instead of another and then for better or worse, that's the way it went." Drew's eyes took on a far-off look. "And now, it's like here you are…getting a second chance to do something else. Does that make sense?"

Amber wasn't sure they were still talking about her, but if they were, she wasn't entirely sure that it *did* make sense.

Fortunately for Amber, before she could say anything at all, Ben's voice, followed by the man himself, interrupted them.

"Something smells good in here." He walked over to the counter where Drew had just piled a fresh stack of pancakes and tried to grab one.

She smacked his hands. "If you're hungry, make yourself useful by setting the table."

"Yes, ma'am."

Amber watched the scene as Ben moved around the little kitchen and did as he was told. He'd been around more and more, and was clearly becoming familiar and comfortable in the space. Just as Drew was obviously becoming more comfortable with his presence. She knew Ben was just being a good uncle to Austin and friend to Drew, but she couldn't help but remember something Cam had told her ages ago about Ben having a crush on Drew when they were kids.

Not that it mattered because whatever the reason, Ben's presence was obviously helping Drew heal. And that's all she could ask for.

A few minutes later, they were all seated around the table, feasting on a breakfast of pancakes and fresh fruit.

"This is awesome, Mom," Austin declared before stuffing another piece of pancake in his mouth. By last count, he'd already eaten at least four and showed no signs of stopping.

"It really is good, Drew," Amber agreed. "I'm so glad you're cooking again. I think we were all getting sick of my toast and boxed cereal breakfast offerings."

Her friend looked down at the table for a moment but when she looked up, she was smiling. "Honestly, it feels good to do it. I never thought it would. I mean…" She shook her head and laughed at herself. "I never thought it would feel okay to do something normal again, but it's not so bad anymore."

Ben took a gulp of orange juice. "Well, if you think cooking pancakes is normal, I bet a pot roast would be just as—ouch."

"Don't push it." Drew gave him a semi-serious look but

there was no doubt she was considering it. Drew had always loved to cook and for good reason. She was amazing at it. "But I am actually thinking of taking care of a few things that should have been done a long time ago." She pointed her fork at Amber. "And I was hoping you could help me."

"I'm sure I can. What's up?"

She almost wished she hadn't asked when Drew said, "Some of the paperwork of Eric's. His will, some estate things mostly. It's all kind of over my head and I could really use your legal mind. Besides, you're the smartest person I know and I trust you with this stuff so if there's anything unexpected, you're the one I want on my side. Besides," Drew added with a wink. "We don't have any secrets, right?"

"Right." Amber shoved a piece of pancake in her mouth. As she struggled to swallow the food that despite being light and fluffy only a moment before had now become thick and dry in her throat, Amber was consumed by guilt. There was no way she could tell Drew or the others the truth about her life now. Not when they all thought she was so irreproachable and trustworthy.

How could she possibly tell them she wasn't who they thought?

She couldn't. And hadn't she always known that?

IT HAD BEEN a couple months already since the adoption had been finalized. Legally as well as bound by the heart, Mya was hers. But that didn't stop the flutter of nerves that took over every time Christy prepared to meet with Mya's birth mother, Becky.

She was a nice girl and she'd never given any indication to either Christy or Mark that she was going to change her mind about giving Mya up for adoption. She hadn't made the decision lightly, and everyone knew it was the right one.

Still, Christy had to swallow her nerves as she approached the park bench where Becky was sitting and waiting for them at Riverside Park.

Almost at once, when Becky stood and greeted her with a warm hug, the nerves were gone. "It's so good to see you," the girl said before turning her attention to the baby. Her fingers fluttered, unsure, over the blanket covering the sleeping infant in the stroller before she snatched it up and moved it away. "She's gotten so big," Becky gasped. "How is that even possible?"

Christy chuckled. "She does a lot of eating." She watched Becky stare at the baby for a moment before she asked, "Do you want to hold her?"

Immediately Becky nodded and then shook her head. "Yes. I mean, no. I don't want to disturb her. I remember very well how hard it was to get her back to sleep."

Christy's smile was kind. She bent over and started to unfasten the buckles that held Mya in place before gently scooping her up. "It's okay, Becky. She settles much better now, and she probably won't even wake up."

She handed the baby to Becky and sat next to them. It took the girl a minute to relax, but soon she was rocking gently without even realizing it, the way most people who hold a baby do.

"She's beautiful." Becky's voice was slightly more than a whisper. "It's amazing what you've done…I mean…she's like a completely different baby. So calm and…" Her voice trailed off as she simply gazed down at the child. After a moment, Becky looked up. "I've registered for school."

"School? What kind?"

"I've decided to go for my nursing degree." Becky's face lit up as she spoke of her plans. "It won't be easy and it will definitely take a long time. And I have to move. The course is in Seattle, which is crazy to even think about. Never mind the whole idea of going back to school for at least four more years. It definitely wasn't top of my list, but that was before. And now…well…I think I can really make a difference. You know, like Doctor Thomas did for me."

Mark *had* really made a difference in Becky's life. Christy blinked hard to keep from crying.

"Do you think it's a stupid idea?" Becky shifted the baby in her arms and eagerly looked to Christy for assurance. "I mean, it's not like I'm going to be a doctor, but I thought that maybe…and there was some financial aid and…it just seemed like—"

"The perfect thing." Christy laid a hand on Becky's arm. "It's perfect and I think it's an amazing idea, Becky. Really. It's going to be a lot of work, but I know you can do it. You can do anything. I'm sure of it."

The girl didn't have a strong parental figure in her life, and just as Christy and Mark had adopted little Mya, in a way, they'd also adopted Becky.

"I'm very proud of you."

Becky held Mya for a few more minutes until she started to fuss and she handed the baby back to Christy. In return, Christy gave her a little photo album she'd put together with some of the pictures Cam had taken. They hugged again and made arrangements to get together before Becky left for school in Seattle.

Christy rocked Mya to settle her down again and waited a few minutes before making her way back into town to take care of the rest of her errands.

After living in Timber Creek her entire life, it wasn't unusual for her to run into someone she knew, so she wasn't surprised when she ran into Logan Myers in the parking lot of the bank.

"Nice to see you," Christy said. "I've been kind of hoping to run into you."

Logan looked around as if to see if she were talking to someone else, but Christy only laughed. "It's not every day that a man manages to snag our Amber," she explained. "And that means that my duty as a friend is to—"

"Interrogate me?" He winked at her, playing along.

"I wouldn't call it an interrogation so much as the…third degree."

They laughed.

"Seriously, though," Christy said. "We've never seen Amber like this, and it's really nice."

It was nice. Christy, like the others, had always hoped that Amber would find someone and maybe not settle down so much as settle in. She'd always seemed a bit restless and agitated somehow. But lately, since she'd been home in Timber Creek, she seemed different in a way. Not so anxious. Christy couldn't help but think that Logan had a lot to do with that shift.

"I was thinking," Christy said, making a snap decision. "Why don't you and Amber come for Thanksgiving dinner? It's Mya's first Thanksgiving, so I thought I'd have a group over and do it up right."

She had most definitely *not* been thinking that. In fact, she and Mark had discussed having a quiet Thanksgiving, just the three of them. Their parents were all out of town, and it seemed silly to do up a turkey just for them. But at no time had they talked about inviting everyone over and having a giant feast. Mark was going to kill her. But he'd get over it. Besides, it would be fun.

"What do you say?" she asked when Logan still hadn't answered. "I'm not going to take no for an answer."

"Well then," he laughed, "I guess that's a yes. What can we bring?"

HE SHOULDN'T BE DISAPPOINTED. It's not like Logan actually thought the bank meeting would go differently than it did. He had no assets, no collateral, and no hope in hell that the bank would give him a loan. He hadn't been the least bit surprised when Leslie Wilson, the bank manager, gave him the news.

"I'm sorry, Logan." She'd looked genuinely sorry, too. Not that it mattered. "I just can't do it. With your lack of credit history, it's just…"

"I understand." And he did. "But I had to give it a shot."

He'd left the bank with the last of whatever hope he had, dashed. The best he could hope for now was that whomever bought Ruby's ranch would allow him to continue to run the therapy practice. Which meant he needed to put together a business plan for Taking the Reins so he'd have the strongest case to present whenever the sale went through.

But first, he had a lunch date with the most beautiful woman in town.

He met Amber at Riverside Grill, where she'd arrived before him and had already secured a table by the window. She had her back to him and was gazing out at the snowy riverbank outside as he approached.

"I hope I'm not interrupting anything." He hesitated a moment before pressing a kiss to her cheek. But the smile on her face when she turned and saw him erased any hesitancy he might have felt about the status of their relationship. Because that's exactly what it was. At least as far as he was concerned. He was falling hard and fast for this woman, and although it was the last thing he ever would have expected to happen, least of all with her, there was no way he was going to deny his feelings.

"Not at all." She grabbed his arm before he could take his

seat and pulled him back to her for a proper kiss that sent electrical shots throughout his body.

Yes. He was definitely falling. That is, if he hadn't already completely fallen.

"I was just looking at the river," she said as Logan took his seat. "Isn't it amazing how it can go from free flowing one moment to completely frozen over? It never fails to amaze me how running water can freeze solid in an instant."

He followed her gaze and nodded. "It's beautiful no matter what."

"It is." She turned to give him her full attention. "How has your morning been? I was surprised when you said you'd be in town."

"Good surprised, I hope?"

She reached over and put her hand on his. "Definitely. I just expected you would be at the ranch taking care of things."

He sighed. "I was in town taking care of things," he said. "Or I guess I should say, I was trying to take care of things." He turned her hand over and squeezed. "I tried to get a loan to buy the ranch." He shook his head and chuckled a little to himself. Even saying it out loud, it sounded completely ridiculous. "But it's not going to happen."

"Oh, Logan. I'm sorry." She looked genuinely upset with the news. "I know I already offered, but is there anything I can do? I mean it. We can—"

"No." He stopped her before she could get riled up with all kinds of plans that probably wouldn't be enough anyway. "It's okay, Amber. Really. The bank was a long shot, but I had to try, ya know?"

She nodded. "I do."

The waitress showed up then to take their drink order, and after she left, they focused on the menus before resuming conversation. "How about you?" he asked after she put her menu to the side of the table. "How has your day been?"

"Good." The grin on her face was so cute, it washed away any lingering disappointment from his meeting. "Drew cooked up a big breakfast, which gave her the opportunity to grill me about you."

"Is that right?" He leaned in because Logan couldn't think of a lot of things that would be more interesting than hearing what she might have said about him to her friends. "And what did you tell her?"

She shrugged and picked up her water glass. "Not much."

"Now why don't I believe that for a second?"

She laughed.

"Did you have a chance to tell Drew about everything we talked about the other day?" The moment he asked the question he regretted it, at least for a second, because her face dimmed as if a flame had been extinguished. But an instant later, the smile was back and she nodded.

"I did."

"You did? That's great."

"You sound surprised."

Instantly, Logan felt badly because he *was* surprised. Of course he'd been hoping Amber would come clean about her secrets to her friends. He felt strongly about everything he'd said to her that night. It was important for her, and for her overall well-being; he really did believe that. And why wouldn't he want Amber to be well? After all, he cared about this woman, a lot. He wanted the best for her. He just hadn't thought she would have done it so quickly. It couldn't have been easy for her.

"I am," he answered honestly. "I mean, you know how I feel about it." She nodded. "But I guess I wasn't really sure that you agreed with me on it and I don't want to force you to do—"

"You didn't force me to do anything." She took a deep drink of her water. "I told her because I said I would. Besides, I agree with you. It was a good idea and I'll tell the others later too."

He couldn't have hid the smile that crossed his face if he'd wanted to. Which he didn't. "Amber, I think that's fantastic." He raised his water glass. "To you and your honesty."

She hesitated, but after a moment, lifted her glass to his.

"I feel like this is the start of something incredible for you, Amber." He reached for her hand again. Things may be going to hell for him, but at least one of them was on the right track with their lives. "You really are amazing."

Chapter Fifteen

SHE KNEW she should have come clean with Logan right away. Or at the very least, she could have gone home from that lunch and told Drew the truth just the way she'd told Logan she already had.

But she just couldn't do it. When Amber got home, Drew had all her important papers spread out on the kitchen table and instead of telling her friend the truth, she helped her work through the legalese of all the documents.

That was more important anyway, right?

And then, a day later, when Christy asked her again if she could help draw up a will for her and Mark, well…naturally she was going to do that.

And then another day went by and she still hadn't said anything, and it just seemed less important all of a sudden. Especially with Thanksgiving coming. She'd accepted the invitation to go with Logan to Christy's house for a big holiday celebration and there was no way she was going to ruin it by telling everyone about her past. It seemed selfish. Besides, what if they were mad at her, or looked at her differently? It would be awkward and uncomfortable and she wasn't going to do that to Christy, who had been working so hard to make Thanksgiving amazing.

She'd tell them afterwards. Another few days wouldn't hurt.

When Logan came to pick her up, Amber felt the now familiar flicker of guilt that she felt every time she'd seen him since she lied. She hated starting their relationship with lies, but…there just wasn't another way.

After, she promised herself. *I'll tell them everything after Thanksgiving.*

"You look gorgeous." Logan kissed her in greeting before holding her out at arm's length to admire her again.

She'd chosen a new wine-colored wrap dress that set off her dark hair. It was far more casual than anything she was used to wearing, but more and more since she'd been back in Timber Creek, she was adopting a new style. Her old suits were a distant memory, and to her surprise, she liked it that way.

"Thank you." She accepted the compliment and fired one back at him. "You clean up pretty nicely yourself." It was the truth. Wearing a button-up black shirt and a dark pair of jeans, his hair still a little damp from the shower he'd obviously recently had, Logan looked incredibly sexy.

"You ready for this?" He led her to his truck for the short drive to Christy and Mark's house. Drew and Austin had left earlier in the day after Drew had insisted on helping Christy with the cooking. No one was going to argue since Drew was an amazing cook and everyone was super aware that it was her first holiday without Eric. If cooking was a good distraction, she could prepare the entire feast, as far as the women were concerned. "It's our first big event as a couple."

Amber laughed. "It's just our friends."

"And family," he reminded her. Christy had taken it upon herself to invite all of their parents, at least those who didn't already have plans, which meant a handful of them, including her own father.

"I seriously don't know what she was thinking," Amber said. "There are going to be so many people there."

"It'll be fun." Logan pulled up in front of the small house and went around to open her door. "Ready or not..."

IT WAS FUN.

Logan didn't even have a chance to knock on the door before it swung open and they were ushered inside to a house full of laughter and chatter.

It was complete chaos, with people everywhere. There was a giant makeshift table that snaked from the kitchen out into the living room so everyone could be seated together, set with an eclectic mix of plates and glasses and decorated with mini pumpkins.

Logan took Amber's hand and they made the rounds together, fielding questions about their relationship. It wasn't until they were seated at one end of the long table, with Cam, Evan, and Cam's daughter Morgan on one side of them, and Drew and Ben with Austin sandwiched between them, that either of them could catch their breath.

"You guys are the worst," Amber said. "I feel like I just ran the gauntlet."

"What are you talking about?" Cam pretended to be taken aback.

"You know exactly what I'm talking about." Amber shook her head and Drew laughed. "You guys have been firing questions at us from the moment we walked in. No wonder I never dated anyone before. It's hard work around all of you."

"It's only because we love you," Christy called from farther down the table. "And we love to see you happy."

Amber shook her head slightly, but Logan could see the smile on her lips. He loved to see her happy, too. And if he had even a small part to play in that, then that made *him* incredibly happy.

From all the way at the other end of the table, Logan caught Joseph Monroe's eye. He'd already chatted with him briefly when they'd arrived, but Amber seemed to be in a hurry to move on from her father and they hadn't spent much time talking with him. Logan offered the older man a smile and made a note to seek him out after dinner and chat with him about the situation at the ranch. He loved the horses too. He deserved to know.

"Don't you think she should, Logan?" He was brought swiftly back into the conversation that he clearly hadn't been listening to.

With a shrug of his shoulders, he admitted his distraction. "Sorry," Logan said. "My mind wandered. What do I think who should do?" The question didn't make sense, but Drew laughed and explained to him again.

"I was just saying how Amber helped me out with some of my legal mess the other day and how much easier she made everything."

"It was hardly a mess," Amber chimed in.

"It *was*." Drew nodded and looked knowingly at Logan. "Anyway, Christy mentioned Amber was going to help her out with a will, too, and it just got me thinking…"

Logan glanced over at Amber, who was shaking her head, but there was still a smile on her face.

"What were you thinking?" he asked Drew.

"That she should move here permanently and open up a legal practice."

"First of all." Amber held up a finger. "There's already a legal practice in town."

"True," Cam jumped in. "But Darcy's getting older. He's already talked about retiring and…"

"And," Drew took over. "You're *so* much better." Cam nodded in agreement. "You actually explain things so they make sense. I haven't had to deal with Darcy Hansen much over the years, but from what I understand, it wasn't unusual for him to be condescending."

"And you are *so* not condescending." Christy wandered to their end of the table with a basket of buns and joined the conversation. "And if you're talking about what I think you're talking about, then I completely agree. Besides, then we'd have you around permanently." She wrapped her arm around Amber's shoulder and squeezed.

Watching all four of them together was a special treat. Their relationship was clearly built on a foundation of trust and support and love. Logan couldn't understand how Amber ever could have doubted that these women would have her back once they learned the truth about everything.

"Are you guys serious?" Amber laughed, but Logan could see that she might actually be considering the suggestion. "I mean, I—" Abruptly, Amber pushed her chair out and stood. "I need to run to the bathroom," she said. "I'll be right back."

"If you think you're getting away from this so easily, think again," Drew called after her with a laugh. When she was gone, Drew turned to Logan. "Don't you think it would be perfect for her? I mean I can't imagine you want her returning to San Francisco or some other big city firm, right?"

"I don't think she'd do that again." Logan shook his head. "Not now. I mean…" He hesitated and looked around at the women, who were all watching him intently. All their parents at the other end of the table were in deep conversation about something and not paying any attention to what the younger generation was doing. He couldn't be sure whether Amber had a chance to talk to her dad yet, but knowing that her friends were so supportive of the truth and her past, he lowered his voice and said, "Not after everything she's been through, right?"

He was greeted by silence and blank stares until finally Christy spoke up cautiously and quietly. "What are you talking about, Logan?"

Maybe it should have been a red flag. Maybe their confusion should have alerted him to something more. But Logan had no reason to suspect that things weren't at all what they seemed, so he didn't think anything of it when he said, "I know Amber said you guys were all really okay about the truth when she told you, but I have to tell you how impressed I am with the support and love you all have for each other." He sat forward in his seat and continued. "I know it wasn't easy for her to tell you about the pills and the addiction and how it all came to a head. And of course, the whole thing in San Francisco and the hospital." He shook his head and didn't even notice the looks on their faces as he kept talking. "Losing her job like that. It was—"

"None. Of. Your. Business." Amber's voice, hard as glass, shattered behind him.

It was only then that he realized the truth. *She hadn't told them anything.*

AMBER HAD to work hard to control her voice when what she really wanted to do was scream, throw things, and run as hard and fast as she could. The entire room had fallen silent. Even the parents at the far end of the table had stopped their chatting. *Oh God.* She couldn't bring herself to look at anyone else at the table, even though there was no doubt in her mind that every single set of eyeballs around that table was locked on her.

Instead, she focused on Logan and his complete betrayal.

"You have no right to talk about me that way. No right at all." She spat each word like venom. There was no point keeping her voice down now. "Anything I told you was in confidence and you had *no right.*" Despite her effort, her voice shook and it only made her madder.

He pushed his chair back and stood so he was directly in front of her. "Amber, it's not like—"

"I'm not stupid, Logan. That's exactly what it was like. If you want to tell stories, tell your own. But leave me—"

"Amber?" Christy stood next to her, the basket of buns still in her hands. "If there's something you want to—"

"No." Amber shook her head. "Seems to me that Logan already did all the talking for me."

It was her opportunity to come clean. Not only to her friends, but their parents and her own… *Dad.* She couldn't bring herself to look at him. No doubt he was shaking his head in disgust. Hell, the letdown might just be the final nail in the coffin that was their relationship. The ultimate disappointment. She'd finally done it. A total and complete failure.

"Amber, I didn't tell them anything you didn't," Logan said.

She shifted her attention to the man in front of her. The one who only a few minutes ago she thought she might actually be falling in love with. Now, just looking at him… How *could* he?

"Just the other day you said you'd told them all everything and they were really supportive and totally cool with it all. I'm sorry if…" He gestured to the opposite end of the table. "I didn't mean for anyone to overhear. I was just…" Logan was clearly confused, and she knew on some level that it was her fault. But there was no way she was going to say that. She could barely *think* it. All her brain could focus on was the fact that everything she'd worked so hard to keep a secret was out there in the open for the world to know.

And there was nothing she could do about it.

"Amber. You *told* me that you told them." Logan took a step toward her, but she shook her head and backed up. "All I did was—"

"No." She couldn't listen to any more. She needed to get out of there. She felt trapped. Her heart raced; the familiar cold sweat started at the back of her neck. She was going to have a panic attack if she didn't get out of there. Soon. "No," she said again. "You had no right…" Finally, she let her eyes drift up, past Logan to Drew. Her expression was unreadable, but tears glistened in her eyes, and that was all Amber needed to know. She'd hurt her best friend at a time when that was the very last thing she needed. *What kind of friend was she?*

"Amber?"

She pulled her eyes away from Drew to Cam, who'd stood up from the table as well. "Whatever it is that you—"

"No." Amber cut her off. "You don't get it. None of you do." She couldn't see through the curtain of tears. She knew her nose was running and she must look like a complete mess, but she didn't care. She swiped at her face roughly. "It's *never* been okay, and it's never going to be. Not now."

She forced herself to look back to Logan even though she thought her heart might crack in two just looking at him. "You've destroyed everything," she whispered, her voice choking over the words before she turned away.

As best as she could, with whatever smidge of composure she could muster, she straightened up and smoothed the front of her dress before addressing the room as a whole. "I'm really sorry. I hope this didn't ruin your dinner." And then she turned and ran.

Chapter Sixteen

SOMEHOW AMBER MANAGED to ignore her phone and generally hide out for two full days after the fiasco at Thanksgiving. Unwilling to go back to Drew's house, she'd walked to the Creekside Inn and taken a suite overlooking the frozen river, where she wrapped herself in a robe, ordered room service, watched Hallmark movies, and generally felt sorry for herself.

She knew she was acting like a child, but she couldn't bring herself to talk to anyone because the only person she really wanted to talk to was Logan and after what he'd done—and more to the point, how she'd reacted—that wasn't going to be an option.

Whatever it was that had started was over.

It wasn't until the morning of the third day when there was a knock on the door of her suite, followed by a deep voice. "Ms. Monroe. It's management. Please open up."

Management? There was no way her credit card had been declined.

With a sigh, Amber dragged herself from the bed, tightened the robe around her waist, and reluctantly answered the door.

"I'm not sure what the—Aaron?"

"Hi, Amber." Aaron Owens, the owner of the Creekside Inn, and a familiar face with their crowd because he was Mark Thomas's best friend, stood in front of her. "How are you?"

"I'm fine."

"You're looking good, Amber."

She knew damn well that she was not at all looking good, and there was no doubt that Aaron had heard all about the Thanksgiving dinner drama. But she smiled and thanked him for the compliment. "What can I do for you, Aaron?"

He pressed his lips together and gave her a curt nod. And in that instant, she knew exactly what he was going to say.

Damn small towns.

"I'm afraid I'm going to have to get you to move out today, Amber."

"Is that right?"

"I'm really sorry to say it is." He nodded and had the decency to look at least a little bit sorry, despite what was actually happening.

"And why is that, Aaron?" She challenged. "Is there some sort of function going on in Timber Creek that requires more than the usual amount of hotel rooms? Because when I checked in, there was no mention of anything. In fact, I believe I told them at the desk that I wasn't sure how many nights I'd need to stay and I was assured that it wasn't a problem."

He nodded slowly. "I'm really sorry about the confusion, Amber. I am. But I'm going to—"

She put her hand on the door and pulled it in closer to her. "Why don't you just tell me what's really going on, Aaron."

"Okay." Aaron crossed his arms over his chest and smiled kindly. "Christy asked me to kick you out."

She hadn't expected him to be so forthcoming. Not really.

"Really?"

"That's the truth." He shrugged. "And I resisted for a day, but you know Christy. She's relentless."

Amber almost smiled. She did know exactly how Christy could be. But the smile didn't have a chance to make it to her lips. "Where will I go, Aaron?"

His smile was genuine and caring. "I was told to tell you that there will always be a room for you at any of their homes."

She let that sink in. She'd ignored her friends for the last few days. Blocking them completely, even with Cam's impending wedding and all the plans that still needed to be made, and this *after* they'd learned that she'd lied to them their entire lives. But even despite her behavior and everything she'd done, when the last thing she deserved was their friendship and love, that's exactly what they'd given her.

"I know it's not my business, Amber." She looked up into his kind eyes. "But they love you and whatever happened, that's not going to change. Go home."

HE MISSED HER.

A lot.

Logan had spent the days since Thanksgiving replaying the events of the evening and what he'd said. He never should have opened his mouth. Especially with her father there. He should have known better. She hadn't said anything about telling her dad the truth. But, she *had* told him that she'd confessed to her friends. How was he supposed to know the truth?

She'd lied.

Maybe he should be mad at *her*?

No.

He'd spent his days at the ranch with the horses. He didn't

have any clients on the weekend, so he busied himself with as many tasks as he could that would leave him too exhausted to pick up the phone and check his messages to see whether she'd returned his two calls.

It never worked. He always picked up and checked, no matter how tired he was.

And it was always the same. She never called.

The idea of spending one more day alone with his thoughts driving him crazy was too much. Which was why when Logan woke up on Sunday morning, instead of burying himself in work again, he jumped in the truck and headed into town.

The sun was shining, and the snow sparkled like jewels against the backdrop of the bright-blue sky. But he hardly noticed the beauty.

He drove straight past the Creekside Inn, where Amber's SUV was parked in the lot, rounded the corner, and pulled up in front of Junky's Auto Shop, where he knew he'd find his dad.

The moment he pulled open the rusty metal door and stepped into the shop, the familiar scent of motor oil mingling with strong, overcooked coffee filled him and he felt at home.

Logan and his sister had spent many hours after school in the auto shop. Sometimes they'd get put to work sweeping floors and emptying garbage and when they were older, Junky put them to work changing oil and rotating tires. But more often than not, when they were little, they'd play tag or hide-and-seek when their homework was done. Or, as was Logan's case, even when his homework wasn't done.

After their parents split when Logan was eight and Kyla was six and their mother had remarried and moved out of state, Junky had done his best to raise them on his own. As far as Logan was concerned, he'd done a great job. It wasn't a *normal* upbringing, but what was? They were happy, healthy, and cared for. Junky had never been the type of father to get emotional, or make a scene of any kind, but they'd always felt loved and as far as Logan was concerned, that was the only thing that mattered.

"Hello?" His dad's voice, cracking and underused, called out from somewhere in the shop. "I'll be right with you."

"It's just me, Dad. I came for coffee."

"Logan?" A moment later, his dad appeared, wearing the same old faded coveralls he wore every day, *Junky* embroidered on his chest pocket. "What are you doing here?"

"I came for a cup of your coffee, Dad." He grinned because it was well known that Junky's coffee was strong enough to strip paint. "I could really use a cup."

His dad smiled and nodded as he walked past Logan toward the tiny office at the back of the shop, understanding what it was that Logan really needed.

His dad.

"YOU KNOW I'd lay down my own life for you, Logan."

They were sitting in Junky's office, the battered steel desk between them. Logan nodded and looked down into the dark black coffee in his cup.

"I know, Dad." He did, too. There was nothing his dad wouldn't do for him. Their relationship wasn't typical, and they didn't need to talk to each other or see each other often, but he never doubted the support his dad would give him. No matter what. "I just...well, I had to ask."

"I understand." His dad nodded sympathetically. "And if I could afford it, I wouldn't hesitate to invest in you. The truth is, Logan, there's not a lot of money in fixing cars and more and more...well, it gets a little harder every day."

"I'm sorry." Logan shook his head and wished he could take back everything he'd just asked for. He should have known better and never have asked his dad for money. Obviously he didn't have the capital to invest in the ranch. "I didn't realize things were tight. Forget I said anything."

"Nonsense." The gruff tone in his voice took Logan back to his childhood. "You have nothing to be sorry for and I'm just fine. Got everything I need. Don't lack for anything."

They sat in silence for a moment, each sipping their coffee. Logan grimaced with every sip he took, but the thick liquid was oddly comforting.

"I have a plan," Logan said. "I just hope whomever Ruby finds to buy her out is open to hearing about it."

"Or you'll figure something else out."

Logan looked up at his dad, who stared at him with the confidence of a man who knew what the outcome would be.

"You will," he said when Logan didn't speak right away.

Slowly, Logan let his father's words sink in. He nodded and stood. "You're right. I *will* figure something out." It was so simple. Not an elaborate pep talk or false platitudes, just simple support and unwavering belief in him. But it was everything that Logan needed to hear.

He would figure something out. At least when it came to the ranch. Amber was a different problem.

"What else is going on, son?"

Logan looked up sharply.

"What?" Junky said. "You think I don't know there's something else? Something like a woman?"

Logan shook his head and chuckled a little, even though he certainly didn't feel like laughing. "I don't know, Dad. I thought maybe it was…well, I guess I thought maybe I loved her." Just saying the words out loud hurt. "No," he amended. "I *know* I love her." That was the real truth. He didn't *think* anything. He *knew* without a doubt of his feelings for Amber.

"Of course you do."

He looked at his dad in question.

"It's easy, son," Junky said kindly. "You don't hurt the way you're hurting if love isn't involved. And if you love her, there's only one thing you can do."

"What's that?"

"Fight for her," he said simply. "Fight for her and don't stop. Make sure she knows exactly how you feel."

"And if it doesn't matter?" The idea of opening his heart to Amber and still having her reject him was too much.

His dad offered him a kind smile, took a slow sip of his coffee, and nodded. "It will, son. It will."

After talking to his dad, Logan was conflicted. On one hand, he was more determined than ever to put together a business plan for Taking the Reins that he could present to any potential buyers. He'd put that on the back burner with everything that had been going on with Amber. But if she wasn't willing to answer any of his calls, at the very least he could focus on something that *could* make a difference.

And that's exactly what he was going to do.

He was so focused on the plans he had that Logan barely noticed the truck parked next to the barn when he pulled up behind his cabin.

Chapter Seventeen

IT TOOK Amber thirty minutes to pack up her few possessions and make the drive *home* to Drew's house. She hesitated at the front door, unsure of whether she should knock or just walk in.

She settled on just walking in. Maybe she could sneak down the hall to her room before running into anyone. She should have known better.

She'd barely set foot in the front entry when thundering footsteps, followed by Austin, who flung his arms around her legs, greeted her. "Auntie Amber." His voice was muffled by her legs. "You're back."

"I am." She smiled and ruffled his hair until he leaned his head back.

"Where did you go?"

"I went…" She looked up to see Drew leaning against the wall, arms crossed, watching them closely. She shifted her attention to Austin again for a moment. "Hey, do you mind if I talk to your mom for a minute?"

"Okay." His answer was reluctant, but he untangled his arms from around her and stepped back. "But then can I show you my Lego tower? It's huge."

"Of course."

He took off running at full speed back into the living room. Amber watched him go and then looked back to her friend, who still stood silently.

"Hi," she offered.

"Hey."

"Can we talk?"

"Always." Drew turned and walked into the kitchen, a cue Amber took to mean she should follow, which she did. They sat across the table from each other. Drew's hands were folded and she stared straight ahead, waiting for Amber to speak.

"I'm sorry," Amber said after a moment.

"For what exactly?" Drew tipped her head. It was clear she wasn't going to be let off the hook easily, but Amber wouldn't have expected anything less. Besides that, Drew deserved a full explanation. They all did.

Yes, Amber was hurting. But if she was being honest, it was more than that. She was embarrassed. Deeply ashamed and more than anything else, terrified that she'd somehow managed to screw everything up even more. And although none of that was an excuse for how she'd behaved, it was honest.

"For everything." She swallowed hard. "For making a huge scene at dinner, obviously. But also, I'm so sorry for lying to you and keeping the truth from you for all of these years. You've always been an amazing friend and I'm sorry I didn't trust you with this…but mostly I'm sorry for allowing my life to spin so far out of control in the first place." She glanced down at the table and swallowed hard. "When I look back at everything, I'm just so incredibly disappointed in myself and I know it might be hard to believe, but I really am sorry, Drew. I completely understand if you don't want me to stay—"

"Stop."

Amber blinked and stared at Drew. Her friend's pretty doll-like mouth was pressed into a thin line. Her eyes blazed with emotion. "Excuse me?"

"I'm just going to stop you before you say something stupid, like you understand if I don't want you to stay here anymore or be your friend or if I don't want you around my son or something equally idiotic."

Amber opened her mouth to object, but closed it again, because that was exactly what she had been about to say.

"I've lost too much, Amber. My *son* has lost too much. We're not going to lose you, too." She pressed one hand flat against the table as she spoke. "Furthermore, you should know me better to even think for a second that I might feel that way. You are my best friend and whatever you have done, or gone through, or secrets you have kept from me, there is nothing that will end this." She gestured between them before pressing her other palm against the table. She leaned forward slightly and stared directly into Amber's eyes. "The real problem here, and as far as I'm concerned, the *only* thing you should be apologizing for is underestimating all of us."

Amber could feel the pressure of tears building behind her eyes. The pent-up emotion that had been trying for days to release caught in her throat.

"We love you, Amber. No matter what. You are family and I think that somewhere along the line you may have forgot that. We don't love you because you're a great lawyer. We don't love you because when we were in high school you could run two committees with your eyes shut, get straight As and organize a birthday party for one of us without a second thought. We don't love you for *any* of that."

Amber nodded, because she had just started, albeit somewhat slowly, to come to that realization as well.

"Do you understand?" Drew stood now, her voice full of determination. "Do you *really* understand?"

"I do." The tears flowed freely now. She stood and a

moment later, her friend's arms were around her, squeezing her tight.

"I'm the one who's sorry, Amber," Drew said through a veil of her own tears. "I had no idea what was going on. I had no idea what you were putting yourself through. I should have known."

"No." She squeezed tighter. "You couldn't have known. I didn't want anyone to know. Besides, it doesn't matter now."

"You're right," Drew agreed. "All that matters now is that you're better." Drew pulled back to look in her eyes. "You *are* better now?"

"I am. So much better."

And she was, too. Especially now that she'd gotten over herself enough to go home. Everything would be okay.

A tight band squeezed around her chest as she thought of Logan and the terrible things she'd said to him. *Almost* everything would be okay.

"JOSEPH?" Logan took a step toward the man who stood next to the barn in a jacket that looked far too inadequate for the weather. It had been less than a week since he'd seen him, but Joseph Monroe looked as though he'd aged at least a decade since he'd seen him at the Thanksgiving dinner. "What are you doing here? You must be freezing."

"Came to talk to you." He ignored the comment about being cold, but Logan could see his efforts to control his shivering. "Got a minute?"

"Absolutely." Logan gestured to his cabin. "But come in and get out of the cold. Weren't you just telling me how your joints hated winter?"

Joseph grunted in response but didn't protest about following Logan into his tiny cabin, where he immediately put on a kettle of water before asking the older man what he needed to talk about. As if he didn't already know.

"Sit down." Logan gestured to the couches. Joseph was still standing by the front door, looking more and more uncomfortable, and he made no move to sit. "Joseph?"

"I'll stand if it's all the same and I won't keep you long, Logan. I know you're a busy man and..." He looked down at his feet, which shuffled from side to side. When he looked up again, his eyes glistened. "Is it my fault?"

The shift happened so quickly that the question took Logan off guard. "Pardon?" He shook his head. "Is what your fault?"

"Amber." His voice trembled. "Her...her addiction." He stumbled over the word as if it caused him physical pain to say it out loud. "Is it my fault?"

"What?" Whatever he'd been expecting Joseph to say, it wasn't that. "Your fault?" he repeated. "No." He shook his head again. "Why would you say that?"

The older man sighed and swallowed hard. "I always pushed her. I put a lot of pressure on her," he said. "From the time she was a little girl. I expected a lot out of her. Maybe too much and then when her mom died...well, I'm afraid I wasn't there for her the way I should have been."

"A lot of kids have pressure," Logan said, but he didn't seem to hear him.

"She's always accomplished so much, done such great things," Joseph continued. "I've always been so proud of her, you know?"

"I believe it." He moved to turn off the kettle but didn't bother with the tea. "Have you told her that?"

"No." He hung his head, defeated. "I don't think I have. At least not enough."

"Come sit down, Joseph." This time he didn't turn down the offer and instead let Logan lead him to the couch.

"You know I've spent the last few days trying to figure all of this out," he said after a moment. "How could I not know she was addicted to drugs?" It was a rhetorical question, so Logan sat quietly. "I spoke with Doctor Thomas about it. Did you know it's a prescription? They use it to treat children who can't pay attention in class."

"Attention deficit hyperactivity disorder," Logan clarified. "Yes."

"Then…how…I mean, why did she feel that she needed to take pills?"

Logan didn't have the answers. Hell, Amber probably didn't have the answers either. Some things couldn't be explained, at least not in a way that would be satisfactory. And the past couldn't be changed. The only thing to do now was understand the best you could and move on. He told Joseph as much.

"Do you think she'll be okay?" The question was so genuine that Logan could see the love the old man had for his daughter.

"No." He grinned. "I think she'll be great."

Joseph finally offered up a small smile of his own. "You're right. But I don't think I'll be able to take any credit for that." He sighed deeply. "I didn't tell her enough that I loved her." His voice wavered. "I've always regretted that." He looked up into Logan's eyes for the first time. "It's not something I can go back and change, but I should have told her more. Hell, I should have told her every day. Little girls need to hear that."

"Joseph?" Logan reached across the couch and put his hand over the older man's briefly until he looked at him. "Big girls need to hear it, too."

Chapter Eighteen

WITH ONLY A FEW weeks before the wedding, Cam, who was usually so calm and in control, was anything but. Which was how Christy found herself sitting in Cam's bedroom, rocking a sleeping Mya while simultaneously trying to settle her best friend.

The roles were almost comically reversed, but Christy had enough sense not to laugh because she was pretty sure that Cam wouldn't think it was nearly as funny as she did.

"It doesn't fit," Cam called from the attached en suite bathroom. "I can't believe it doesn't fit."

"There's no way it doesn't fit." Christy stroked Mya's soft cheek and shifted her in her arms. "Come out here and show me." She knew damn well that Cam's wedding dress fit because a few weeks ago she'd been there when Cam purposely selected a dress with plenty of give in the stomach for the baby bulge that was growing by the day.

A moment later, the door to the bathroom opened, and Cam appeared. Her dress was a simple, full-sleeved cream lace that gathered under the bosom to float beautifully over her stomach. It fit perfectly, except for… "Wow," Christy said. "Your boobs have—"

"They're enormous!" Cam spun to look in the full-length mirror that hung on the wall. "They're popping out all over the place. The dress doesn't fit."

Christy shifted the baby again and got to her feet. She went to stand behind Cam and together they looked at her reflection in the mirror. "You look gorgeous, Cam. Really. And your boobs…well, Evan will love them." She couldn't help it, and thankfully Cam burst into laughter.

"You're right about that."

"The dress fits fine," Christy said. "I mean, there's definitely a bit more cleavage than last time, but I'm sure we could sew in a little lace right in the front if you think it's too much."

Cam twisted and turned in the mirror, assessing her reflection. "I kind of like it." She blushed and burst out laughing again. "Do you think it's wedding appropriate?"

"I think it's your wedding, so whatever you want is appropriate. And I meant what I said. You look amazing. You're glowing and you're going to be a radiant bride."

Cam's smile wavered and her hand wiped a tear away.

"Don't cry," Christy ordered. "You're not allowed to cry until the actual wedding day."

With her pregnancy, Cam had been more emotional than ever and was crying at the slightest things. Christy had taken to turning off the radio whenever she was around because even the songs on the local stations could set off a round of tears.

"Okay." Cam pulled herself together. "I'm good now. I promise."

"Good." Christy put the now sleeping baby into her car seat. "I have a good few hours while she naps if you want me to help with centerpieces or something."

"Done." Cam presented her back. "Unzip me and we'll start drilling holes."

Christy stared after her friend as she disappeared into the bathroom again. "Holes?"

A few minutes later, she discovered exactly what Cam had been talking about when she led Christy out to the garage, where she thrust a drill into her hand and presented a huge box full of small logs.

"Centerpieces," Cam announced. "We're going to use this drill to put some holes the size of a tea light into the logs. Then I'm going to bundle three logs of different sizes up and tie ribbon around them. Like this." She produced a sample of what she was talking about. "We'll tuck some red berries and pine boughs under them on the table for a bit of color."

"These are actually really nice," Christy said. "Very rustic. I like it."

"Cool, right?"

"Very cool," Christy agreed. "It's going to be a beautiful wedding." They spent a few more minutes looking at the various pinecones, pine boughs, and red accents that Cam had gathered for decorations. They were having both the ceremony and the reception at the Creekside Inn, which would already be decorated for Christmas, so Cam's decorations would only add to the festive ambience. Simple, but elegant.

"Let's get started."

"What are we working on?" Both Christy and Cam spun at the sound of Drew's voice in the doorway. "Whoa." Drew held her hands up. "Don't point that at me."

Christy lowered the drill and laughed. "Sorry. I'm not even sure I know how to use it."

"There's nothing to it." Amber stepped out from around Drew and walked into the garage. "I'd be happy to show you if you'd like?"

No one spoke. It had been almost a week since Amber had more or less self-imploded at Christy's Thanksgiving table and ran off without so much as a word to any of them.

"Hi," Amber said after a moment of silence. "I'd really like to help you guys, if that's okay?"

Cam moved forward and nodded slowly. "But..." She looked from one woman to the other, obviously not sure how to proceed.

"I brought her," Drew jumped in. "Because I knew that you'd both want to see her, and I think we all had a few things we needed to say."

Drew was right and her words shook Christy out of the mute state she'd fallen into. "Yes." She took a step forward, put the drill down, and took Amber's hand. "Of course we want to see you. We've been worried." She looked to Cam, who nodded.

"Very worried."

"You didn't need to be worried about me. I was just..." Amber swallowed hard. "I was feeling sorry for myself," she said. "I was so worried about what you'd think of me if you knew the truth and Drew said something that...well, I should never have underestimated you. Any of you. I'm so sorry. For everything."

Christy chuckled. "No," she said. "If there's one thing I know about all of us...don't ever underestimate us."

"Oh hell no." Cam wrapped her arms around Amber and Christy. A moment later, Drew was there, and they all swallowed Amber in a tight bear hug. "We love you, Amber. No matter what," Cam said into the circle, her voice choking on her tears.

Christy's tears came next and pretty soon they were all crying and then laughing. Finally, they all pulled apart and wiped their faces clean.

Cam picked up the drill and held it in the air. "Now can we please make some centerpieces? This wedding isn't going to get ready for itself."

EVEN THOUGH IT was the last thing she would have expected, spending the afternoon building centerpieces with the girls was exactly what Amber needed. They laughed and talked and created beautiful decorations for Cam's big day. Amber's heart was close to bursting by the time Drew excused herself to pick Austin up from school.

"We should probably wrap this up anyway," Cam said. "I need to go through some client photos before dinner and I promised Evan I'd cook a real meal tonight. We've been so busy we haven't had a chance to sit down at the table all together in ages."

"I can totally relate to that," Christy said with a shake of her head. "And it's just going to get busier in a few months."

Cam rubbed her tummy. "But in all the best ways."

Amber watched her two friends who'd both just recently come through major life disruptions only to be happier and more in love with their lives than ever before and smiled. She'd never before considered having a child of her own, but looking at Christy and Cam, suddenly the idea didn't seem so crazy.

Maybe one day.

"Are you walking, Amber?"

They'd waved good-bye to Cam at her front door. Christy had Mya bundled in her stroller and was pushing it down the path.

"I guess I am." Amber looked around and shrugged. "I came with Drew, but…"

"Good. Let's walk together."

She wasn't going to argue with that. It was a cool afternoon, but the crisp, early winter air was refreshing and it wasn't a long walk.

They'd only been walking a few minutes when Christy asked, "So, have you spoken to Logan yet?"

The question froze Amber in her tracks. She recovered quickly and shook her head. "No."

"Are you going to tell me why?"

"There's nothing to tell."

It wasn't quite a lie. There was nothing to tell Christy because she didn't know why she hadn't reached out to Logan yet. She wanted to. Very badly. Every time she thought about him, her heart ached and she missed the sound of his voice and his arms around her and...she missed *him.*

This time it was Christy's turn to stop walking. Amber turned and Christy shook her head. "Are we doing that again? I thought we were past that thing where you didn't tell us what was really going on."

"Ouch." The comment stung, but she deserved it. "Christy, I'm sorry," she said. "I really am. About not telling you everything and you have to know that I'm so sorry about Thanksgiving." The guilt she'd tried to push down when it came to the actual Thanksgiving dinner resurfaced. "I am *so* incredibly sorry about ruining your beautiful dinner, Christy, and—"

"You didn't ruin it," she said matter-of-factly. "It was delicious and despite the unplanned entertainment, I think everyone had a good time. At least most people." She shrugged. "I'm pretty sure Logan didn't, which brings me back to my question. Are you going to tell me why you haven't spoken to him yet?" She stared pointedly at her. "And this time maybe we can go for the full truth."

"Ouch again." Amber pressed a gloved hand to her chest. "But I deserved that. I'm not going to lie to you, okay?"

"I hope not."

She took a deep breath and swallowed hard. She'd just promised Christy she wouldn't lie, but she also didn't know exactly how to put into words what she needed to say. She hadn't spoken to Logan because she didn't know what to say.

Should she apologize? For what? He'd told her secrets. It was him who'd…

She knew that wasn't true.

She'd been the one who lied.

He'd done nothing but try to help her almost from the moment they'd met.

"The truth is," she started. "I don't know what to do."

She could feel the tears building again. She wasn't a crier. Or at least, she never had been before coming back home to Timber Creek. She was pretty sure she'd cried more in the last few months than in her entire life. Maybe because she'd been too busy. But now that she had time to think and more importantly, just *be*, the tears were definitely coming more frequently and she couldn't decide whether that was a good or a bad thing.

"Oh, Amber." Christy started to close the distance between them but Amber shook her head. She didn't need another hug. She needed to face the reality.

"I think I really screwed things up, Christy. But the thing is, even though I know I need to say something and apologize to him, at the same time, I just feel so confused."

"I'm not going to pretend to understand what you're going through," Christy said. "But I do know what it's like to be afraid you've lost the man you love."

Love? Did she *love* him?

Maybe. How would she know? She'd never been in love before. Was it supposed to feel like a million emotions all jumbled up? Was it supposed to make you feel like laughing and crying and jumping up and down all at the same time? Was it supposed to make you feel warm and safe inside but the next minute leave you feeling empty and wrung out when you thought it was all slipping away?

If so, then she was unequivocally, head over heels, completely lost in love.

"Come on," Christy said after a minute. "We can't stand out here forever. Let's get home."

Home.

The word hit her. Timber Creek had always been home, even when she'd tried so hard to get away. But now...

"You know what?" Amber said as they started walking, slowly, in the direction of Drew's house. "I kind of feel like I *am* home. Is that crazy?"

Christy laughed and wrapped her scarf tighter around her neck. "What's crazy is it's taken you so long to realize it."

Amber thought about that for a moment.

"You know what I think, Amber?" Christy didn't wait for a reply. "I think that maybe the pills made you *think* that you could accomplish all the things you needed to, but I don't think you really needed them."

"What?" She shook her head, ready to argue with her friend although it was quite possibly the last thing she wanted to do.

"No," Christy continued. "I mean it. I've been thinking about it and doing a little research. And from what I understand, Adderall doesn't change who you are fundamentally. Instead, it just kind of amplifies you. So you've always been an overachiever who can accomplish anything you set your mind to and that hasn't changed. I think you *are* home and I hope you realize it. I also meant it when I said that I thought you should open up a practice here. You could really help people. It might not be the glamorous lifestyle you had in San Francisco, but it would be a real one."

Stunned by Christy's impassioned and unexpected speech, Amber stayed quiet.

"But mostly," Christy reached over with her mittened hand and grabbed hers, "I really hope you realize how many people here love you. Don't think that's a small thing because it's not."

She stared at her friend and thought her heart might

completely burst. Not because she didn't believe what Christy was saying, but because she *did*.

They turned onto Drew's street. "It's never too late to fix things," Christy continued as they made their way up the street. "In fact, the only way you can lose right now is if you do nothing."

"But what do I do?" The reality set in again and Amber's shoulders slumped.

"You know all those steamy books you like to read?"

Amber laughed. "Those aren't real."

"Maybe not," Christy admitted. "But what happens in those stories?" She stopped walking.

"Usually the hero has screwed up somehow and he makes a big grand gesture to win over the…oh." Amber's focus was drawn from the topic at hand to the front porch of Drew's house that they'd stopped in front of and the man who stood there.

Christy turned, seeing her friend was distracted. "Oh." She turned back to Amber. "It looks like you might have more than one relationship that needs attention."

HER DAD HAD CALLED and left a voicemail two days after her Thanksgiving meltdown, but like most of the messages she'd received, Amber had ignored it. Because just like all the others, she had no idea what to say to him.

Hell, on a good day she didn't know what to say to her father. But after hearing the truth, he must hate her or at the very least, be incredibly disappointed in her. How could he not?

"Dad?" She left Christy on the sidewalk and walked toward the house and her dad. "It's freezing out here. What are you doing?"

"Waiting for you."

"You'll freeze out here."

"I wasn't about to let that stop me."

She looked at him. Really looked at him and couldn't help but notice how much older he looked than just a few weeks ago, as if the events of the last few days had aged him.

It was her fault.

"Come inside, Dad." Amber reached around him and unlocked the door. She pushed it open and led the way into the house. It had already been an emotional day and all she really felt like doing was crawling into bed with one of her books so she could forget about the reality she didn't want to deal with. But that was the old Amber. She'd come too far and made too many changes to stop now.

Besides, she owed it to her dad to finally have this conversation.

"Can I make tea?"

"That would be nice." He followed her into the kitchen and took off his jacket, which from what Amber could see, was woefully inadequate for winter in the mountains. He was thin under his coat. *Had he always been that thin?* Or maybe she just hadn't noticed.

They made small talk for a few minutes while Amber fussed with a kettle and prepared two mugs with tea bags. She chattered on about trivial things like the weather and the upcoming holiday season. Her dad mostly nodded and grunted to everything she said. It wasn't until she sat across from him at the table and slid a tea mug over to him that he had something to say.

"Was it my fault, Amber?"

Taken off guard by his question, her hand jerked and hot tea sloshed over the mug. "I'm sorry?"

"The drugs, Amber," he said, as if neither of them knew what he was talking about. "Was it my fault?" He held up a hand before she could say anything. "And you don't need to answer. I already know the truth. I pushed you too hard. I expected too much and I was never there for you. Not really. Not the way a father should be."

He dropped his head, and somehow looked even smaller and more fragile than before.

"Dad." Her voice was soft, as if she could break him by speaking. "It's not…it was never…I'm sorry." Tears filled her eyes.

"It was never about you," she said after a moment. "Not really. It was always about me."

He nodded. "But I…I was…I *am* your father. I should have known. I should have seen it. I should have *stopped* it, goddammit." With force that didn't match his current physical state, he thumped a fist down on the table. More hot tea splashed over the edges of the cups, but neither of them moved to clean it up. "I should have gotten you help," he said, softer this time. "It was my job. And I failed you." He reached across the table and took her hand.

Amber startled a little at the touch. She couldn't remember the last time her dad had taken her hand or held her in any real way beside the obligatory hugs they occasionally shared. His hand shook slightly, as if he were struggling to contain his emotions. "I'm your father, Amber, and I failed you. I will never forgive myself for that."

"Dad."

He shook his head, unwilling to hear anything else, but she tried anyway.

"I know it doesn't matter what I say right now, but I do hope you hear me when I tell you that this was not at all your fault. I made the decisions I made. It was on me. And I should have told you earlier. I just didn't want to disappoint you." The tears started to flow down her cheeks. "I'm the one who's sorry,

Dad. I'm so sorry I disappointed you. I know how—" Her words were lost in a sob that rose up from her throat.

"Oh, Amber."

She heard him muttering, but didn't open her eyes to look at him. He'd never liked it when she'd cried, which was probably why she'd stopped with any emotional demonstrations long before.

But this time she couldn't have stopped the tears if she wanted to. Her vision blurred, so she dropped her head into both of her hands, and let herself cry. She was done bottling up her emotions and holding back tears. Really and truly done.

She was so consumed by the release of her guilt, anger, and disappointment that she didn't even notice when her dad got up from the table. She didn't notice until she felt a gentle tugging on her arms, pulling her out of her chair and up to standing. He wrapped his arms around her and held her tight, letting her cry until there were no more tears.

It couldn't have been the first time Amber had cried on her father, but it was the first time since she was a little girl. When her mother died, she wasn't even given that level of comfort. Likely because back then, he didn't know how to give it. But now, he clearly did know how to offer the comfort she so desperately needed. Maybe he always had, and she just hadn't let him. And as he rubbed her back, let her soak his shirt with her tears, and even occasionally whispered comforting words she couldn't quite decipher, she found herself, for the first time in years, actually feeling better.

As Amber dried her tears and finally sat across the table from her dad and their now almost cold tea, she finally saw clearly what she needed to do. It was finally time to have a real conversation.

BY THE TIME they were done talking, Amber had told him everything, and he'd listened. Really listened. And then it was her turn to listen—about how hard it had been for him to lose her mother so young and how alone, sad, and completely scared he'd been to find himself a single father of a young teenage girl.

They both drank their tea, neither of them caring that it had long since become cold. Amber shed a few tears when he told her the story of how he'd met her mother, how much they'd enjoyed being young parents together and how she'd taken such a large piece of him when she'd died.

"I know it wasn't right," he said gruffly. "I shouldn't have let myself be so consumed with grief. You needed me."

"It's okay." She offered him comfort, but still he shook his head.

"It's not," he insisted. "I should have been there for you. You were just a girl and you needed me."

"It's okay, Dad." Amber could see the pain on his face. "It's in the past and there's nothing we can do about it now."

He nodded slowly before looking up into her eyes. "You're right. But there's something I can do about it now." A slow smile crossed his face. "Tell me about Logan." It was an unexpected conversation turn, but then again, they'd been talking about his own love; maybe it wasn't too big of a leap to talk about hers.

Her love. Love?

Yes. The word sat well in her heart. Despite everything that had happened, maybe because of it, she loved Logan.

Because it finally felt right, she did as her father asked and over another cup of tea, this one fresh and hot, she told him all about Logan and the horses—which he of course already knew about—but she told him about how they'd helped her and how she wasn't sure whether they were going to be able to continue helping people if Ruby sold the ranch.

"Is there anything you can do?" he asked when she was finished. "What did Logan say?"

"He said the only thing that could help him was a million dol—that's it." The idea hit her so fast and hard she almost laughed. How could she have not seen it earlier?

She knew exactly what she should do. What she *wanted* to do. And not just for Logan, but for *her*.

"I know what to do now, Dad." She jumped up from her chair, unable to contain her excitement. "I know how to fix things with Logan."

He tilted his head and looked at her with a mildly indulgent smile. "How's that?"

She was so excited, she could no longer sit. Adrenaline rushed through her. It was going to take some work, and it might take a few weeks. She'd have to be patient and wait. And if it was going to be a surprise, she'd have to force herself not to reach out to Logan. But it would be worth it. As long as the time didn't make everything worse between them.

It was a risk she had to take.

"My grand gesture, Dad." She clapped her hands together. "I know exactly what it will take. But I might need your help."

Chapter Nineteen

AS CHRISTMAS APPROACHED, the days grew shorter, darker, and colder. And Logan didn't think it was just his imagination that they also got a little bit heavier. Everything felt hard and sad and…lonely. He missed Amber with a ferocity that he didn't think he'd ever be able to shake, but she'd made it clear that it was over.

He hadn't left a message since right after Thanksgiving, but he'd sent a few text messages and then, with whatever was left of his pride, he'd somehow resisted reaching out again. One time he ran into Cam in the grocery store and he'd asked about her, but she wouldn't tell him anything more than, "She's doing fine."

It was frustrating and hurtful, and short of standing on her front step to wait for her and force her to talk to him, he didn't know what else to do. Besides, if she didn't want to see him, he could take a hint. The ball was in her court; he could accept that. No matter how hard it was.

With the prospect of another lonely day stretching out in front of him, Logan decided to start with the best part: the horses. A little time talking to his horses would do him good. The chores could wait.

But when he got to the barns, it was clear he wasn't the only one who'd had that idea. A familiar face greeted him from inside Peanut's stall. "Good morning, Logan."

"It's good to see you, Ruby." He meant it, despite the trickle of concern that threaded its way down his spine. If Ruby was here, she probably had news about the ranch and there was a good chance that he wasn't going to like it. "What brings you out here this morning?"

She turned and rubbed the horse's nose. "The same thing that's brought me out almost every morning of my life. I just love these animals." She spoke almost to the animals themselves. "I'm sure going to miss them." Her voice was thick with sadness, but a resignation as well.

Logan had a thought. "I don't have any clients for a few hours this morning," he said. "And it's been awhile since I've seen you go for a ride… Maybe we could…"

"Oh, I couldn't." She shook her head. "I'm sure you have things you need to be doing."

"I do," he answered with a laugh. "But just like you, I love these animals, and sometimes the best thing to do is clear your head. What do you say?"

She shook her head, but Logan could see the hesitation. "The truth is…I'm not sure I can get in the saddle anymore," she confessed after a moment. "I'm not as young as I once was and…" Her words drifted away as she focused on the horse in front of her.

"Don't give it another thought." Logan quickly developed an idea. He knew the woman was proud, but he hoped he was right that she'd let him help her. "I have an idea."

"Logan, it's fine."

"No," he said firmly. "I was hoping to go for a ride this

morning and I'd much rather have you join me than go alone." He beamed at her and finally she smiled back and nodded.

Twenty minutes later, he had both the horses saddled and ready to go. Logan brought Peanut up alongside the fence and used a stepladder on the other side of the horse. Ruby looked skeptical, but fortunately trusted Logan enough to climb up the ladder and use him—perched on the fence—as a support to scramble up on the horse.

"I could build something a little more stable if you'd like?" he asked as he mounted his own horse. "It could be easier and then you would be able to get up on your own."

"It's fine." She waved away his offer. "I don't want to be a trouble."

"No trouble." He smiled brightly at her, and couldn't help but notice it was the first time he'd felt okay since Thanksgiving. A ride was definitely a good idea.

The air was crisp and bit at his exposed face as they moved along the pasture. As soon as they took the trail through the pines and had a bit more protection from the wind, things warmed up and they started to settle into their ride. The peace of the forest was exactly what Logan needed to soothe his restlessness and he hoped that behind him, Ruby was feeling the same sense of calm.

After about twenty minutes, the horses, who knew the way, turned almost automatically back for home. Before they arrived at the barns, Ruby drew her horse up next to his. "Thank you, Logan. I can't remember the last time I'd been on a horse and I wasn't sure if I…well, I guess I didn't know if it would ever happen again." There were tears in her eyes, and Logan nodded, understanding finally the real reason she'd come out to the ranch that morning. "I have buyers," she finally said, confirming Logan's thoughts. "The deal should be finalized before the holidays."

That was only a few days away. Logan's heart sank, but he smiled. "I'm not going to lie, Ruby. That's not the news I was hoping for. But I understand why you have to sell."

"I haven't heard yet about your offer," she added. Almost a week ago, Logan had complied a formal offer for Ruby to present to any potential buyers about the opportunity to continue running Taking the Reins, but he wasn't hopeful it would actually work. "But as soon as I do..."

"Don't worry, Ruby." He forced some optimism into his voice and tried to regain some of the tranquility he'd felt earlier. "This isn't on you," he assured her before spurring the horse on. "But we should get back before we freeze to death."

And before my heart breaks completely.

A FEW DAYS LATER, the morning of Christmas Eve, there was a knock on the door and a courier presented Logan with a simple envelope.

A Christmas card.

But the message wasn't one of cheer or good tidings. Inside, the card adorned with a photographed Christmas tree was a handwritten note from Ruby.

THE SALE IS COMPLETE.

The new owners take possession January 1.

I'm sorry, Logan.

Merry Christmas.

HE HELD the card for a minute and stared at the message as if it would change if he looked at it long enough.

It was over.

All his hard work, the good the horses had already done for people, the potential for the future.

Done.

Chapter Twenty

CAM LOOKED radiant and Amber swore she had never seen a more beautiful bride, a point that everyone agreed with.

Her dress fit her perfectly, the fabric skimming the top of her growing baby bump before falling to her feet in cascades of fabric. She'd been worried about her cleavage, but Christy had sewn a little panel in the front of her dress so she was slightly more modest, although Amber was pretty sure Evan would appreciate the display anyway.

All four friends, along with Morgan, Cam's teenage daughter, were putting the final touches on the bride, and themselves, at the Creekside Inn. The ceremony was set to start in less than thirty minutes. Just as she had been in the last few weeks, Amber was thankful for the distraction of the wedding. Being apart from Logan, knowing how close they could have been to having the type of happiness she never even knew she wanted, had been harder and harder to bear every day and she'd had to force herself to stay away from him until she had a proper apology. Even if going to him was the only thing she really wanted to do.

"There," Drew announced, bringing Amber back to the

present. Drew had tucked the last of the holly berries into Cam's pulled-up hair. "You look amazing."

"You really do," Christy gushed. "I can't believe this day is finally here."

"Don't cry," Cam ordered. "If you start, I have no chance and I'm not going to ruin this makeup until *after* the vows."

"More like *during* the vows." Drew laughed. "There is no way you're going to make it through the ceremony without bawling your eyes out."

"Truth," Morgan said from the corner of the room, where she was applying another layer of lip gloss. "Mom, you're going to be such a mess."

Amber laughed. "Something tells me that we all are." She was coming to embrace this new, more emotional version of herself and there was no doubt that she'd be wiping a few tears.

About forty minutes later, as Amber sat in the front row of chairs, watching one of her best friends, surrounded by two beautifully and subtly decorated Christmas trees and huge red pillar candles, stand with the love of her life, she was doing just that. And as predicted, so was everyone else.

Morgan stood next to her mother as her maid of honor, looking so grown up and poised for her young age, but even she wiped a few tears as they exchanged vows.

"Cam, I have loved you for as long as I can remember." Evan held his bride's hands and gazed deep into her eyes. "Over the years, we've been through it all, but even when you weren't by my side, you were in my heart. Fate had different plans for us, but I wouldn't have changed a thing," he continued. "Because fate also brought us back together, stronger than ever. My love for you only grows deeper every day, my commitment even more unwavering." Cam sniffed and Amber knew she was working hard to keep from losing control completely. "Cam," Evan continued. "I promise to choose you every day. I promise to put you, our love, and our family, ahead of everything else. You are my world, my life, and my home. I love you."

Cam couldn't control her tears any longer, nor could anyone else. All around Amber, guests were dabbing at their eyes. It took the bride a moment to gather her thoughts, and when she spoke, Amber couldn't help but feel their love profoundly in her own heart.

"Evan, I—" Cam broke off and took a second to collect herself before continuing. "Today feels like a dream come true. You were and will always be, the love of my life." Cam pulled Evan's hands, still clenched in her own, to her chest and dropped a kiss on them. "We have the kind of love that comes along once in a lifetime. I have never been happier than I am today, knowing that in a few moments, I will finally be your wife. I promise to love and care for you, to wake up every day and tell you how much you mean to me and never go to sleep without telling you again. I even promise to let you cut the green peppers *wrong* without complaining. *Too* much." That got a laugh from everyone. "I love you, Evan." She grew serious once again. "Thank you for loving me the way you do."

As soon as she finished speaking, Cam broke down in tears and without waiting for the officiant to say anything, Evan took her face in his hands and kissed her gently before pulling back and staring deep into her eyes. Despite the fact that almost a hundred sets of eyes were trained on them, the couple was completely unaware of anyone or anything. The way they looked at each other sent shivers through Amber's body. *Would she ever experience a love like that? So strong that everything else melted away?*

She turned in her seat and almost at once her eyes locked with Logan's, three rows back and to the left. Her heart simultaneously stopped and sped up. Heat flooded her and she knew her face was flushing red enough to match the dress she was wearing, but she didn't care. When he lifted his hand in a tiny wave, it took everything she had not to jump up in her seat to go to him.

Maybe she *could* experience a love like that. *Maybe* she already had.

AFTER RECEIVING RUBY'S MESSAGE, the last thing Logan felt like doing was going to the wedding. But the moment he saw Amber, dressed in a long, form-fitting red dress, her dark hair pulled back and piled up on her head, he knew there was nowhere else he could have been.

He sat in the middle of the crowd, and just like everyone else in attendance, was consumed by the emotions of the ceremony. But even though he was listening to the bride and groom along with everyone else, all of Logan's attention was focused on Amber. He saw the way she dabbed her eyes when Evan proclaimed his love and the way her shoulders shook ever so gently when Cam started crying during her own vows.

Even though he was watching her intently, he still wasn't prepared for it when she turned around and locked eyes with him.

God. She was beautiful.

She didn't look away. She didn't look angry or sad or anything but…perfect.

He raised his hand in a little wave when all he really wanted to do was jump up from his seat and pull her into his arms. Of course he couldn't do that, but it didn't stop him from wanting to. Instead, he smiled and when she smiled back, just a little, a surge of hope rushed through him.

Her attention was taken by something happening in front of her and she turned around as the officiant declared Evan and Cam husband and wife. The whole room cheered and

Logan joined in. He turned and watched as the new couple made their way down the aisle and then once again, he turned and searched for Amber, who was following the crowd and falling into line, aisle by aisle, behind the bride and groom.

She wasn't looking at him though; instead, she was laughing and smiling with her friends as they walked down the aisle together. Short of pushing everyone out of the way so he could get to Amber sooner, there was nothing Logan could do but be patient. And that's what he did.

But the moment he was free from the chairs, he dodged and weaved through the crowd and made a beeline directly for the woman in the red dress standing next to the river stone fireplace in the lobby of the hotel. *Was she waiting for him?*

No.

A moment later, Drew and Christy joined her, laughing and smiling. He stopped walking, unwilling for a moment to interrupt their happy moment. He wasn't going to cause a scene, or create any drama on Cam and Evan's wedding day.

He shook his head and fought against the tightening in his chest at the thought of not talking to Amber. Of not finally understanding what had gone so terribly wrong on Thanksgiving that it had destroyed everything they'd been building.

He was surrounded by people, as the rest of the guests spilled out from the ceremony and gathered in the lobby to greet the happy new couple and toast them with champagne before the reception started. But Logan didn't notice anything else except the woman he knew without a doubt that he was desperately in love with. It was torture not to go to her, but he'd told himself it had to be her choice. She had to be the—

"Screw it." He muttered the words and without letting himself think about it too much, he strode across the room and stood in front of her.

"Excuse me, ladies. I really need to borrow Amber for a

second." He didn't wait for an answer but took Amber's hand in his and led her through the crowd out a side door.

"Logan, what is…it's freezing out here."

The sun was starting to go down, and the temperature was falling fast, but a thick cloud cover that meant impending snowfall kept it from being unbearably cold. "This won't take long." He turned to face her. "I just wanted to tell you…how gorgeous you look tonight." It wasn't the only thing he wanted to say, but somehow it seemed easier to lead with it.

"Thank you." She smiled, but her eyes still held a trace of sadness. "That's really—"

"That's not the only thing," he interrupted her. "I miss you." He blurted out the truth, because it was the only thing he could do. "I told myself I wasn't going to do this." He shook his head, no longer caring about pride or whose ball was in whose court. "I tried to be patient and wait for you to realize… well…Amber, everything that happened…" He shook his head. Nothing was coming out the way he wanted it to. The way he *needed* it to. "Amber…" He took her hands in his and to his surprise and delight, she didn't pull away. There was too much they needed to talk about. Things they both needed to apologize for. But all of that could wait until later. There was only one thing that needed to be said. "Amber," he started again. "I love you."

She looked about as surprised by his words as he was that he'd said them out loud. He'd come to the conclusion weeks ago that he was in love with her, but he sure as hell hadn't planned to say it. Not that way. But a moment later, the surprise on her face faded and her lips twisted into a smile.

"Logan," she began. "I—"

"Amber! There you are!" The side door flew open, bringing with it a gust of warmth, and Christy. "Sorry to interrupt, but Cam needs us for some unofficial bridesmaid pictures."

Amber glanced between him and her friend and then back at him. “Save me a dance?”

“Of course.” He wanted to add that he’d save all his dances for her because there was no one else he ever wanted to have in his arms, but she’d disappeared inside with Christy and once again he was standing alone in the cold.

Chapter Twenty-One

HE LOVED HER.

He'd said it.

And she'd...

"Smile," the photographer ordered, pulling Amber back into the moment. They did as they were told before striking another pose. Despite the fact that they weren't official bridesmaids—the position having been saved only for Morgan—there was no way they weren't going to have a photo shoot together.

For the next few minutes, they took a series of pictures as a foursome, just the way they had at Christy's wedding and Drew's and high school graduation before that. And just like all of the previous occasions, they laughed and smiled until their faces hurt.

Finally, when they must have filled an entire memory card of images, the photographer declared it enough, and stole the bride and groom away for a few more shots before the reception was to begin.

"I'm sorry I interrupted you guys out there." Christy spun

on her the moment she had a chance. "I hope I didn't interrupt anything important."

I love you.

That was important. That was *very* important.

"It's okay." Amber shrugged. "We'll talk later."

"Talk about what?" Drew asked.

She looked between her friends. She didn't want to keep any more secrets from them. "I think I'm in love with Logan."

Drew burst out laughing and after a brief look of admonishment from Christy, she, too, couldn't help it, and stifled a smile.

"What?" Amber stared between her friends who were being anything but supportive. "What's so funny?"

It was Drew who pulled herself together first. "Obviously you love him, stupid."

"What?"

She still couldn't wrap her head around what was happening. It had taken Amber so long to come to the conclusion herself, and even longer to admit it. Let alone say it out loud. She couldn't see what was so funny about that. In fact, there was *nothing* funny about it.

Christy put her hand on Amber's arm. "Sweetie, we're not laughing at you."

"Sure sounds like it."

Drew swallowed another giggle and forced herself to be serious. Amber could see the effort it took. "Honestly," she said. "We're not. It's just…Amber, you're so cute. We could all see ages ago that you were in love."

Amber took a step back and shook her head.

"It's true," Christy confirmed. "Even more so since Thanksgiving. You are head over heels, girl. Why do you think you were so upset with him?"

"That doesn't even make sense."

"It totally does," Drew said.

Amber's head spun. *They all knew? They knew before she did?*

"I mean, I knew I liked him," Amber said, trying to sort the feelings out in her head. "And I enjoyed spending time with him, but…" Had it always been love? The racing heart when he kissed her. The warmth and excitement every time they were together. The ache that had been a constant since they'd stopped talking. Her hand flew to her mouth. "I'm such an idiot. How did I not see it before? I mean, I guessed that maybe that's what it was, but I *just* realized it. Really realized it. Like, just now."

"For a smart woman, you're pretty clueless sometimes." Christy laughed.

"Why didn't you say anything?"

"It wasn't for us to say." Drew's smile was sweet. "You needed to see it for yourself."

AMBER DIDN'T GET another chance to talk to Logan until after the dinner and speeches were done, which was probably a good thing because it gave her a chance to sort out her feelings in her head and figure out exactly what she wanted to tell him. She'd been looking forward to seeing him for weeks. It had been incredibly hard to keep herself from calling him or texting him, but she'd needed to wait. And she'd known exactly how she was going to do it, but now, with his declaration… everything was different.

Now that the day was here and it was time, everything she'd thought she would say to him had completely gone from her head.

When finally the band started up, and Cam and Evan went to dance their first dance, Amber stood on the edge of the dance floor and watched them along with everyone else. They truly were the happiest couple she'd ever seen, and she didn't know anyone else more deserving of their happy-ever-after than Cam and Evan. As the music played and she looked around the room at all of her family and friends, Amber's heart was full. Timber Creek was exactly where she belonged. It always was. It had just taken her a long time to figure it out.

Her eyes landed on Logan right as the first song ended, and the band invited everyone to take to the dance floor. Amber didn't hesitate. She walked directly to Logan, who met her halfway.

"May I have this dance?"

"I can't think of anything I'd like more." Amber slipped her hand in his, her body reacting at once to his touch. He pressed his other hand to her back and they started to move slowly to the beat.

"It was a beautiful wedding," he said. "Everything has been so—"

"I'm sorry," she blurted. "I'm sorry I lied to you. I was scared and—"

"It's okay." They'd stopped moving but Logan's arms were still around her. "You don't have—"

"No." She shook her head. "It's not okay. I was scared and you were trying to help and…I lied. I shouldn't have done that. And I never should have gotten mad at you that way. I…" Tears filled her eyes, but she couldn't cry. Not until she was done telling him what she needed to tell him. "I've missed you too."

He pulled back a little so they could see each other properly. "Why didn't you answer my calls?"

It was such a simple question, but not one she could answer completely. At least not yet.

"I just…I couldn't."

He nodded, somehow accepting her non-answer.

"Logan?" She took a breath. It would be so easy to continue to protect her heart, and keep living a solitary life. It would be safer. But with him standing so close to her, his scent that was somehow both peppermint and cinnamon, filling her senses, Amber knew she couldn't run. Not anymore. "Did you mean what you said?"

He nodded, not needing any clarification at all. "Every word. Amber, I—"

"I love you," she interrupted him. "I have for a while now, but I didn't realize it," she said quickly. "I love you, Logan. It's the craziest thing and I've never—"

He silenced her with a kiss. His hands came to her face, holding her, and she pressed her hands to his chest, absorbing every beat of his heart, and together, they fell completely and totally into each other in the middle of the dance floor.

THEY STILL HAD SO much to talk about, but Logan knew there'd be plenty of time for that later. Together they enjoyed the wedding, dancing into the night with their friends and absorbing the fun and festivities. Finally, when the newlyweds made their exit, Logan took Amber's hand. "All I want for Christmas is for you to wake up next to me tomorrow," he said. "Will you come back to the ranch with me?"

He didn't add that it might be one of the last times he'd be able to say that since the ranch had been sold. There'd be time for that later. For the moment, he just wanted to hold her in his arms and make love to the woman he loved.

Amber glanced toward Drew.

"Give me a moment?"

She slipped away from him and went to Drew, who was struggling to scoop a sleeping Austin into her arms. Naturally she'd be concerned about Drew and Austin. It was their first Christmas without Eric. He was about to go after her, and tell her it was fine—Drew needed her, and she should stay with her

—when Ben joined them and took Austin from Drew's arms. He shifted the child to his shoulder easily while the three of them had a brief conversation.

A moment later, Amber was back.

"It's okay," he said. "We don't have to—"

"It's fine." She cut him off. "We're all pretty sure that despite the fact that he's exhausted, Austin will still be up super early to see if Santa came." She laughed, her eyes sparkling. "And Drew doesn't want to subject me to an early wake-up. Besides, I think it's important for them to do this alone. Ben will take them home and make sure Austin is settled. Besides, I promised we'd be over for brunch."

He laughed, happy to know he'd have her for the night. "Sounds good. I look forward to it. Now let's get out of here."

"THIS IS PERFECT." Amber cuddled closer to Logan on the couch. The first thing they'd done when getting back from the wedding was to light a fire in Logan's stone fireplace, change out of their fancy clothes, and cuddle under a blanket together. "Except, how will Santa get down the chimney if we have a fire?"

"The only gift I need this year is you." He stroked her hair and in that moment, Amber couldn't remember having ever been so happy before. And she'd almost let it all get away.

Never again.

"Is that *all* you need?" She sat up a little so she could look at him. She still had one more gift to give him. "Because I have a present for you."

His eyes flashed with desire and Amber laughed. "Not that," she said and then added, "At least, not yet."

Logan pretended to look disappointed. "I was serious," he said. "You're the only thing I need."

"Well, I kind of hope you don't mean that." She unfolded herself from the couch and went into the bedroom, where she'd left her bag with the change of clothes she'd taken to the wedding. When she returned, she was holding an envelope. "I hope you like it."

Her hand shook as she held it out to him. She could only hope he'd be happy with what she'd done.

Logan glanced at her again before turning his attention to the envelope. "You really didn't have to—" His voice broke off when he saw what she was holding. "What is this?"

"It's a business card." Her breath caught in her throat while she waited for him to connect the dots. "For Taking the Reins Treatment Center." She remembered the night he told her about his dreams for the ranch. With more horses and the way he wanted to expand it to an entire center where he could host more than one client at a time and really immerse them in the horse experience so he could help more people.

She saw the moment he realized what it meant, his eyes lit up, but a moment later, he squeezed them shut and shook his head. "Amber, I don't know what to say."

"Say that you're excited," she offered. "Say that's great."

He wasn't smiling.

"But it's not." When he looked up, he looked immeasurably sad. "Remember when I told you that Ruby was putting the ranch up for sale?"

She nodded. "I do, and—"

"It's official," he interrupted her. "The new buyers take over on the first of the new year. I didn't want to say anything tonight. I just wanted to enjoy this without bringing it up, but…well. Anyway, I tried everything I could. I put together a business proposal for her to present to prospective buyers, but it wasn't enough." He shook his head and tried to hand the card back to her. "It's not going to happen."

"Yes, it is." She put her hands on her hips and refused to take the card. "Logan, you don't—"

"I'm not trying to be negative, Amber." He stood. "Really, I'm just—"

"I bought the ranch!" she blurted. "That's what I'm trying to tell you."

"You bought the ranch?" He blinked once. Twice. "What? How?" He shook his head. "No, *why* would you buy the ranch?"

"Because…" She took the card from his hands and pressed it to his chest over his heart. "I believe in what you're doing here and the difference you're making. I believe in the difference you can make to so many more people if you're given the opportunity and most importantly, I believe in *you*, Logan."

He looked down at her hand pressed to his chest and then back up at her. His eyes were still clouded with confusion, but the realization was starting to push through the fog. "But…I don't…"

Amber took his hands in hers and together they sat on the couch. "Remember when I asked you what I could do to help?"

He nodded.

"Well, it got me thinking. I had some investments and savings from too many years of working and having no life, so…"

"You did this for *me*?"

"No." She laughed. "Not really. I mean, yes. Obviously. But mostly I did it for all the people you're going to be able to help and because the world needs more of that. A lot more."

Logan pulled the card out again and stared at it. "Really?" He looked up. "This is happening?"

She nodded. "It's happening. Ready or not."

"Oh baby, I'm more than ready." He wrapped his arms

around her then and kissed her hard before leaning back. "Now, seriously. Tell me how you pulled this off."

It wasn't nearly as hard as she thought it would be, and she told him as much. About how after their fight, she realized how stupid she'd been—that she'd been thinking of a way to make it up to him, and the idea was born, but how it quickly became so much more than that. "Once I realized I could afford the investment—along with a partner—I started thinking about how amazing it really could be. Plus, since I have no real interest in cattle or ranching in any way, I've decided to sell whatever herd Ruby had left to Thundering Hooves Ranch. They've already been leasing most of the land for their own herd anyway, so we've kept that arrangement, which means I only need to worry about the barns, the cabin, the main house, the horses, and about twenty acres that you can use to develop the center. That's about how much your proposal said you needed, right?"

"My proposal?"

"That's the one." She laughed. "Ruby showed it to me, and I was very impressed. We can draft an agreement for leasing the space and—"

"You've thought of everything, haven't you?" Logan shook his head, clearly still in disbelief of the entire situation.

"Almost everything," Amber said more seriously this time. "I honestly wasn't sure if you would forgive me, or want to get involved with me in any way again. So, I was prepared to walk away and hand over control to my partner."

"Your dad," Logan guessed correctly.

She nodded. "Yes. So if you aren't sure about this, about me, or getting involved in a business venture with me, I understand."

Logan shifted on the couch and took her hands. "You need to slow down," he said. "I'm still trying to catch up with what's going on here." He squeezed her hands. "Let's go back to what you said about you not being sure I'd forgive you or wanting to be involved with you again."

Her heart sank. Maybe the last few hours were too good to be true; maybe they wouldn't be able to get past everything that had happened. "Can you understand why I didn't reach out to you before now?" she said quickly, desperate to make him understand. "I needed to be sure that this…that everything…I needed to make a grand gesture so you knew how I felt. And that was even before *I* knew how I felt. But it was—"

"Ssh." He pressed a finger to her lips. "I understand," he said slowly. "But now I need you to understand something, okay?" She nodded and he took his finger away. "You didn't need to do this. You absolutely did not need to make a grand gesture, Amber. Not for me. That's fiction and this is…" He gestured between them. "This is real. I don't need all this to know how you feel."

"But, I—"

"No buts, Amber. You told me you love me. Is that true?"

She didn't hesitate a second. "Yes. Without a doubt."

"And I love you. That's all I'll ever really need." He kissed her then and all further discussion of Taking the Reins Treatment Center, or grand gestures, were forgotten, because all there was was the two of them.

Chapter Twenty-Two

"AUNTIE AMBER!" The moment Logan and Amber walked through the front door of Drew's house the next morning, Austin came flying down the hall and into Amber's waiting arms while Logan side-stepped out of the way.

"Merry Christmas, buddy. Did Santa come?"

The boy wiggled out of her grip and started jumping up and down in front of her. "Did he ever! Come see." He grabbed Amber's hand and led her down the hall into the living room, leaving Logan to trail behind.

The scene in the living room was one of chaos, with piles of wrapping paper on the floor with toys scattered throughout.

"Merry Christmas, Logan." Drew greeted him with a hug. "I may have gone a little overboard," she said with an apologetic smile.

"Not at all." Ben joined them from the kitchen. "He needed to be spoiled this year. It's all good." He handed Logan a cup of coffee. "Merry Christmas, Logan."

"Merry Christmas," Logan said with a toast of his cup. "I know it's a hard one for you guys..." He trailed off, not wanting to make Drew sadder than she already might be.

"It's okay." Drew smiled. "It's always going to be hard, but seeing Austin so happy and…well, honestly you guys all really help too. It's been rough. But it's going to be okay." A tear slipped down her cheek then, but she didn't wipe it away. "Eric would have loved all this," she said. "We should have come home more."

Ben slipped an arm around her shoulders and squeezed. "Don't do that, Drew. You can't change things now."

Logan watched while she closed her eyes and took a deep breath. When she opened them again, she was smiling. "Enough tears," she announced. "It's Christmas." She turned to find Amber, who was sitting on the floor, playing with cars of some kind. "Amber, do you need a coffee?"

"Do I ever! This kid is exhausting."

TWENTY MINUTES LATER, Amber had managed to extract herself from the toys and convince Austin to have some of his mother's delicious Christmas waffles. Which he ate as fast as possible before returning to his new toys, leaving the adults alone at the table.

"This is delicious, Drew," Amber said. "I am so glad you're cooking again. Lord knows how we survived on my food."

"It wasn't so bad." Drew was lying and they all knew it. "Well, some of it was pretty good."

"Like the cereal and milk?" Amber laughed. "I got pretty good at that. But cooking is definitely not my specialty."

"You have other strengths." Logan put his hand over hers and Drew groaned.

"Seriously? You two are way too sweet." She rolled her eyes. "But I love it. It's crazy seeing you with someone, Amber. And I mean that in the best way."

"I know exactly how you meant it," she said. "And I totally

agree." She glanced at Logan out of the corner of her eye. She never would have thought she'd be sitting here like this with a man she was totally and completely in love with. "You know what else is crazy?"

Logan looked at her sideways. "I might be scared to ask, but what?"

"I decided to take everyone's advice," she announced. "I'm opening a law practice in Timber Creek." Saying it out loud made it feel real, but instead of being scared, she was excited. "I didn't have a chance to tell you yet," she said to Logan. "But I decided just last week. Along with everything else, I guess I just thought…well, maybe I really can have that second chance you were talking about, Drew."

"First of all," Logan said. "I think that's fantastic news. You'll be the best lawyer in town and I think you can really help a lot of people."

"I agree," Drew chimed in.

"And second," Logan continued. "You didn't ever need a second chance with me, Amber."

She nodded. "I know that now. But that's not really what I meant." Amber had no idea whether how she felt would translate into words, but she wanted to try. She took a breath. "Before coming back to Timber Creek, I felt broken, as if I'd wasted my life and made choices that would forever define who I was. I was stuck and I never thought it was possible that I could have anything else." She turned to look at Logan. "But then I met you, and your horses and…something changed. I started to believe that I could have something else. That I *could* have a second chance to live my life the way I really wanted to and not the way I'd told myself I wanted to. A second chance to write the story. Does that make sense?"

She was looking at Logan as she spoke, but it was Ben who responded first. "I think it makes perfect sense."

“So do I,” Logan said. “And I for one am glad you came back home, even more pleased that you opened your mind enough to the horses…and to me.”

Amber laughed. “That one took a little more convincing.”

Across the table, Drew stood abruptly, her chair pushing back roughly against the tile floor. She picked up a stack of dishes and moved to the sink.

Amber exchanged a look with Ben that she hoped conveyed the need she had to talk to her friend alone.

Ben, thankfully, got the hint and nodded to Logan. “Why don’t we let the ladies clear up in here and we can take the living room mess?”

She waited for the men to make their exit before picking up a stack of plates and joining Drew at the sink. “You okay, sweetie?”

She didn’t answer, but shook her head.

“I wish I knew what to say.” Amber wrapped her arm around her friend’s shoulders and steered her away from the sink and in for a hug, but Drew shook her head and stepped away from the embrace.

“No,” she said. “It’s fine. I’m just having a moment.”

“Of course you are. It’s Christmas. It’s—”

“So hard,” Drew finished the sentence. “I never thought it would be this hard, Amber. This morning when Austin was opening his presents from Santa, ripping the paper off and throwing it in the air, all I could think of was that Eric would never be there for a Christmas morning ever again.” Drew shook her head. “And do you know that last night, after Ben helped me bring Austin home and tuck him into bed, he offered to help with all that? With all the Santa stuff so I didn’t have to do it alone.”

“Oh, Drew. I should have been—”

“No.” She shook her head. “I made him leave. I wanted—

no, I *needed*—to be alone. I poured myself a big glass of wine and I did it all myself." She shook her head with a sad laugh. "I cried throughout the entire thing," she said. "But I couldn't bring myself to let anyone else be Santa. It was bad enough that it had to be me. It was always Eric's job." She looked up at Amber, her eyes full of tears. "But he's gone, Amber. He's really gone."

Amber nodded slowly. "Yes," she said gently. "He is."

"I think that finally hit me last night." Drew dabbed at her eyes. "Like, *really* hit me. I mean, I know he's gone. But…" She dissolved into tears and instead of reaching for her right away, Amber let her cry for a moment because she knew that's what Drew needed.

"He'd be so proud of you," Amber said. "It hasn't been easy for you, but you're doing an amazing job, Drew. Today is going to be hard, but then you'll wake up tomorrow and know that you got through it. And then the next day, and the day after that. And maybe one day—"

"It won't be so hard anymore," Drew finished.

Amber nodded. "I really hope that's true." She hugged her then and squeezed her friend tight.

"Me too," Drew mumbled into her shoulder. "Me too."

AMBER WAS STILL full from the brunch at Drew's when they pulled up to her father's house later that afternoon. She still wasn't sure she'd be able to eat another bite, but she'd promised her dad they'd have Christmas dinner together. The first one since she'd left home.

Earlier that morning, Logan called to invite his own father over, too, and for the first time since Amber could remember, she was actually looking forward to Christmas dinner.

When they arrived at the house, the smell of roasted turkey greeted them on the porch. Instead of knocking, Amber opened the door and called out, "Merry Christmas. We're here."

Her dad appeared, looking younger and brighter. He wore a Santa suit apron and held a spoon in one hand. "Merry Christmas." He smiled, but she could see the hesitation in his eyes. Their relationship had made leaps and bounds in the last few weeks, but there was still a lifetime of uncertainty and old habits.

Amber made the first move, crossing the space between them and pulling her dad into a tight hug. "It smells fantastic in here, Dad. I didn't think you were going to make a turkey."

In fact, as far as Amber could remember, her dad had *never* cooked a turkey. Their tradition had always been Christmas macaroni and cheese. Nothing special, but Amber came by her cooking skills honestly, and it was the best they could usually come up with.

"You'd be surprised what you can learn on that internet." Joseph laughed. "Logan." He waved him out of the door and into the house. "Did you know there's a video for everything?"

Logan laughed. "I have heard that, yes." He stuck his hand out. "Merry Christmas, Joseph. Thank you for welcoming us."

"It's nothing." He grumbled, and Amber tried not to laugh at his attempts to downplay the occasion. "Come in already. Your father is here. He brought the potatoes. Look pretty good, too."

Logan laughed and caught Amber's eye with a wink. "My father always did make some mean mashed potatoes."

Amber couldn't have anticipated that sharing dinner with their fathers would be so enjoyable, but it turned out to be one of the nicest Christmases she could remember. Besides the turkey and stuffing, which her father perfected, Junky's mashed potatoes, and a bowl of carrots and peas, her father had also cooked a pot of macaroni and cheese. Logan and his father looked confused by the unusual side dish, but Amber had to blink back tears when she saw it.

Junky's presence brought out a lighter side of her dad, and when the meal was finally served, he started to relax, and actually even laughed a few times. More than once, Amber found herself sitting back and watching the little group and marveling at how this now was her life. These people, her family.

"I got you kids something," Joseph announced suddenly when the dishes were cleared from the table. "Wait here."

"Dad," Amber protested when he returned and handed them each a box. "You didn't have to get us presents. We haven't exchanged gifts for—"

"Maybe it's time for a new tradition," he interrupted her. "A lot of things have changed—maybe this should too." Amber smiled, but before she could say anything, her dad said, "Besides, it's not much. Open them."

Logan looked at Amber and nodded. Together, they removed the shiny paper he'd wrapped them in and removed the matching lids. Inside Amber's box was the most beautiful hand turned wooden pen she'd ever seen. It was a deep red wood and had been sanded until it was so smooth it was almost silky. It was stunning.

"Dad…" She lifted the pen from the box. "You made this? It's…"

"Gorgeous," Logan finished for her. Amber looked to see him holding an identical pen in his hand. "Joseph, these are outstanding."

"They're made with bloodwood," he said with a nod. "First time I've used that wood and I thought…well, I thought maybe you'd both be needing pens with your new businesses." He grunted, obviously uncomfortable. "So, there you go."

“Thank you, Dad.” Amber got up from the table and wrapped her arms tightly around him. She held on until he hugged her back and then she just kept on hugging, unwilling to let him go.

Chapter Twenty-Three

THE CROWD GATHERED in the Log and Jam for New Year's Eve was one of the biggest that Timber Heart had ever performed for, maybe *the* biggest. Either way, the energy in the room was incredible and just like she was during every show, Christy was energized. They'd just finished their first set, and had escaped to the little storage room in the back of the bar that they'd claimed as their dressing room.

"This is great," she said to Jamie. "Can you believe all the people out there?"

"It's pretty crazy," Josh, the drummer, agreed. "What a perfect night to show off some of our new stuff. I'm really glad we decided to change up the set list."

"Me too." A few nights ago, at their last rehearsal before the New Year's performance, Christy had campaigned the guys to add some more of their original songs into the set list. Usually they focused on some popular cover songs that got the crowd going, and only mixed in one or two originals, but more and more Christy couldn't help but think they were missing a real opportunity to showcase what the band really could do. "I'm glad you all agreed."

"You're hard to say no to." Jamie laughed. "I mean, you have met yourself, haven't you?"

"You are pretty persistent, Christy."

She laughed and took it as the compliment it was intended. She knew she could be a bit overbearing when there was something she wanted. But so far, that determination had been paying off and she couldn't wait to tell the guys just how much it had paid off. But that would have to wait.

"I'll be right back, okay?" She hopped off the stool she'd been perched on. "I'm just going to go say hi to Mark. I'll only be a few minutes."

"Sounds good," Jamie said. "But let's meet back in ten, okay? That'll give us enough time for a good long set before we ring in the new year."

"Perfect." Christy slipped out into the busy bar and headed straight for the table full of her friends.

"There she is." Mark jumped up and gave her a quick kiss on the lips. "You're amazing tonight, Christy. I mean, you're amazing every night, but…"

"Thanks, babe." She took a seat next to him and joined her friends. "Are you guys having a good time?"

"The best." Cam smiled at her from across the table where she sat with her new husband. "You guys are awesome. I love your new stuff."

"Me too," Amber agreed. "It's great. And the crowd seems to be into it, too. How is it you don't have a record deal yet?"

Christy laughed and next to her Mark winked, because he knew the secret. "Hopefully soon," she said. "I can't stay long, though. We're going to start our new set soon. I just wanted to come say hi and propose an early toast in case things get crazy later."

"Sounds good to me." Drew, who already looked as if she'd had a few drinks, picked up her wine glass.

Christy shot Ben, who'd just arrived with another tray of

drinks for the table, a look that she hoped he would pick up on, but ultimately she knew Drew would be okay even if she had a few too many drinks.

"To us." Christy raised her glass. "May the new year bring us all even more happiness, more adventure, and more opportunities than the year before."

"To good friends," Amber said.

"And family," Ben added. "And friends who feel like family."

They all toasted, glasses clinking together before Cam let out a loud cheer and they all laughed. All but Drew, who, after draining her glass, was refilling it from the bottle on the table.

Before Christy slipped away, back to the band, she went to give Drew a hug. "Hey," she said quiet enough so only her friend could hear. "This year is going to be better."

"Well, it can't get any worse," Drew said, a slight slur to her words.

Before Christy could say anything else, although she didn't know what it would have been, Ben reached between them and put a glass of water in front of Drew.

With one last kiss for Mark, she rejoined the band in the back room. "Are you guys ready to do this?"

"Absolutely." Josh tapped his sticks together. "Let's do—"

"Just one more thing before we go." Christy stopped them before they could leave. "I have some news."

"News?" Jamie crossed his arms over his chest and Caleb turned to stare. "Please don't tell me that you've finally had enough of us after all and you're quitting."

"Are you kidding?" Christy laughed. "Totally the opposite, actually." She had to keep from jumping up and down with excitement. "I was going to tell you earlier, but I wanted to wait for the right moment…"

"Just tell us already."

"Okay, okay." She rolled her eyes. "Remember those demos

I sent off awhile ago with our original stuff?" She didn't bother waiting for an answer; they all knew what she was talking about. "Well, we got some replies. Two, in fact."

"Two?" It didn't sound like a lot, but it was and they all knew it. "From who?"

"Bryce Bengston and Derrick Webb. They're both agents out of Los Angeles."

"We know who they are," Caleb said. "They replied?"

"Not only did they reply," Christy said. "They want to meet with us in the new year. They're both very excited about our potential as a band. Isn't that awesome?"

She looked around the small group while they absorbed the news. It was Jamie who reacted first with a yell, and pretty soon they were all yelling and hugging and celebrating what the new year could mean for Timber Heart.

AMBER FELT a twinge of guilt leaving the Log and Jam before Christy's last set, but she knew her friend would understand. She and Logan had something very special to celebrate together, and that's exactly what they were going to do.

It was a cold night, but after Logan got a fire roaring in the fireplace of the cabin, they grabbed thick blankets and a bottle of champagne, and bundled themselves up on the porch swing that Logan had cleared of snow earlier in the day.

"Are you cold?"

Amber shivered, but it wasn't enough to complain about. "I'll be fine for a few minutes," she said. "Besides, this will only happen once and I'm not going to miss it because of a little chill."

Logan responded by wrapping his arm around her and pulling her closer. "This is perfect," he said after a moment. "I mean, I enjoyed the bar with everyone but—"

"This is better."

"This *is* better. Can you believe how much has happened?"

"And how far we've come."

"Exactly." They were quiet for a few moments. "You know how some people are always in a hurry to say good-bye to the old year because it was hard or bad things happened?"

She nodded.

"I don't feel like that."

Amber turned to look at him, curious. "Do you mean, you're sad to see this year end?"

"Not at all." He chuckled. "It's just that I've learned over time that even when a year is particularly challenging, there's good that will still come out of it, and I don't think that should be disregarded. There were a whole lot of challenges this year, for both of us, don't you think?"

Amber nodded, completely in agreement. The last year had knocked her to her knees. It definitely hadn't been easy.

"But even so," Logan continued. "It also brought a lot of good." He snuggled her close. "It brought me you."

She tilted her head up and kissed him on the cheek. "That's a very good point. But if you're not sad to see the year end, I guess I'm confused."

He laughed. "I guess what I'm saying is, for all the crap the last year brought us, it also brought us a lot of good and I think we've both learned that it's because of the hard stuff and the challenges that the good stuff happens."

"Right," she jumped in. "Like, without all of that, we wouldn't be sitting her together right now."

"Exactly."

"So you're saying we should celebrate the last year."

Logan nodded. "Don't you think so?"

Amber thought about it for a moment. "I guess, but I'm not going to lie, Logan. I've never been so excited for the start of a new year and all of the possibilities it will bring us." She shifted in her seat so she faced him. "So, I'll tell you what, how about we toast early?" She gestured to the bottle of champagne that sat next to them. "Before the countdown. We'll toast the end of the year and everything that brought us to this moment. And then at midnight, it's all about the future."

"I love it." He grinned broadly and reached for the bottle. "And I love you." He gave her a quick kiss on the lips before manipulating the cork. "Ready?"

"Like for a mini countdown?" She laughed. "Like to say good-bye?"

"Is there another way?"

She laughed again. "Okay. Ready." He nodded, so she counted down for three and with a quick push, Logan sent the cork flying through the air.

He quickly poured them a small glass and Amber raised it in a toast. "To the year that was," she said. "And all of the challenges it brought with it."

"And the opportunities that followed," Logan added and raised his glass. "To last year."

They clinked glasses and drank deeply. The bubbles popped and fizzed on the back of Amber's throat. "Do you feel better now?"

"So much." Logan chuckled and tucked the blanket around them a little tighter. "And just in time, too." He glanced at his watch. "Are you ready for this?"

"For our future?" Amber shivered, but not because of the cold. "I've never been more ready."

"Here we go." Logan looked straight into her eyes and together they counted down.

"Five...four...three...two...one."

"Happy New Year, darling." He whispered the words against her lips before swallowing her own well wishes in a deep kiss.

Overhead, there were pops and booms as the fireworks

from town blasted in the night sky, ringing in the new year. Logan and Amber leaned back in their seat to watch the celebration while Logan poured them another small glass of champagne.

This time, Amber knew her toast would be different because as the clock struck midnight, not only had it become a new year, but her ownership of the ranch also became official. She raised her glass. "To new years, new beginnings, new businesses, new relationships, and new starts."

"That's a whole lot of newness." Logan grinned. "How about one more?"

"What's that?"

"What about a new place to live?" he asked. "For you, I mean. This cabin has never felt more like home since you've been here with me. I want to wake up every morning with you next to me. I know it's not very big, but…"

When Amber had finalized the deal with Ruby, they'd made a special concession that would allow Ruby to keep living on the ranch for up to three years, or until she was ready to move off. It turned out that after she'd gone riding with Logan before Christmas, she was feeling a rekindled connection to the horses and preferred to stay close. Amber had happily agreed. After all, Ruby and her generous dealing had made everything possible. Besides, Logan didn't mind staying in the cozy cabin.

"Are you asking me to move in with you?" She laughed, suddenly feeling like a kid again. She'd never lived with a man before, and she hadn't really stopped to consider it as a possibility. But to her surprise, the idea didn't scare her—not at all.

"That's exactly what I'm asking you," he said. "And really, technically it's your cabin now."

"No way." Amber shook her head. "It's *our* cabin. Besides, it's kind of where we began, don't you think?" She thought about it for a moment. This place, this ranch—it was more than just a place. Everything had changed when she first set foot on the ranch and agreed to talk to Logan's horse. *She'd* changed that day. "No," she amended. "It was *when* we began. Does that make sense?"

He laughed. "It kind of does, but you know what? Whether it was where, when, or even *why* we began, it's just that—the beginning. And you and me," he reached one hand out of his blanket and laced his fingers through hers, "we're just getting started."

There was no disagreeing with that, nor could she disagree when he stood and led her inside to their cabin to start out their new year and new beginning together.

Chapter Twenty-Four

MARCH

"I STILL CAN'T BELIEVE you're moving out." Drew plopped on Amber's bed instead of helping her pack. "I mean *really* moving out."

"I'm not sure why you can't believe that." Amber gave her friend a sideways look. "I've only spent one or two nights here since New Year's. I technically haven't been living here for the last two months." She picked up a sweater and folded it before putting it on the top of a pile on the bed. "Besides, we both knew this wasn't going to be a permanent living situation, right?"

"I guess." Drew picked up the sweater and held it out to look at it before tossing it next to her on the bed. "But I thought, well…it doesn't matter. I really am happy for you and Logan."

Amber picked up the sweater again, folded it and placed it back on the pile. "I know you are," she said, and meant it. Drew had been nothing but supportive of her relationship and more importantly, of her. "And I really want to thank you, Drew."

"Thank me?" She moved to grab the sweater again, but Amber picked up the entire pile and dropped it into a box. "For what?" She shot Amber a look.

"For everything." She sat down on the bed across from her friend. "Mostly for letting me live here with you and Austin to help you out when you needed it."

"Oh my God, Amber. I should be thanking *you* for that. You saved me." She shook her head. "I don't know if I could have made it through those first few months after losing Eric if you hadn't been here. You were...you were huge, Amber." She blinked back tears. "I don't know how Austin and I would have made it through. Honestly."

"Sweetie." Amber reached over and hugged Drew hard and fast. "You would have been fine. You are so much stronger than you think you are."

Drew sniffed and wiped at her face. "You know, sometimes I think it would be nice to not be strong. I mean, just for a minute."

"I get that." Amber laughed and stood again. "But it is what it is and losing Eric was shitty and hard and something I wish you never had to go through, but—"

"It happened."

"Yes." Amber nodded thoughtfully. "It happened."

They were quiet for a few minutes while Amber resumed packing.

"Do you remember what you said on Christmas Day?" Drew asked after a moment. "About second chances?"

Amber stopped, two books in her hand. "I do. It was your idea. Why?"

"I've been thinking about that a lot. I mean, what you said about getting a second chance to do your life over again."

"Well, not really *over* again, but a chance to do something different with it." Amber put the books down and examined her friend. "Do you want to do something different? I mean…I guess I don't understand what you're saying."

She knew Drew couldn't mean that she didn't want to be a mother or a wife, that she hadn't loved her life. *Or did she?*

Beside her, Drew shook her head. "I know it doesn't really make sense, and I don't regret for a minute anything I've done. I mean, marrying Eric and being a wife and a mother—I wouldn't give that up for anything. It's just that…now that's gone." She looked as though she might cry, but to Amber's surprise, no tears fell.

"It's not gone, Drew. You're still a mother and you'll always be Eric's wife."

"No," Drew corrected her. "I'll be Eric's *widow.*" She closed her eyes and dipped her head for a moment before she lifted it. "Don't get me wrong, that is what it is. But I guess what I'm really saying is that maybe there's a second chance for me in all this, too? I don't know if I'm ready yet, or if it's even going to be a thing. But, watching Cam and Evan find their second chance and Christy and Mark—they got a second chance at their love, too."

"I didn't get a second chance at love."

"Yes, Amber. You did. But your second chance wasn't *just* love. It was life."

Amber wanted to reach out to her friend, hug her, and tell her everything would be okay. But that's all Drew had heard for the last few months since Eric died, and maybe the time for that was over? Maybe it was time for more?

"Drew? What are you saying?" she asked softly.

She dropped her head in her hands and rubbed her eyes before looking up again. This time when her eyes met Amber's, there were still tears that shone there, but there was something Amber hadn't seen in a long time. Hope. "I think that maybe my life didn't end when Eric died."

Amber opened her mouth to agree, but Drew stopped her with a gentle shake of her head.

"I mean obviously I've always known that, but it's hard to believe something when your heart has been shattered."

"I can't even imagine."

Drew nodded gently. "So maybe it's time for my second chance."

"Or maybe just a new chance?"

"Yes." Drew smiled. "A new chance. I like that."

It was then that Amber moved across the bed and pulled her friend into her arms. "I love you, Drew."

"I love you, too." Amber could feel the tears soaking her shoulder. "I'm going to miss you so much."

"Hey." She pulled back and held Drew out at arm's length. "I'm moving five minutes away. It's not like you'll be rid of me that easily."

"You know what I mean." Drew grabbed a t-shirt from a different pile and used it to swat at her. "But I am happy for you. And maybe …"

Amber paused and waited.

"Well, I was thinking that maybe," Drew continued, "I could come out to the ranch and check out the horses." She stood quickly and looked away. "I mean…I know they helped—"

"Definitely." It was a great idea and one that she'd thought of herself once or twice. Logan and the horses would go a long way in helping Drew heal. Amber had just needed Drew to be ready for it. "I think that would be a great idea. And maybe Austin would benefit, too. At the very least, he'd probably enjoy going for a trail ride." She smiled and Drew laughed.

It wouldn't be easy, and there was still a lot of healing to be done, but Amber knew in her heart that Drew would be okay.

Amber stood and pulled her friend into a tight hug. "Now, are you going to help me with these boxes or what?"

Drew laughed but before she could answer, her cell phone rang. She pulled it from her pocket and Amber watched as her friend's eyes lit up. "It's Evan!"

"And?"

"Cam?" Drew looked at her as if she'd missed something completely obvious, which apparently she had. "The baby?"

"Oh my God," Amber screeched as it finally hit her. "Answer it!"

"Right." Drew shook her head and turned her attention to the phone. "Hello?"

"Put it on speaker."

Drew pushed the button and Evan's voice filled the room.

"It's happening. We're on the way to the hospital."

"Right now?" Amber looked at Drew. "I thought her due date wasn't until the twenty-eighth. It's too early."

Drew laughed. "It's only two weeks early. It's fine." Then, to Evan, she asked, "What can we do?"

"Can you come?" Normally so calm and self-assured, Evan sounded frantic and…like a first-time dad. "I'm not sure I know what—"

"We'll be there," Drew answered for both of them. "I'll drop Austin off at my parents' and we'll meet you there. Right, Amber?"

Amber looked at her stack of half-packed boxes. She was supposed to move later tonight. But it could wait, because clearly Cam's baby wasn't about to.

"As if we'd be anywhere else," she said. "Stay calm, Evan. You've got this."

IT WAS a good thing that Amber didn't have a lot of things from her old life in San Francisco. She'd always been so busy working that she hadn't bothered to actually collect a lot of stuff and things she did have were mostly donated when she moved back to Timber Creek.

Either way, Logan still felt as if he'd been carrying boxes into their tiny cabin for hours.

"That was it," she announced right as Logan put the box he'd been carrying onto a stack behind the couch. "I'm officially all moved in."

"Well, I don't know about *all*." He put his arms around her. "I think you have a bit of unpacking to do." He kissed her easily on the tip of her nose. "But as for officially? Definitely. And it's about time, too."

She wiggled out of his grip and winked at him. "Hey," she said. "It's not my fault Theo made his appearance early. And," she continued, "it's also not my fault he's so stinkin' cute that I couldn't stop cuddling him."

Logan laughed. Cam and Evan's baby *was* pretty cute, which is something he never thought he'd even think, let alone *say* out loud. But he had. A few times. *Maybe one day…*

"Okay," he said, not letting his brain go down the rabbit hole that was the future. "It wasn't your fault and it doesn't matter anyway because now you're here." He pulled her back in for another kiss. He'd never get tired of having his arms around her and having his lips on hers.

Logan held her for a few minutes longer, unwilling to let her go despite the fact that he knew she wasn't going anywhere. Except maybe outside to the building site where they were supposed to be meeting the general contractors in only a few minutes.

The building site.

Logan didn't think he'd ever get tired of hearing those words. After Amber officially took possession of the ranch and they signed the documents leasing him the land and buildings for Taking the Reins, the real work began and in the last eight weeks, they'd both been busy.

Plans had been drawn up for a lodge building that would house private bedrooms, a large kitchen, and general meeting rooms. It wasn't huge, but there was the potential to expand at a later date and it would be big enough that they could start taking on clients almost as soon as the build was completed. After all the planning stages, it was finally time to see exactly where the building was going to go.

Everything was about to get very real.

"Are you ready for today?" Amber asked, as if she'd read his thoughts. "It's going to be pretty incredible."

The fact that she totally understood the magnitude of the day made him love her even more. "It is going to be incredible. Even more than it already is. I mean, now I have you officially." She giggled as he tried to kiss her again.

"Silly boy. You've had me from the moment you met me."

That wasn't true and they both knew it, but he kissed her anyway. "As for the center, I am more than ready to break ground. Should we get going?"

They hadn't wanted to make a huge deal about the ground-breaking ceremony for Taking the Reins Treatment Center, at least not at first. But when their friends and family heard the good news, they'd all insisted on being there and of course they'd relented, because as Amber had said, "It's important to celebrate all the things, especially the ones that changes lives. Either yours, or someone else's."

And she was right. Taking the Reins had already changed his life, and of course Amber's. With the opening of the center later that year, there was no telling how many lives they could impact for the better. And that was definitely something to be celebrated.

Together, they went outside to meet with the contractor who had the area staked out. The ground was still not entirely thawed, but he assured them they'd be able to start the process anyway. A few friends had already gathered, and Logan looked over to Joseph Monroe, who stood to the side, watching them with a smile on his face. Logan hardly recognized him as the cantankerous old man he'd first met. Another person Taking the Reins had helped. He offered Joseph a wave, and the old man grunted and shrugged into his coat in reply.

Okay, maybe some people never *really* changed. Logan couldn't help but laugh.

He took another look around the crowd before his eyes landed on the one person he'd been hoping to talk to. Leaving Amber chatting with a small group of friends, he moved across the yard.

"I'm glad you came today," he said.

"Oh, Logan. I wouldn't have missed it for anything." Ruby reached out and took his hands in hers. "What you're doing here…it's just so special and I couldn't be prouder that it's here on the ranch."

"None of this could have happened if you hadn't—"

"No," she interrupted him. "None of this could have happened if it hadn't been for you and your kind heart. And let's not forget your young lady over there." She winked.

"Never." He returned her wink.

"You're both very special, Logan. I hope you know that."

"Thank you, Ruby." Impulsively, he pulled her into a hug. "For everything. I really mean it."

He released her and was about to go find Amber when they were joined by his father.

"There you are." Junky clapped Logan on the back. "Quite a turnout today for you."

"It's a pretty big deal," Ruby said. "You should be very proud."

Junky turned to Ruby, and Logan watched as his eyes lit up and a broad smile stretched across his face.

"Dad, have you met Ruby Blackstar? She's kind of the—"

"We have, in fact, met." Ruby cut him off. "You worked a

miracle on my old truck a few years back. I don't know how you did it, but I got another few years out of it before it finally gave up."

"Well, I do remember that." Junky chuckled and extended his hand. "It's nice to see you again, Ruby."

"Ruby is…" Logan drifted off as he became aware that neither Ruby nor his father were paying him any attention at all. They were already chatting and laughing, and Logan laughed to himself as he walked away. It was an unlikely pairing, but who was he to make that type of judgment?

A moment later, he was standing next to his own unlikely match. Together, they chatted with a few more people, discussed the details of the dig, and then it was time. Amber handed him a shovel with a bright-red ribbon tied to the handle and he stood in front of the small crowd.

"Thank you all for being here today." Logan cleared his throat and took a minute to gather his thoughts. "It means a lot to me that you'd come out today because I think today marks an important day not only for me, but for the community as a whole. Taking the Reins has been a dream of mine ever since I realized the power that animals had to heal." The memory of Tina filled his heart. It no longer hurt him to think of her, but made him smile to remember.

"They healed me," he continued. "And from that moment on, I knew it could be something very special and I've been working toward this moment." He looked to Amber, who watched him with a smile on her face. "I've had a little help in making this dream a reality and I wouldn't have it any other way." He winked at her and she blew him a kiss. Logan turned back to the small crowd and held the shovel up. "I'm so incredibly proud to break ground today on the Taking the Reins Treatment Center." He plunged the shovel into the ground and a cheer rose up from the group.

Amber joined him and placed her hands over his. Together,

they lifted the cold soil from the earth. "This is going to be amazing," she whispered in his ear.

All Logan could do was smile, because it already was.

Thank you for reading When We Began! I hope you loved Amber and Logan's story as much as I did! The love in Timber Creek isn't over yet! It's finally time for Drew to have her story and her second chance at life...and love in When We Fell. You can read a sneak peek of her story right after this...

For more love and happily ever afters, I have an exclusive sweet novella that's not for sale anywhere. You can read it HERE!

When We Fell

PLEASE ENJOY **this excerpt from Drew's story—When We Fell**

THE SECOND DREW ROSS opened the garage door, she wished she hadn't. When the door rolled up, the only thing staring back at her were boxes. Piles and piles of boxes.

"Awesome." Drew rolled her eyes and put her hands on her hips but there was no help for it. If she was going to find her son's baseball glove, there was only one thing to do.

Start opening boxes.

"Here goes nothing," she said aloud before taking a step into the garage. Her long, dark hair was twisted up on the top of her head in a messy bun and she'd managed to find a bandanna that she'd tied around that. Dressed in an old t-shirt and a pair of cut-offs, she at least looked as if she was prepared to do a little organizing and cleaning.

Which was good, because she certainly didn't feel ready to face the lifetime of stuff the cardboard boxes and rubber totes held. Not that she had a choice.

Austin was going to start Little League, and he needed a glove. He was just barely five. He needed stability. He needed everything to be as normal as possible.

He *needed* his glove.

That was the thought that propelled Drew forward and into the garage full of boxes and memories.

She held her breath and opened the flap of the first one. It wasn't labeled. Most of them weren't. When she and Eric had decided to pack up their entire lives and move back to Timber Creek so he could live out his last few months in their hometown, there hadn't been much time to pack up properly or label anything. In fact, it would be a miracle if half of their things weren't broken and smashed inside those boxes.

Not that she cared all that much anymore.

Drew did most of the packing herself, with Eric helping out as much as he could. He was already so weak, even then, that he spent most of his time resting in a chair, keeping her company and trying to make her laugh while she threw things in boxes so they could uproot their entire lives that were about to be shattered completely.

"You might want to wrap that in bubble wrap," he'd said when she picked up his overstuffed trout pillow. He'd owned it for years and for reasons Drew could never understand, insisted on keeping it on the living room couch.

Drew paused, the pillow in her hand. "Seriously?"

He nodded, a grin on his handsome, but way too pale face. "Deadly. It's very special."

"I was actually thinking maybe we could donate this." She held the printed pillow up. "I mean…really?"

"No way." Her husband of eight years pushed himself to his feet and made his way over to her. He took the trout out of her hands and kissed it before turning and using it to kiss her. "This is my most prized possession." He laughed and before she could protest, wrapped his arms around her, and pulled her into him.

There were times when, if she didn't look close, Drew could forget that cancer was ravaging his body, and just for a minute she could pretend that it was just an ordinary day. When he pressed his lips to hers, and dipped her backward, just a little, it was one of those times.

Maybe the doctors were wrong and as soon as they got home to Timber Creek, Eric would finally beat the cancer and they'd live to be old and gray together.

The memory washed over Drew as she stood with the box open in front of her, surrounded by their memories.

The doctors hadn't been wrong. She was the one who was wrong. Being home in Timber Creek hadn't saved Eric. It had been almost nine months since he'd been gone. Nine months that Drew had to adjust to the idea of a new future.

For the most part, she was succeeding. With the help of her friends and family, she was starting to live again. More and more each day, it got a little easier to breathe without wanting to cry, kiss their son—who looked so much like his father—without thinking of all the things Eric would miss out on, and just get through the day without having a total meltdown.

Yes. Most days were easier.

But most days she didn't have to go through their boxes.

Drew wiped a tear from her cheek and shook her head. "Come on, Drew. You've got this. They're just boxes." She scanned the garage again, a new determination steeling her resolve. "And one of them has Austin's glove in it."

She took a deep breath, held it and opened the first box.

The rush of air came out in a laugh as she realized she was looking at the very same trout pillow she'd just been remembering. She should have thrown it in the donation pile before they'd left Nevada. After all, it was completely ridiculous. She lifted it out and held it in her hands for a moment before putting it aside.

Maybe she should have donated it, but Drew was glad she hadn't. It was ugly and ridiculous but it had been Eric's. She had no idea what she was going to do with it, but for the time being, it was going to have to live in the garage. She had more pressing issues than redecorating the house. Although the time would come where she would have to go through the boxes and actually do something with them, it was not on that particular warm day in the middle of May.

Drew shoved the fish back in the box and reached for another one.

Nothing but photo albums and old books she'd never read again.

Next.

Mercilessly, as if each box that turned up without the glove fueled her toward the next, Drew reached for box after box. She dug through the contents, sometimes pulling them out to the floor around her, before shoving it to the side and reaching for the next as if the contents of each container didn't hold the intense power to hurt her.

They did.

But she refused to let the pain in. Not today.

She had to find the glove.

After too much fruitless searching, Drew finally stood and wiped her arm across her brow.

"Come on." She groaned and stretched her back side to side. "It has to be here." She straightened up and looked at the stack in front of her. It was the highest pile of boxes, mostly Rubbermaid totes that were leaning against the back wall. The glove had to be in there. She was running out of options. Austin's first practice was that night and— "Dammit." There wasn't much help for it—she was going to have to get to the top of that pile.

She didn't have a ladder, so she moved a few of the larger boxes to the bottom of the stack, put her foot on the lip of a tote and hoisted herself up. For just a moment, it looked as though it would work. Her hands brushed along the top box, the one she was aiming for, and then…the entire stack wobbled to the right and then swayed to the left. And in the split second before the entire tower of totes fell with her still clinging to the side, instead of panicking, all Drew could do was laugh.

BEN ROSS LIFTED the last of the oversized planters out of his truck bed and hauled it to the brick patio at the back of the Log and Jam. He set it with the others he'd just unloaded and used the edge of his t-shirt to wipe the sweat from his face. It was only the end of May, but it was already hot for the mountain town of Timber Creek, a fact that boded well for the new patio he'd just finished constructing behind his pub.

He'd opened the Log and Jam almost ten years ago and it had quickly become the favorite place for locals to hang out. The problem, at least as far as Ben was concerned, was that the cozy timber-framed interior, decorated with local logging antiques, was cozy and perfect during the snowy winter months, but during the all-too-short mountain summer months, he just wanted to be outside.

And if he wanted to be outside, then his customers likely wanted the same thing, which was why he'd spent the last six weeks getting permits and loans and then finally, building the huge outdoor patio at the Log and Jam.

Ben leaned back against the log wall of the building and surveyed his work. It had been a huge job and one that had taken a whole lot of collaborative effort from his friends and people in the community, but it was almost done.

He'd taken the empty space next to his building, which had

served as overflow parking, and had created a combination of decking and brick-laid patio space. Because the weather could be unpredictable in the mountains, he'd covered half of the space with a huge timber-framed open-sided roof, which not only served as shelter in case of inclement weather, but also held his lighting and industrial space heaters, which would be perfect on cool evenings and extend his patio time well into the fall months.

He'd been able to leave most of the trees around the space, which gave it a feeling of privacy and intimacy, but he'd been told by almost all of his female staff members that planters full of bright flowers were an absolute must. Which was why he'd just spent the last few hours unloading the massive ones he'd bought in Seattle and hauled back earlier that morning.

Soil and plants could wait though, because as much as he'd like to finally see the space ready to go, Ben had other matters he had to take care of that afternoon.

He left the patio and entered his pub through the side door.

"Something smells amazing," he called into the kitchen at Michael, his head chef. "What's the special today?"

Michael appeared a moment later from the swinging door. He wiped his hands on his apron. "Roasted chicken club sandwich with a loaded baked potato soup. Want some?"

He hadn't had a chance to grab anything to eat, and Ben's stomach rumbled. But a quick glance at the clock over the bar told him that as much as he'd love to sit and enjoy a meal, he didn't have time.

"Maybe later," he said. "I'll be back for the evening shift, but I have to run right now."

"I can't promise a sandwich," Michael said. "But I'll save you a bowl of soup."

Ben laughed. Even as the boss, he didn't seem to have any pull when it came to enjoying the amazing food Michael created. Ever since he'd started working at the Log and Jam, the pub had become one of the most popular lunch destinations in town, and the dinner crowd was picking up too. Business was booming. Which was a good thing, considering the loan he'd just taken out in order to make the patio happen in time for the summer season.

But he couldn't think about that right now. It would only stress him out and there was nothing he could do about it. Sometimes you needed to spend money to make money, and the pub business wasn't any different. The patio would pay off; he knew it would.

Ten minutes later, Ben was across town in the childhood bedroom he'd shared with his older brother. It never failed to hit him how much things hadn't changed inside this room, with the matching twin beds, various posters tacked to the walls—mostly cars because their mom wouldn't let them put up anything that might be considered *too provocative*. Good thing she didn't know about the *Playboy* Eric had stolen from a friend's dad when he was thirteen.

Ben chuckled a little at the memory of how Eric had given him the contraband magazine two years later when he'd turned thirteen. He'd treated it very seriously, as if it were a rite of passage for his little brother. Things had been different then. They'd been close when they were young. Inseparable. Ben's chest ached with the familiar pain of loss that had dulled, but not disappeared in the months since his brother passed.

He didn't think it would ever go away completely. *How do you fill the hole your brother leaves behind?* It was a question he couldn't even begin to answer.

The idea of searching for the box where he'd hid that magazine crossed Ben's mind. No doubt it was still under his bed where he'd left it all those years ago. But he shook it off. That's not what he'd come to find.

"What are you looking for, Ben?" His mother's voice from the doorway startled him out of his memories and Ben turned around to see Sylvia Ross, a dishtowel in her hands, watching him.

"Sorry, Mom. I didn't think you were home." Ben crossed the room and gave his mother a quick hug and kiss on the cheek.

She looked tired. Older. She'd aged at least ten years since Eric had died. It wasn't easy to lose a brother; Ben couldn't even imagine how hard it had been for his mom to lose her oldest child.

"You look good, Mom."

She gave him a look that made it clear she knew he was lying, but she managed a smile anyway. "I've been sleeping a little better these days."

"It'll come, Mom. Maybe you should go see the doctor about some sleeping pills. You really do need to take care of yourself."

She shook her head and waved the dishtowel to dismiss the idea. "The best medicine for me is seeing you. Can I get you a cup of tea?"

Ben instantly felt guilty. He knew he wasn't spending enough time with his parents. But there was only so much time in the day, and…well… "I'm sorry, Mom. Not right now. I came to grab something. But I'll come for dinner tomorrow," he added when his mother's face fell.

"I'll make roast chicken." Her face once more lifted, but Ben's guilt didn't disappear. "And I'll see if Drew and Austin would like to come by as well. There'll be plenty for everyone."

"It sounds perfect." Ben made a quick mental note about making sure the bar was staffed properly for the following night. He wouldn't let his mom down.

"What is it exactly that you are looking for?" Sylvia asked as Ben got down on his hands and knees and started rooting around Eric's old bed.

"I'm hoping that you still haven't cleaned under here," he teased.

"If you're talking about that dirty magazine, I got rid of it years ago."

"What?" Ben lifted his head so quickly, it made a sharp, hard contact with the bed frame. "Ouch." He turned around, his hand on his head to see his mother grinning at him.

"Don't tell me I don't clean under there."

He couldn't help but laugh as he resumed his search. A moment later, it was Ben's turn to smile as his hand landed on the item he'd been hoping to find.

"Got it." He held the item up over his head in triumph. "I'm glad you're so sentimental, Mom. Because I know one little boy who I'm hoping will be pretty excited to see this when he gets home from school."

"Oh, Ben." Sylvia put her hand to her mouth and bit her bottom lip. "I didn't even think…you're so thoughtful."

He shrugged. "Anything for him, Mom. Anything." He gave his mother a kiss on the cheek. "Don't cry, Mom. Please."

Sylvia wiped her tears, but Ben was sure she'd be crying again the moment he left. He knew in his heart that it would have broken Eric's heart to see his mother still so torn up about his death, but she'd always been an emotional woman. Strong, but emotional. She was healing; it was just taking her a bit longer.

"I'll be fine." She waved him away. "You get going and I'll see you tomorrow."

Ben left his mother at the front door, and made the quick drive down the street. Not even five minutes later, he was parked in front of the low-rise bungalow where he'd spent more time in the last nine months than his own house.

SHE MAY HAVE BEEN LAUGHING as she fell from the boxes, but Drew definitely wasn't laughing a second later as she toppled to the ground. Fortunately for her, she landed in one of two oversized cardboard boxes where she'd packed a variety of throw pillows that Eric had always complained were more of a pain in the ass than decorative.

At the moment, considering her somewhat soft landing that could have been a lot worse, Drew couldn't think of anything negative at all to say about the blue and yellow throw cushions she'd bought a few years earlier to brighten up their living room, despite the way Eric used to toss them to the floor whenever he wanted to watch television.

"It's a good thing I wasn't very good at donating much of anything." She laughed and rubbed her hip that had connected with something a little less soft that must have been hiding under the pillows.

"Jesus Christ! Drew?"

She tried to swing her head around toward the voice, and the front of the garage, but Drew was somewhat stuck in the box. Like a turtle on the back of their shell. The image made her laugh again.

"Are you okay?"

She leaned her head farther backward, stretching until she could make out the image of her savior. Her eyes landed first on the work boots before traveling up to the muscular legs clad in worn denim, the narrow waist, untucked t-shirt and finally familiar dark hair and green eyes. Her laughter caught in her throat as she sucked in a sharp breath.

Eric.

Drew froze in place, not that she could move very much anyway, as her eyes focused on the upside-down man.

She blinked once and then again.

No. It wasn't Eric. Of course.

"Drew? Are you okay?"

Ben.

A second later, Ben stood over her, his face twisted in a frown. "What the hell? Did you…" He glanced up and took in what was left of the precariously stacked totes. "Were you *climbing* that?"

She opened her mouth to answer, but ended up closing it again and shaking her head in an effort to clear the image of Eric—her late husband and Ben's older brother—from her mind. It wasn't even that they looked anything alike. Eric had been fair and slighter in stature—even before he got sick—than Ben, who had dark features and a much more muscular build. But every once in a while, Drew was struck by some similarity. Something Ben said, those deep eyes, or the way he stood, or… something else.

Just like Eric.

"I'm fine," she said after a moment. "But I seem to be a little stuck."

Ben reached for her arms and lifted her easily out of the box and set her upright on her feet as if she were a doll. "Were you seriously climbing up that stack of totes?" he asked again.

She tilted her head in answer and raised an eyebrow.

"What the hell, Drew? You could have killed yourself."

"But I didn't."

"I don't think that's the point."

She took a step toward some of the totes that had toppled down with her and winced in pain, her hand flying to her hip. Whatever she'd landed on was definitely not a throw pillow.

"You okay?"

"I really am." Ben was sweet and had been nothing but amazing since they'd come home and then especially after Eric had passed. She didn't know what she would have done without him over the last few months and the way he'd taken care of her and Austin and made sure she was eating properly, getting out of the house, and of course taking care of some of the random jobs around the house. Along with Amber, one of her best friends, Ben had been an absolute rock over the last few months. But as amazing as the care and attention was, more and more Drew had been looking for opportunities to stand on her own two feet without depending on anyone else.

Even if she should have asked for help.

Ben was still looking at her with disbelief on his face. "Really," she said. "I'm okay. I just landed a little funny. I'll probably have a bruise is all."

Fortunately, Ben didn't press the issue but instead put his hands on his own hips and looked around the disaster of a garage. "What are you looking for anyway?"

She sighed. She'd been looking all afternoon and still hadn't found Austin's glove. "Austin starts Little League tonight," she said. "Eric bought him a glove last summer and they'd tossed the ball around a little bit in the backyard before…well, before we moved. I need to find it."

A shadow passed over Ben's face but it was gone as quick as it came. "Okay then," he said. "We'll find it." He grabbed one of the totes that was now laying on its side. "I assume you were reaching for these?"

She nodded as relief washed over her. Something about Ben's presence, despite her desire for independence, was comforting and strong and just made her feel as though everything was going to be okay. For the first time in hours, Drew actually felt as if they would in fact find the glove in time for Austin's practice.

With Ben's help, they sorted through the last few bins and in the second to last one, finally found what they were looking for.

Drew held it up triumphantly. "Thank you so much."

He shrugged the way he always did, brushing off how helpful he was. "You know I would have helped you from the beginning, right? I mean, I know you're perfectly capable of looking through boxes," he said quickly before she could object. "But sometimes these things are made a little easier with two sets of hands. Especially considering…" He waved his arms around.

Drew knew he was referring to how hard it probably was to go through all of their things, or, more specifically, Eric's things.

"It was fine." It wasn't totally a lie. It hadn't been nearly as hard as she'd expected it might be. "What are you doing here, anyway? Don't you have a patio to put together?"

"I do." He grinned and gestured outside. "Come on," he said. "Let's get out of here."

Drew laughed and shook her head. "I can't go to the Log and Jam right now. I have to go get Austin from school right away and an early dinner and—what's that?"

Ben stood on her driveway, proudly holding a wooden baseball bat in his hands. He gave her a sideways look.

"I mean, I know what it is." She smacked his arm. "But *what* is it? As in…where did it come from?"

"I went by Mom and Dad's earlier. By the way, Mom wants you to come for dinner tomorrow."

Drew nodded. Absolutely they'd go for dinner. Spending time with Sylvia and Mitch had been good for everyone after Eric died. She'd even noticed Sylvia crying less and less.

"This was Eric's bat when he was a kid," Ben continued. "I think he got some sort of record number of home runs or something with it. It was under his bed, just where he'd left it."

Heat rushed to her face. "It was…" She reached for the bat. "It was Eric's?"

Ben nodded. "He never let me use it. Well, except that one time. But that was different." He shook his head and his smile was back. "It was his lucky bat and I'm absolutely positive he'd want Austin to have it."

Drew took the bat from him and held it in her own hands.

It was way too big for Austin. At least it would be for a few years, but without a doubt it was an incredibly special gift. "Ben, this is perfect. He'll love it. Thank you."

To Drew's surprise, she wasn't going to cry. The tears threatened, but then they were gone. It was getting easier and easier to control the sadness that still washed over her with a regularity that was exhausting.

Read the rest of Drew's story When We Fell!

About the Author

Elena Aitken is a USA Today Bestselling Author of more than forty romance and women's fiction novels. The mother of 'grown up' twins, Elena now lives with her very own mountain man in the heart of the very mountains she writes about. She can often be found with her toes in the lake and a glass of wine in her hand, dreaming up her next book and working on her own happily ever after.

To learn more about Elena:
www.elenaaitken.com
elena@elenaaitken.com

Made in the USA
Columbia, SC
03 October 2023

23761673R00164